WITHDRAWN

Date Due

The King's Vixen

Pamela Hill

THE KING'S VIXEN

G. P. Putnam's Sons

New York

Contents

Part One

THE KINDLING

1491

I

JAN grasped her skirts more securely in one hand and craned sideways so that she could see beyond the man-at-arms' broad back to where the street was thronged with people, all hurrying towards the Castle. If any-one tried to turn and go back, he would be crushed, she thought. The fact registered in her mind as a thing to be remembered without surprise, and made use of later. There had been many such facts, all learned in the past day or two, since she had ridden into Edinburgh from the west.

Detaching herself for an instant from the nearness of the crowd, she allowed her mind for a brief, heady moment to recapture the experiences of the last few days; closing her eyes, so that the acrid smell of the serv-ant's leather jackcoat mingled with other smells—the flesh of the horse they rode, reeking now a little in the summer heat, even though it was not further than walking distance from the lodging in Mint Street whence they had come; the smell of the offal in the roads, foul-trodden beneath hundreds of hurrying feet so that sometimes the mount stumbled and then one could be thankful one rode and was not compelled, like the eager, hurrying, squabbling commons, to go on foot. Even so it had taken her a while to get used to the filth of the streets, fresh as she was from the clean gray air of Galloway and the hills where one could walk barefoot. And the smell of townsmen, differing in some way from the smoke-and-worsted shepherds' smell that she had left behind; secret, alien, exciting, a compound of sweat and laundered linen and leather and cheap essences bought at the shops, and tallow and the faint, all-pervading presence of the salted fish they ate here at every meal. And the houses, many of them still made of old wood, smelled too; the sourish,

musty-damp smell in the timbers swept, as one rode by, from the stair-
ways and alleyways, through the alcoves that fronted every house toward the street so that at ground level further back there was room for
little hidden shops, like caves.

Jan opened her eyes and tried to attract the attention of her half
brother David, riding in front. David had promised before she returned
home to take her one day to the shops, but he had not done so; and
although it was unlikely he had forgotten on purpose, being freer with
his money than her father, he was dreamy and would have to be prodded.
Since he took a wife she allows him to do as he wills, thought Jan impatiently, and he is growing fat and stupid. No, she would not let David
slip out of his promise.

A smile came to her lips, curving the corners triumphantly. Hadn't
she pestered him with regard to this very visit, till he cried for peace?
And even then the battle had been only half won, because her mother
had said she was too young to see a tilting, and her father had been un-
willing to find the price of a new gown. Well, she'd got the new gown,
and to Edinburgh also, although not without a deal of scolding and
being beaten twice. She moved her thin body slightly, easing the fit of
the gown; she could see it in her mind's eye without looking down at
it. They had made it too big, to allow for her growth, and when she
walked the skirts had to be held bunched high almost to the shoulder.
But it was a green gown and new and the color became her, and Agnes,
David's wife, had made her a little hood of the same to set off her red
hair.

"Am I a passable fine lady?"

She had asked Agnes that and Ag had laughed. Jan frowned. How
long would they treat her as a child? Surreptitiously she watched the
women in the streets, seeking an answer to her question. Their faces
were pale, she thought, like wax; some had raddling on the cheeks and
lips. She had thought at first that these must be harlots, but David said
they were not all so and that many of the commons' wives now painted
their faces in imitation of the ladies at Court, in the same manner as
they copied their clothes. Therefore it should be possible to know from
watching them if oneself were fashionably dressed or not. She had already seen that few of them here still plucked their brows and left their
foreheads shaven, as her mother and many ladies did who never came to
town; and also that no one wore horned padding now, several having
hoods like her own.

Reassured, she looked again in front of her. She was glad in a way, of the horses' slow pace; it gave one a chance to see. She drew a deep breath and thought how the excitement did not all begin with the tilting, and how it doubtless would not end when one had seen the King.

The King. It was odd, when one said that, to think only of a boy, and not of the very tall dark man who had once ridden down into Galloway on a pilgrimage to the shrine of St. Ninian at Whithorn, when she had seen him. That had been before the troubles came and they had all ridden past in a jangling of little bells and with the gay colors of their silks and pennants cast back on the wind. But after that the King had been killed when he lost a battle somewhere and his gray horse ran away and threw him. Then they had made his son king in his place, as they had been going to do even before he was killed. No one knew exactly what had happened. But now that was over and everyone spoke of the new young King and how gay he was, and openhanded as his father had not been; and of his bravery in the late wars and how he could handle a lute and love a woman, even though he was still so young. Was he not known to be already the father of a bairn by Marion Boyd, the niece of the Countess of Angus, whose lord the Earl was at feud with Jan's father, their estates marching close, so that they heard all? And yet with all that they said the new King was bookish and devout and so greatly sorrowful concerning his own sire's death, having himself by his part in the rebellion aided it, that he wore forever about him a heavy iron chain.

"How can anyone be gay and yet sorrowful?" Jan asked herself. Her eyes fastened on a great solid gray building as they rode past, with a newly built spire surmounting it like a crown. "David, David!" she called again.

David Kennedy turned, a little impatiently. The long ride and the slow pace irked him. Was it worth this flocking like a drove of sheep to do the King favor? He would by far sooner have been at home in Lesswalt, only the child had made such clamor to come that he—Agnes—which of them was it that had promised, in a rash hour, that she should accompany them? Never again, he swore!

"St. Giles," he told her, following the pointing finger. Soon they would come to the Baresse, the tilting ground, and after that the great horseshoe of green turf where the mounts would be left guarded. He dared say there would be lifting. Whom was one to trust in a large town? His Grace had summoned Islesmen, who were to take part in the contest, and everyone knew from the sight of a saffron shirt that there went a thieving devil. For now it was of no avail to speak, but woe betide any

lout of his who wandered so far forward to watch the fight that there
was a saddle missing at the time of their return. . . .

Janet's smile caught him and he felt contrition tug at his heart. Poor
lassock, she'd given all to come; he didn't envy her, left at home with
that mother of hers and the whole stirring of them. He and Agnes must
do what they could . . . his thoughts flew back to Agnes again and he
wondered if the crowds and the heat of the day might not upset her, as
she was expecting a child. But she rode beside him placidly, and the
sight of her passive, gentle face caused him once again to thank his
stars he had married such a woman, who never gave anyone trouble, and
not a pebble-eyed bitch such as his father had brought home from his
second venture out of Aberdeen. The late Earl of Erroll, who had had
her first, had, he thought, been the more fortunate in that it had not
been for long. But where in God's name had either that woman or his
father got that flamelike, eager-alive creature who rode behind? Why, as
long as he could remember, small things—a new mammet or a dog, even—
had been enough to send her crazy for joy. And how she had looked
forward to this!

David suddenly reached back his arm and drew the servant's mount
alongside. "Looking over from here, you can first see the Castle," he said.
"Press on, now, with me."

Jan's breath of delight deepened. "David, David!"

She was taut in the saddle and ready as whipcord, shining-eyed, with
a strand of vivid hair escaped from under her hood and blowing back
from her face. David thought he had never seen such intensity of colors
in any creature. Irrelevantly, he thought of a strange wild bird that his
uncle, Walter Kennedy, who was a poet, had brought from France a
year or two back. It had had bright flamboyant feathers in various hues,
and a shrill cry. It died with the winter's cold here, he thought, and that
was the end of it. In any case the analogy was farfetched. He sensed
Agnes beside him and tried not to think of her as brown and dull. Why,
to marry such as Jan would be a torment! He wondered whose would
be the hand, for a strong hand it would need to be.

"The pavilions," said Jan. "I can see the King's pavilions."

The great tents, mushroom-colored, and hung with pennants in red
and blue, lay spread before them as they emerged from among the
clustered walls of wooden makeshift inns and bothies that had been
erected, many of them, for this very tilting. Beyond, the high dark bulk
of the Castle sprang. As they drew nearer there came a wailing sound:
a piper, walking up and down on the outskirts of the crowd, would

pause occasionally to collect his money in a catskin bag. At the edge of the ground the bothy women sold confectionery, marchpane and French sugar for those who could afford them, little cakes flavored with honey for those who could not. Out of the crowd a woman stepped, her skirts held high to display crimson stockings. In one hand she had an orange stuffed with cloves to ward off the stink of the crowd. Jan laughed. "David, David, the woman's stockings! Oh, she is going to faint."

Agnes murmured how glad she was that they had places reserved in the pavilion. Jan heard her half with impatience, thinking how dim and lifeless she was. Like a mouse, she thought. She herself wanted to be among the crowd, sucking fruit and telling bawdy stories, elbowing one another to get the best view, throwing coins to the piper to make him play louder. But Agnes could never forget she was David's wife and that David was Lord Kennedy's son and that the Kennedys were lords of Galloway.

A sudden wild elation possessed Jan. Who was she, then, if not herself? But stepping across the tufted ground after they had left the horses under guard and gone to find their places, she found herself humming a song. It was a boastful song, about her family that had fought and wenched and hunted and killed enemies, serving themselves rather than the King at all times, so that now my Lord Kennedy sat in his castle and there were few in those parts would gainsay him.

> " 'Twixt Wigtown and the town of Ayr,
> Portpatrick, and the Cruives o' Cree,
> No man need think for to ride there
> Unless he court wi' Kennedie!"

sang Janet.

It was a long way from Portpatrick, a long way from Luce where the gray sea coiled and threatened. A long way from her father's castle where the poultry straggled in the yard, and the men-at-arms quarreled in idleness and her mother beat her often for nothing, and the twin lochs, the White and the Black, reflected the colors of day and night because of the way the rocks lay about their sides. A long way . . . and this was Edinburgh, the King's town, where she was nobody, or almost nobody, and as green to many things as the hood she wore, as the humblest apprentice boy about the streets. But she would learn; she was quick at learning things. And she was happy being nobody, at any rate for now. And today she would see the King.

The place they had was in the lesser pavilion for country lairds and such visiting nobility as were not of the Court. Jan found that by looking across she could make out the figures in the greater, which lay across the ground. About her the voices rose and fell; the arrival of some great lord would be an event to call comment from that country knight, the dress of some fine lady from that padded dowager. If she had cared she could have known more of the details of their private lives for the trouble of asking. That nobleman was Lord Lyle, he had been a rebel against the King last year, but His Grace put him down. And then the King's clemency was exclaimed at, which allowed Lord Lyle now to sit there in his place, instead of on a block with the head struck from his shoulders. But was not that very clemency like the blessed late King his father, who had landed in all his troubles through forgiving too readily and too often? But then the voices of dowagers and knights would recall how this King had still not spared Drummond's son, who had burned six score souls alive in Monzievaird church.

Jan heard it all idly, neither shocked nor intrigued. Of burnings she had heard often, and of murder, down in Galloway. As long as it did not touch oneself there was no call to attach too much importance to it: if one did so, there would be few peaceful nights for any subject in the kingdom. She shifted her gaze slightly, watching a plump lady in a gown of honey-color, who had just made her way into the pavilion with a lazy, languid grace; the white hand, raised many times to acquaintances, showed her a person of consequence. The sleeves she wore were richly barred with fur.

"The Lady Daisy," someone said. There was a slight stir in the pavilion. Jan listened again and heard one tell another that this was the Princess Margaret, James III's sister, who had led them a weary life in Haddington Convent when she was a girl.

"She would not marry into England, no, not for king nor priests nor governesses, and in the end they had to let her have her way, and for the gallants that climbed Haddington walls at all hours of the night she was left, to be sure, with a bastard, a girl that goes everywhere with her, but I do not see it today."

Jan felt laughter rise and overwhelm her. She knew an admiration for the gay princess. Wouldn't she have done the same, placed to school with stuffy nuns? Oh, the joy of knowing that there were others like herself, who would bear a bridle for no man! If a princess could do so, against all principalities and powers, then she, *she*, could, when she was grown. . . .

Lady Daisy laughed and lolled in the pavilion, yellow skirts kicked aside to show tiny, pointed feet. Although she was stout and no longer very young she had a dozen lords about her, all eager to touch her hand, to give her sweetmeats, to tell her about the tilt. Chief among them was a tall nobleman in dark garb, his heavy brows closely drawn so as to give a stern air to his face. After a while it was his turn to be discussed and Jan heard that that was Patrick Hepburn, the new Earl of Bothwell—"*he* has the kingdom in his hand!"—and then came a recital of all the Earl's new titles that the King had given him, because, it was said, Patrick Hepburn had once shown kindness to the weary and bewildered royal boy they had forcemarched against his own father on the long road from Stirling to Linlithgow, four years back. The King, they said, never forgot a kindness.

The King. The King. Insensibly, curiosity was growing in her to see him. It did not seem to matter what everyone talked of, sooner or later it would bring them to a mention of him, an act, a memory of him. What manner of King was this that had made such an impression on all minds as never, through all, to be forgotten?

She looked at the crowds. They would be waiting, too, for the King. Some must have waited since before dawn of day. They pressed against the barricades that divided the tilting ground from the common grass; the thin high sounds of the piping still floated from among them. Their faces, at this distance, were all identical; flatly upturned, and waiting. She felt their power.

Others had power too. Just before His Grace's pursuivants rode out there was a stir in the greater pavilion, and a tall broad nobleman in a blue cloak thrust his way in, late, to one of the chief seats. He had long hair, silver-gilt, and a heavy beard flowing over his chest; the broad Flanders hat he wore was pulled well down over his eyes. His coming caused some comment, both in his tent and their own; heads craned to look at him, and there was a buzz of talk.

"The Earl of Angus! Bell-the-Cat! He is back from Amiens!"

Some one else bade the speaker be quiet because they must not say that name here.

Bell-the-Cat, thought Janet. Bell-the-Cat.

She said the name over and over to herself, its very danger adding spice to her enjoyment. *She* knew who the Earl was, and why they called him that. Our neighbor, she thought sardonically. She'd seen once, against the skyline, a troop of armed men riding, and her mother, who never showed fear, had gone white as chalk at sight of them, and then

sworn roundly, to show she was still mistress of herself, that the Red
Douglas rode not over his own land now. And Jan, who had been small
at the time, had seen in that instant a huge figure on a black horse, the
vizor down, and the standard borne in front of him; and had known that
that was the Earl.

Bell-the-Cat. Other things she knew about him, besides that he neglected his wife and quarreled with his eldest son and had more bastards
than any man in Scotland. She knew how he'd come by that name. During the late wars, when he had changed sides from King to lords and
from Scots to English and back again, as he thought would reward
him best, my lord of Angus had had occasion at Lauder Kirk to hold a
session. It was in the kirk at dead of night, thought Janet, hearing it half
as told to her by servants, who made every detail fearsome, and half in
her father's little, dry, cracked voice, coming so strangely from a man
who was the greatest lord in Galloway. And in that kirk at dead of night
had been assembled all the lords who meant to have the life of Cochrane,
the King's friend. But Cochrane was so powerful (having made himself
greater than the King) that there was a question how it was to be done,
for if the plot failed there would be death for the nobleman who had
attempted it, and their meeting was compared to one of mice who sought
to rid themselves of a troublesome cat, by hanging a bell about the cat's
neck to warn everyone of its approach. "But who," the mice said, "is to
bell the cat?" And it was said again at that meeting, for no man alone
dared risk what it might mean to fail. But then the Earl of Angus had
risen and said that he would be the one to do so; and he had gone from
there to the King's tent and seized Cochrane and his friends, and he
and his men took them out every one and hanged them over the bridge
at Lauder.

Bell-the-Cat.

She stared at him, forgetting to watch for the heralds. It came to her
fancy that he saw her, and devilment made her stare on. To stare out
Bell-the-Cat, as though *she* had been the cat! Who was he? He was a
prideful old man, a conceited old man, who came in late and sat there in
his place with his arms folded as though he were the King.

The King. The King.

The heralds rode out and she switched her attention abruptly from
Angus and listened to their fanfare. The liveries they wore this year
were blue and white. David had told her that every year at Yule the
King made his servants gifts of new liveries, every year a different color.
Last year they had been black and rowan-tanny.

All around her the voices still went on. They were lower now and
waited for the cry of the heralds, when there would be silence. They
talked about the knight who would appear who was called Clockwise.
He was a knight of Holland and was said to be so brave that no champion
in Christendom could match him. It was said the King himself had
wanted to try, but on persuasion had given place to Sir Patrick Hamilton,
who would fight today.

The King. The King. Back in the crowds they were beginning to
shout for him. She wished he would come.

The shouting grew louder. "They are coming," said David. Everyone
in the two tents had risen and she could hardly see above the heads in
front. The trumpets shrilled again and one could hardly hear them. Janet
craned in her place, thrusting aside the shoulders of the man in front;
she must see, she must! Ah, some had seen the King already and they
were cheering and waving their hats in the air. She struggled and pushed
at the shoulders in front, determined to see.

In the end she saw. A boy had come out on to the stone balcony that
abutted from the Castle above the tiltyard. He had his cap in his hand
and was bowing, gravely, and smiling right and left to the crowd. The
noise they made was deafening. The women called loudly, their shrill
voices rising higher than the men's. The boy raised his hand and bowed
again and settled himself in his place in full view of everyone. He wore
a black velvet short-gown and white hose and his hair, like her own, was
red. He was slight, with a pale oval face, and neither short nor very tall.
The straight hair fell about his face as he leant forward.

It is the King, thought Jan. Settled again in her place she found that
her hands were trembling. She heard the trumpeters again and then the
wrestlers ran in, for it was not considered a good thing to start a jousting
with the choicest item on the list. And then again they sounded, for
swordsmen, and again; and last of all the Black Knight rode into the lists,
somber plumes tossing on his helmet, and his horse caracoling, magnificent in sable trappings. There were cheers for him and for Sir Patrick
Hamilton, whose armor was dinted and his build slight by comparison,
so that it was thought by many he would not win. The King sat chin
on hand while they rode to lance, as though it were hard for him to sit
there when he would rather have been in the lists. The lances broke and
they rode a second time, and then discarded their horses and fought
hand to hand. His Grace grinned like any boy, following every move of
the swiftly hacking blades; the crowds called on, some for Hamilton
and some for the Black Knight. Jan heard them in a dream.

Later, she looked at Angus again. She could not think what had compelled her. To her discomfort he was looking not at the lists nor at the
King, but at herself; the blue eyes shifted slightly in the shadow of the
hat. Jan felt anger rise; how dare he look at her as though she were a
cow for sale? Swiftly, under cover of the fact that David and Agnes were
watching the tilt, she put out her tongue. Immediately giggles stifled her
and she choked them down. The Earl moved restively in his seat and
she saw the flush mount darkly above his golden beard. Elation filled
her, as it had done when she had sung crossing the ground. They'd never
frighten *her* with tales of the Red Douglas. A pompous old man, a plaything!

The champions contested the ground. Each would fight to exhaustion,
and in the end the winner was determined by the King himself, who
threw down his plumed hat into the lists at the end of the long day.
But of the thudding of armed feet swiftly and hard on the turf, she
heard less than most, and of that most famous fight of all when Sir
Patrick Hamilton beat the Black Knight of Holland, she remembered
not the fight but other things. One was the King; she was to recall the
pale boy on the balcony as long as she remembered anything. The other
was Bell-the-Cat, but him she remembered with annoyance. She could
not know, for no astrologer had told her, what they would bring to her,
and she to both men.

Part Two

BELTANE

1494–1497

I

WIL KENNEDY the groom waited motionless, the knotted reins dangling from his hands. Behind him was the soft cropping of the horses at grass, and during the hour he had waited this had become so familiar that his mind no longer heard it. But now at last twenty yards away he had heard the sound of laughter, and knew that the two girls had come.

Wil was aware of the sharp hammering of his heart in his breast. For a little longer he stood still, taking this moment, so seldom available, of seeing without being seen (for my lady's sharp eyes were everywhere) and waiting, half-hidden, behind the hillock, where the light Galloway summer wind tugged at the moor-grass, so that it showed as a thousand little dark heads, bobbing and dancing. That I should wait here, he thought, and she coming!

Lady Jan strode in front, like a young animal, skirts kilted high above the knee. She was like a boy, he thought, the way she took the ground; brushing lightly through the long grass with her red hair blown back from her face. And so she had been a boy, almost, until this thing had happened to him one day last year, and he had come to think of her not as the wild thin stick of a thing she had used to be, but someone silvery and unattainable as the moon, so that she had only to appear thus, on the moors, or about her father's yard, for the voice in his throat to die in him and this weird thudding of his heart to make him ashamed. Ah, but why should he be so? He was as good a man as the fleshy young lord to whom they had betrothed her, and who did not, he dared swear, know of their meeting now or of the ploy that was afoot this day.

He grinned, admiration flooding out the pain in his heart. Flaming

Janet! They said she was afraid neither of man nor devil, and certainly there would be the devil to pay for this, once my lady got wind of it. The only thing as he saw it was to ride fast away from here, for at any moment they might be followed or prevented, but he would undergo any number of strokes on his back as long as they allowed him his hour with her. Already, he thought, it is almost noon.

He heard Jan's voice, cast back in scorn to her sister Helen, who followed behind. "Mother of God! Had I known you were such a cry-baby, would I have brought you to see the needfire at all? Keep your ills to yourself!" she called sharply. Wil's half-rueful grin broadened. "To shout of needfires over half the moor!" he grunted, thinking of the furtive, half-pagan ceremony the priests frowned on, for which they were bound. He himself had seen many a needfire lit, but it was no place for a girl. All the same, she'd pestered him to take her, and so he'd do.

"Wil! Wil!"

She had seen him; was calling him. He came out from his concealment, flushed and sheepish. The small curved smile of triumph that he knew so well told him that she had been aware of why he was hiding behind the mound. Almost, he hated her.

"I knew you would not fail us," she told him. Wil set his teeth; she was to be gracious today, then, Lord Kennedy's daughter, and he the groom. He fixed his eyes on Helen Kennedy's blubbered face, knowing the sullen pudgy child had been dragged against her will across the moor, and knowing why.

Jan laughed suddenly. Always she was torn between gusts of fury and gusts of laughter. "Up, cry-baby," she said to Helen, indicating the horses with a jerk of her chin. Behind the dropped lids her eyes sparkled. This was St. John's Eve, the time of Midsummer, and today she would see the kindling of the year's new fire from green wood, and the choosing of the carline, the bearer of all the year's ills, by lots from a broken bannock. If she had not escaped from the dreary castle for this one day she would have run mad, she felt. Who cared about what would happen on their return?

She heard Helen sniveling, her twelve-year-old dignity in tatters. "I do not wish to soil my hands and gown dancing with swineherds. It is out of place for ladies of our station. If our mother knew—"

"Ho!" said Jan. "What makes you think you will get even a swine-herd?"

Wil Kennedy laughed and Jan put her hand in front of her face. She began to give a splendid imitation of a pig, one finger pushing up her nose while the other two dragged her eyelids down. Helen sniggered angrily, furious at being made to laugh. Always it was so in everything, never could she have any matter her own way. Had she wanted to come over this moor? Bewildered, she tried to remember the manner in which Jan had cozened her: Jan, she thought, had said she did not wish to be left alone with Wil. But when had Jan ever been afraid of any man? She was as strong as a horse, and feared nobody, not even my lady.

Helen surveyed her own plump body ruefully. She had never managed to accept whippings with the philosophy of Jan. That there would be one was certain, and she had torn her gown in the scrub and bracken hurrying after her sister across the moor. She had not dared lose her; Jan always knew where to put her feet to avoid the dark sour patches of bog that lay across the way without warning. And now they were so far from home that Helen was afraid to return by herself. She began to cry again.

"Promise we'll not go by the Green Lake," she quavered.

Wil was leading the horses forward. He had eyes for no one but Jan. It was, thought Helen angrily, as though *she* did not exist. Jan answered briefly, one hand on the saddle. "It's quicker," she said. "Why not?"

"There are spirits there," said Helen. Fear made her voice prim. She had been afraid, ever since she could remember, of Soulseat, the Green Lake where the water was foul with greenish scum, and ghosts of drowned men were said to rise at dusk in pale spirals.

Jan's high laughter cut the air scornfully. "What a gowk you are," she said slowly. She turned and faced Helen for an instant, bright-eyed. "You shall ride with me tonight the round of the lake and see these spirits, which are white flies," she said. "Clouds of them, hundreds of them arising—God's my pity, but you are a grown woman, very near! What man will wed a scary-cat that fears her own shadow? Not even a swineherd! You'll be an old maid."

Helen burst into tears. "Your Sandy Gordon had to be paid well to take you! And our mother says he is no great catch, and has boils on his neck besides, and that either he must marry you soon or—no, Janet, don't, don't, no, oh, oh!"

A fury in whirling skirts had flung itself about her; fingers pinched hard at every part of her body. "Let be your filthy talk, you little adder, or I'll skin you! Ah, by God, I'll stuff you in the bog so that ravens will come and pick out your eyes!"

Helen wriggled and squealed with pain, fighting wildly to escape those cruel, dexterous fingers. "Squealing pig!" said Janet. Wil jingled the harness patiently. This was his lady in one of her set-tos, like her mother. It was best to say nothing, and things would remedy themselves; he had no wish for a cut across the face from his own stirrup leather. He waited till a sobbing Helen turned wretchedly to her horse. Jan, in the saddle at one bound, was off and away before he could help her.

There was a narrow track that they were to follow; it led across the moor. The horses picked their way carefully; Wil allowed himself time to dream, with his eyes fixed on his lady's straight slim back. Helen followed, swollen-eyed. Jan thought of none of them. She had allowed herself deliberately to ride a little ahead, the wish for solitude—so rarely hers nowadays—becoming a crying need. Here, with nothing before her but the moor and the sky, she could imagine that she was indeed alone. The bleakness of the scene exhilarated her, who had known it since childhood; it was as though she had never really seen the round gray cairns and the unbroken miles of moor before. The fancy took her that it was Midsummer madness, working in her blood; the old dark faith that a simpler folk knew, who had once dwelt in Galloway. Little squat men, she thought, with round skulls and long arms; they said that if you were to open the gray cairns you would find their bones there, earthenware jars, and maybe the ashes of a fire. Why was it that everyone was always afraid to find out? If you were like Helen you believed that the cairns were fairy hills and goblins lived in them, so that you were filled with fear if you rode more than a mile from home.

She smiled. She wasn't troubled with goblins, any more than the Red Douglas had troubled her. Once she had ridden alone by Soulseat for a wager, and found out about the flies; and she had bathed naked in the Black Loch in the dark of the moon. She was uncertain why she had done it, unless to give everyone a chance to say that she had sold herself to the devil. Closing her eyes, she remembered the cold caress of the black water, and the pale gliding smoothness of her own body in the dark. It had been a thing queer and unsharable, and she had spoken of it to no one; only the watching eyes had seen and soon after they had betrothed her to Gordon of Lochinvar for a matter of four hundred merks, to be paid in installments.

Remembering Gordon, she felt a sullen resentment rise. To combat it she laughed aloud, and Helen, left far behind, heard the laughter and saw the tossing hair. She thought Jan laughed at her discomfiture and was filled with helpless fury. Oh, if Wil would tumble Jan in the heather and give her what she deserved!

It's always like that with any man, she thought savagely. They make sheep's eyes at her and moon after her, but they're afraid. Even Sandy Gordon's afraid of her, although he won't admit it; running home to that mother of his who tells him that he must wed. Jan orders him and all of them as though they were dirt. She thinks she owns the whole of Galloway.

Her mouth drooped at the corners. She wanted to go home, and if they were all to be whipped at the day's end she would rather her share were over soon. If she turned her horse's head now the beast would find its way. Why should she be bumped and jolted over the moor after Jan and her lovesick groom?

Home, she thought. The rhythm of the horse's hooves sounded the word to her. They stepped more firmly now, over the hardening ground. She still could not summon courage to go back.

And then, quite suddenly, they were cresting the rise, leaving the scrub and heather and gray stones behind. A dip in the hills revealed green grass, on which little figures moved and ran. They looked like the fairies, and Helen was afraid. Then she saw that they were real enough; country folk in gray and drab, gathered about a greenwood frame. In the middle was the axle for the needfire, which was not lit yet. Helen caught up with Jan and Wil who had come to the edge of the rise and were paused waiting, taking in the scene and the busy gnomelike figures. The three of them, against the sky, were outlined blackly, and suddenly a great shout of welcome came. Jan, rose-flushed, waved from the saddle. To Wil Kennedy, watching, it seemed as though she were made from head to foot of fire.

"Jan, you've let your hood slip," said Helen sharply. "You will be known."

Jan laughed. The carping little voice went on.

"We will be spoken of, and you have seen it now. I did not want to come and you made me. I am going to tell our mother. I am going to tell everyone. Why should I be punished for you? I want to go home."

Jan turned a glowing face from contemplation of the needfire mound; the little figures had begun to draw the axle toward it. From the periphery of the crowd hands wavered, beckoning them down. "Go, then," she said, as though addressing a stranger. She turned suddenly and galloped down the slope, red hair streaming after her.

Wil followed his beacon, deaf to every voice but one. Helen, watching him go, began to scream and twist the reins. It seemed to her that everyone in that hateful crowd was laughing at her, hands pointing in her direction, eyes that leered. Surely that was a cowherd scrambling up the slope toward her? Jan was in the midst of the vulgar, drunken crowd, slipped out of the saddle with her hair tousled loose. She was laughing, mad. Everyone was detestable. Ah, she, Helen, would tell such a tale as to have the skin flayed off both their backs, Jan's and Wil's, when they returned!

She gave a small sob of outrage and wrenched the reins about. To be lost on the moor, the immense and alien moor, was a less frightening thing than going down there with them. The crowd was like no crowd she had ever seen. Already the vision of a saturnalia was replacing reality in her mind, as the hoofbeats sounded. She rode desperately, caught between the fear she had left behind and that which was to come.

Down in the ring of watchers by the mound Jan turned to Wil Kennedy and laughed. Her eyes sparkled at him with an intensity of color; the life in her seemed to have lit a fire behind them. Before her the mound rose, encircled by its deep ditch; it had been there so long that not even the oldest of the old men present could tell who had dug it down, in this place where every year they would come as they came today.

There was cloud today, Jan thought. That meant that there would be no long sun-shadows on the stone. This festival was bound to the very old world, the prayers for sun and rain and for the fire that was needful for all. She laughed, wondering what her confessor would have thought. The quietness in the Castle chapel seemed alien and shallow-rooted now.

She turned and found Wil gazing at her. "There go the teams," he muttered, for something to say. Jan felt an urge to be rid of him. "Where?" She avoided his arm. A group of young men, the nine times nine, who were to rax the bough, were forming themselves. Almost every man in the north of Galloway must be here. The ropes hung slack in the hands of the leaders; the crowds began to withdraw.

"Where's Helen?" She had suddenly turned and realized her sister was missing. Wil kicked at a tussock of grass, and shook his head. Anger with him rose in her.

"Where's Helen, I said? Answer me, you clout!"

As she said it, she rejoiced for an instant in her own power over him. His dark face, so well-known, today puzzled and intrigued her; he was like, she thought, a ferret, long and lean, eyes narrow in his head and bead-black like my lord's. She wondered if it was true that he could be her bastard half brother. The skin to his shirt's edge was tanned as a nut, and below that, seen through the opened folds as he moved, creamy and thatched with dark hair. It was a pity he was a fool. He was gauping at her now in the way he had; if he had struck her, or answered her, she thought, she could have loved him.

Wil had flushed at the sharpness in her voice. "How do I know the way she went?" he answered sullenly. The moment the words were out, he regretted them, knowing, by some means other than wit, that he had lost her, never having had her; that now, by the hold she had over him, he would allow her to be so lost; would go, blindly, and would obey her command. Mistress and servant, not lover and lass; and so for evermore.

She swung round and faced him. "What in God's name, Wil Kennedy, allowed you to forget yourself so? Would you have my sister sunk in a bog, or ravished? I'd have you mind your ways before I take my girth about your sides. By God, are you my father's servant or his master?"

Her voice, cruel and clear, pierced his wretched mind. In all his idle thoughts it had not come to him that she could make him so ashamed; every word, every cool epithet, that she applied, cut him like a whip. Ah, if she'd lost her calmness, raved and stormed at him as she sometimes did, he could have caught her in his arms, he thought. As it was, standing there, placid as a nun in the folds of her cloak, calling him worm, clout, fool, what was he to do? He heard, acutely conscious of them, the folk nearby snigger. Oh, if he were her equal, to seize her with strength and drown her words with his mouth!

"Go now," finished Jan softly. They looked at one another and his eyes fell.

He turned and went.

She was alone. She was alone. She was alone.

Sitting on the tussock of grass, hugging her knees in the delicious power of solitude, she drew deep breaths of air. Suddenly the laughter that lay in her rose up, overflowing control. She threw back her head and let the laughter escape from her throat as a bird sings, seeing the tilted curve of the soft flesh and the back-dragging weight of her hair in the eyes of the women, who looked at her curiously. She did not care what they thought. Already they said that Flaming Janet was a wanton, and for all she grieved so let it be.

When was it that she had last been alone? Not, at any rate, since her betrothal to Lochinvar; not since the night in the lake. No one could say what this day would bring. She watched the teams. They were making ready now for the pull, the crowds about the circle crying them on, and the rope taut in every man's hand and coiled about the shaft, ready for the signal.

Into the air came a breathless silence. It was unlike anything she had
ever known. In it the events of all her life lay before her, the memory of
Gordon bringing such revolt that she had to clench her hands hard on
the grass to stem it down. Others might dance at Court, and some would
make banefires, but she, because her father was close with his silver, must
stay here buried in the Galloway hills, bearing to Gordon year after hum-
drum year his lumpish, flat-faced children, till she grew heavy and old.
Ah, but she was not old yet, and the faces that were turned away now
as though to a magnet would be toward her again, once the flames leaped
high.

A sharp shout came—the signal. Instantly there was a long groaning,
and the whirl of wood on wood, as the raxing started. The men's backs
strained hard, naked to the waist as they were and oiled, so that the
muscles shone as they pulled at the ropes.

"Back! Forth! Back! Forth!" The timekeeper stood on top of the mound
with his cap in his hand. Not a man moved from the place where he
had first stood; firmly planted, toe to the heel of the man in front, they
wrought and heaved at the wood.

The watchers crept nearer and nearer, and Jan rose to her feet the
better to see. She knew of the things they would be saying to one another,
the callings of good luck on the unborn fire, the saying that if it did not
come there was a hearth still lit within three miles about, which would
bring a murrain on the cattle. The sweat was pouring down the raxers'
faces, and still the green wood had no spark struck. An old woman in the
crowd began to jeer and curse. "Is it mother's milk ye were reared on?"

The crowd began to laugh, but there was small goodwill behind the
laughter. It was as though this needfire were suddenly the most urgent
need on earth, a stronger force than birth or death which would come
between one Midsummer and another. They looked, Jan thought, like
a pack of wolves. She knew no fear, only a queer exhilaration. The men's
bodies were drenched with sweat. The wood groaned and squealed. If
they obtained no spark, she thought, the rest would tear them to pieces.

She shook her hair back; was she a fool, and were they in the Dark
Ages? But the power for evil in the hollowed hills made it seem as if
the very sky had darkened, and she could not rid herself of the feeling, or
the awareness of it.

"Back! Forth! Back! Forth!"

They were not separate any more, they were a molten mass, waiting
for the power to shape them back into identity. She forgot her name
and everything except that she was standing there, by the ditch about

the mound, swaying and calling aloud with the others. The god was
angry; he had sent no sun to dry the green wood. A curious beating
rhythm seemed to pervade the air; the men still heaved.

There was a man watching. She saw him once when she raised her
eyes, dazzled with watching the pass and repass of the wood. He was not
among the others, but stood motionless, a little way back from the
crowd. His cloak was wrapped about his shoulders and his hat pulled
forward over his eyes. It was as something dark and alien that she looked
for him again. Suddenly her heart leaped, turned about in her breast
and then settled again. Later she could feel it beating wildly.

For the King was here.

When had he come?

Had he seen her and the two others crest the rise with the horses and
stand watching, so that they were outlined blackly against the sky?

Was he really the King? Had her mind played her a cruel trick?
What brought him here?

She remembered hearing how he went much about the country,
dressed as a common man. He went into the inns and cottages and talked
to the common folk and sometimes healed them, for he had knowledge
of herbs. Often he would ask about the King and what they said of him.

Green devils leaped in her eyes, and she smiled. Let him ask *her!* She'd
shake James Stewart in his opinion!

"Your Grace, they say that the King is lazy, bad. They say he hunts
all day and wenches all night. They say he is not handsome really. They
say . . ."

He was no boy now, she saw, but a man. The red beard made him
look older than his years. Under the shadow of the hat the eyes looked out
darkly; she could not tell what he was thinking, or what he saw. One
long hand, white-fingered, with the tips turned back, grasped his cloak.
He wore no rings.

She had forgotten the men, and the groaning mound. She took no more
account of place and time. It might have been seconds or hours that she
stood there, while the crowds swayed and shouted round her. They
jostled her and she did not feel them, looking across and up at James
Stewart, as motionless as he.

He had not seen her. Inwardly she resolved that he should do so. She
framed a wish to herself, secure in the knowledge of the power that was
in her. "When the fiddles start and the dancing begins, he shall dance
with me and no other."

But now he watched the crowds, as he had done that day at the Baresse. She felt that like herself he would be at one with the crowds. How was it that none of them knew him for the King?

A tiny murmur had risen in the midst of the shouting, swelling at last to a roar. From that wildly whirring wood a spark had struck, and then another and another so that the joints, stuffed fast with linen, caught swiftly alight. The crowd, the sullen wolfish crowd, was suddenly off its head with joy, stamping and cheering. The teams, exhausted, fell back and grinned; everyone, once again, had resolved into fisherfolk and shepherds and their wives. The King smiled faintly, watching, and still she watched the King. The flames gained strength, leaping into the air as if they would feed there. And still the people roared.

"The wind is right, praise Heaven! All will be right this year!"

God see to it, thought Janet. The thought of her own late preoccupation amused her. To be brought to that state by a log, which might or might not kindle!

Swiftly, shrugging back her cloak from the fire's heat, she elbowed her way out. She knew what she would do, and the way to do it. Behind her, the men were stoking up the peat and dry bracken that lay ready-piled by the fire. Moving, she knew of the picture she made; wishing she had worn her blue gown of fine wool, although the one she wore was square necked, fitting well, and showed her breasts gracefully. She could feel a purpose in her every movement, even to the way her hands hung empty and loose by her sides; oh, let him turn, and see her!

Will ye not wake, and turn to me?

the old song came to her. Why should she think, at this moment, of a song? There had been once, that time, crossing the Baresse in Edinburgh, when a song had come to her lips quite as foolishly.

She focused her will in her eyes, knowing of their shining. James Stewart, turn to me. My sleeping prince, turn to me. Was this the way the girl in the song had felt, who had toiled seven years to win her prince and found him, at last, in a sleep that knew no waking, at the top of the glassy hill?

A tongue of flame shot out, making a wall between him and her. He turned to look at the flame, and saw her; she watched one eyebrow shoot up in the shadow of the hat. She was standing still now, certain with all the mind she had that she would brand his face on her memory; the bearded mouth sweet-lipped, not full, as many men's were; the jutting nose, and high cheekbones with the pallor that she remembered. The brows were arched, thin and mobile above eyes curiously bright; they were fixed on her now, but not, she felt, without reserve; why was it that she had the feeling of a veil drawn behind the eyes?

She stood, neither smiling nor moving, nor dropping her own.

"Good day to you, mistress." He took her, then, for a country woman. She was glad, feeling relief for her drab cloak. Time enough to tell later! But now she knew what she would say.

They had a hangman's rope about the wood, it was said, from the King's ayre at Kirkcudbright.

As she spoke she fixed her eyes on his face, hardly able to contain her laughter. "They say he hanged nine," she said. "Do you believe that?"

"He would hang those who deserved to die, and let the rest go."

His voice was deeper than she had expected, arousing a queer little shiver in her. Swiftly she smiled, to give the feeling pause. "Is the King just, then?" she asked him, hoping he would reply "Do they say so of him?" But he did not and was watching the bonfire. Jan began to laugh. Mingled with it was her anger that she could make so slight an impression on him.

Her laughter intrigued him; he wheeled round. "Why do you—" he began, and suddenly he smiled; she had heard that many women were in love with him. "You have the key of life," he said, "and in that way you may unlock any door."

"All but one, for Your Grace will take no heed to me."

She saw a flicker, a hint of weariness, pass like a shadow across his eyes. "Ah, what the devil is that to me?" she said in an undertone. "I have no court to pay, except that I wish Your Grace would dance with me."

James Stewart flung back his head and laughed aloud. "Why, then, let us say for today that I *am* the devil," he told her, "and as such the name you give me has ill place."

She could see his eyes now, raking her; the sight of them brought to her an odd yearning. They were strange eyes, neither hazel nor gray; the leaping lights of the fire behind made little flecks dance in them. "You are no devil," she told him, "any more than I am an angel; and certain it is that I am none."

"So?" he said, and his mouth twisted in appreciation. Always, she thought, there was a shadow behind his smiling, and grief behind his laughter; he was like a man in constant inward anguish, less of body than of soul. She remembered the legend of the chain. Did he wear it now beneath his tunic, chafing his flesh?

A shudder took her; she could not have told why. Was this herself, Jan Kennedy, afraid of shadows? She tried to shake the feeling free and assert her own robust common sense again. This man did not move like one bowed down, he was lissom and alert like a young tree. Even the way he stepped over the ground was different from other men.

But now she found herself tongue-tied. A Court lady, she thought angrily, would have known what next to say. He had not promised to dance with her, and thinking of it now it seemed an impertinence to have asked. Jan put her hand on her shoulder and fingered one of her stray locks of hair. This King who went about the countryside as a common man could not, then, shed his kingship.

"Shall we stand by?" said James Stewart.

She saw that the crowds were withdrawing. This, then, would be the casting of the bannock, that she had so longed to see, and which mattered now less than nothing; but she allowed herself to be withdrawn. Standing by the King, close enough for the russet weave of the cloak he wore almost to brush her cheek as the wind stirred it, she thought: Does anyone know of him here? They all know of *me*. . . .

She raised her head. If they knew, no one was looking their way. Everyone was watching the preparations for the bannock and caudle, which would decide the devil's own. They had taken him, if they thought at all, for a sprig of the Douglas down from Luce. In any case it was no one's concern if Flaming Janet got herself a lover.

He is taller than I, she thought. Looking up at him, she decided, though, that he was not as tall as many men. David would overtop him by half a head, and the Earl of Angus (why had she thought of him?) by two hands' span. Yet he was tall enough, she reckoned, and with a quality that none could name. Was it because he was consecrated, a king? Or was it because of the blood in him? They said his mother had been a saint and his father a martyr and that he was descended from the old Norse gods. Looking at him, the jutting profile outlined above her against the sky, she saw the likeness in him to an eagle.

"Look now," he said, "they are finding the carline."

His voice sounded wistful and she was suddenly transformed from her late estimate of him; he was a boy, a well-mannered but truant boy. The laughter gushed up in her again as it might have done for one of her own brothers. "Then do you also go and find the carline, and come—"

She had been going to say "come back to me" but did not. When had she ever had to beg a man's return to her? It was hard not to feel chagrin as he took her hand, raised it, kissed it, and then was gone. What was it he had said as he went?

"I shall call you Astaroth, the fire spirit out of the old Arabian books. Pray that I find a worthy carline."

Pray to whom? she had wanted to ask, but he had not given her time. Standing alone where they had been, she watched the dance begin, this time for men only; a fierce running round, without music, or any sound but their own padding feet. The steaming caudle stood on the fire; James Stewart ran with the rest in the circle, devoid of his cloak and hat, between a swineherd and a Douglas dairyman. Jan saw the coating of the bannock, the breaking into the caudle of eggs and milk. Still there was no reality for her but that running, slight figure. Ah, it was untrue, she thought, the talk about the chain! No chained man could run so lightly, and laugh as he ran.

Behind him and all of them the flames rose high, for the fire was well started now. Quietly, from all sides, the women and children watching began to creep down the slope. The old man who had acted as timekeeper waved testily, but without heeding them; he, like every other, was watching the dance, wondering which man would draw the marked piece of bannock and be carline, to have the worst of all pestilence, death and ill luck to himself and his house all through the coming year till next Midsummer, if he leaped not through the flames thrice.

Jan heard voices, coming as in a dream. Her head whirled with the noise and movement. When she shut her eyes tonight in sleep she would see the flames dance still, and hear the talk that went on of how the carline last year squealed because the fire had been piled too high.

They took the bannock and divided it. The old timekeeper had ready his bonnet. Each man as he ran round dipped a hand into this, bringing out a piece. One piece would have a nipple on it and that would be the carline's. No one looked into the bonnet, with its trailing ends; nothing must be that was not left to chance.

Again the silence fell, as it had done before. Again she felt the nearness of evil, of the power akin and yet alien to her, and the queer rhythm of the running feet, as though someone beat upon a drum. Then a yell arose, and she shivered. They had found their carline. The devil had come, she thought, and chosen in his own manner his own.

There was a surge toward the banefire, and she moved with it, eager to be again near the King. Twisting, running, using her elbows and

hands, she fought her way to the front; the press of the crowd surrounded
her, she found herself wedged between a farmer from the Rhinns and a
farrier who smelled of horse leather. Everyone laughed and jostled and
roared; she could no longer see the King.

Then she saw him. He stood in a clearing with the fire between them
again. He had taken off the dark doublet he wore and the fine linen of
his shirt blew lightly in folds against his body with the draft from the
fire. A man stood on either side of him. Janet began to laugh again. The
laughter rose and choked her and she heard it herself, high-pealing across
the space that divided them, so that as before he looked and then he
laughed too.

God in heaven, thought Jan, he's the carline. The ridicule of it beset
her. Such things did not come to common men.

Afterward, when she remembered that time, it came to her as a series
of things seen, jumbled together in her mind's eye in no order that
would make sense to God or man. The carline's leap she remembered,
the hurtling with a practiced twist of the body through the flames and
landing, a dark shape out of them, clear on the other side. The yells of the
crowd she remembered, and how they cheered him on; a good carline this,
a falcon, a bird, so that for the third leap they piled the flames higher,
and some women shouted that it was a shame. But James Stewart shook
the straight hair back out of his eyes and leaped again, as though he had
a wager with himself, and won the wager; and her pride in him brought
tears to her eyes, as though she had been his. And then at the back of
the crowd a fiddler had begun to tune for the dancing, and she had been
afraid of being taken up by some of the men who were shouting and
flinging their caps in the air, as though they had drunk strong ale. Afraid?
He had not said he would dance with her . . . and then she had felt
herself seized round the waist from behind, and lifted and swung round.

"Good fortune all the year!" someone had called out. And the fiddler
then was scraping out a reel. The red beard laughed down at her; was
ever anyone like this King? She flung herself into the reel with the
abandon of an animal, swinging down the long lines of formal pairs,
catching first one arm and then the other, and always back again to his.
She could feel the hard muscles taut beneath his shirtsleeve; heard, almost, the beating of his heart as they swung round, bodies closely pressed
together, so that the world had faded. She had the fancy that his heart
and hers kept time, so that it was like the other rhythm she had thought
she heard; the unseen hand beating a great drum.

Then a rough grasp was on her shoulder wrenching her away, and the fiddling stopped and the dancing died. She staggered for a moment, regaining her balance, and then saw that it was Gordon, her betrothed, and his face was white. She had no idea how he came to be here.

Grinning sheepishly, the dancers parted. Later they would begin again, when the quality had gone. For now, they were content to watch the set-to, if there was to be one, between Flaming Janet's new young sprig of a lord and their own laird of Lochinvar, whom they knew well enough but liked little, and feared not at all. They looked at the stranger's shoulders and calves and judged him, as a man, more likely to win. He had been a brave carline and they wished him luck, and the lady for prize if he desired it so. They waited, while the two young men stood staring at one another; the carline pale and calm, and my lord of Lochinvar white as a whelk, and gaping. Dear God, was he not going to put his fists up, then, for the lady? They said he was a mother's coddle, old Annabella Boyd back at the gray stone tower had fed him on pap too long, and he had no strength in him. What a lover for Flaming Janet! She'd have him on a string within a week of marriage, and meanwhile look for others. So it was foretold.

"There's no fight," said a woman, disappointed. Were they friends, then? My young lord of Lochinvar had pulled off his cap, and made as if to lout down, but the other prevented him. And then the truth of the thing dawned, and the name of their carline came to them; and after the first hush of awe and surprise for the nearness of king's flesh, the joy of the truth surged up in them and they clustered every one nearer, as near as might be, and cheered and shouted for the King.

Later, the fiddler tuned up again. There would be talk at many firesides that night of His Grace's coming, and of how he danced, in the end, with every wench there and kissed many. And the men, too, had tales of how he had talked and laughed with them and later drunk their ale. None could be ill at ease with him, so gracious was he. "Ah, the bairn!" the women cried. "A true hand and a straight eye," the men said. "A good fellow."

There was that and much else of which to tell; the departure of Flaming Janet and her angry young man was scarcely noticed, except for the stir Gordon had made when he found her horse was stolen. He had rated her like any common chiel and she had answered him in kind; there had been laughter but not between the two of them, and in the end

Gordon had put her on his own saddle and ridden with her away. It was wondered how they would fare and how he had known to come here; and then someone remembered having seen Helen Kennedy ride back across the moor. If she had met him, that poor-spirited little partridge, she would have poured out the tale to him and sent him flying hither. Stout countrywomen shook with laughter; what a tale to tell! And to end it all His Grace, on parting, and before my young codling's very eyes, had kissed Flaming Janet's cheek.

Janet, riding back with Gordon over the moor, preserved a sullen silence. It had been a fitting end to the adventure that her one horse should have been stolen; circumstances conspiring with all else to brand her as a child and a fool. If Gordon's unbearable smugness had not been increased she could have borne it. She stared ahead of her, trying not to picture his face, with that other so vivid in her mind. What had the King said, courteously, as they parted; standing there with his white shirt-sleeves blowing in the wind?

"Bring her to Stirling when you are wed." And the kindly, amused glance. That had infuriated her too, proving that he thought of her now as a child. Small wonder, after what had befallen! And Gordon, who had the manners of a herd, had replied nothing at all but that her mother would have a switch waiting for her when they got home and it was time they were getting there. And then the King had kissed her good-by, but not as he might have done a half hour since. Yet that, at any rate, she could say; he'd kissed her. No one could take that from her as long as she lived.

How hateful Gordon was! She had never been able to endure him even when he was a little spotty-faced boy. The nearness of his body in the saddle irked her; she wanted to draw away.

"When shall we be going to Court?" she said idly. She had been anxious to hit on some topic that would annoy him and also satisfy the ache in her mind, which wished for nothing but to think of the King.

She heard the smug voice. "Those who go to Court do not make hoydens of themselves. You are unfit to go to Court."

"Then you will never take me?"

"Never."

She glanced idly up at him. The flesh of his neck and jaw were beginning to run together in a little roll of fat. His eyes were close-set and the linen at his throat needed changing. She wondered at how little she had thought of these things before she met the King.

"I can't marry him," she thought suddenly. The horse plodded on.

Gordon stared woodenly ahead and she wondered what he was thinking. Probably of the four hundred merks' tocher, two hundred of which had lately been paid. She wondered if he had ever considered her as other than a purchase, put to it by his masterful old mother's urging and the fact that Kennedy blood was the best in Galloway.

Well . . . the King had not known who she was, till Sandy told him. And now he would never see her again. Or perhaps, if he rode in a year or two to the shrine of St. Ninian, he would look to see her as a country nobleman's wife, thickened and dowdy, with her hair shoved under a cap and an infant, two, burping and goggling on either arm. That was what came to women.

And then rebellion rose in her, strong as all other emotion ever felt; and with the awareness of her own power in her she swore, irrevocably, so that no one but herself could hear, and still uncertain of the whole means she would employ.

"I can't marry him."

If she had known, Lochinvar was indeed thinking of the tocher, hurt and bristling, as an animal is, with a series of slights which he imagined and which were brought to culmination by this, the escapade which Helen had related to him when he met her, sobbing and lost, on the moor.

Was Janet a wanton? He had begun to believe that she was. The episode of the Black Loch, of which he had heard only after they betrothed him to her, implanted suspicions in his mind. The placid pink-cheeked women of his own kind that he had met would no more have thought of behaving so than of taking wings to fly, or—or mixing spells as crones did, to be mistaken for a witch! And he, the son of a younger son, had been chosen thereafter to mate with the proud daughter of Kennedy, the foremost lord in Galloway. He didn't like it, and he liked still less the way the Kennedys behaved, as though they were doing *him* the favor in parting with their silver, for the pleasure of ridding them of their wanton girl. He was glad of the presence of his mother at Lochinvar; old Annabella would school her! There'll be no riding out to dance in a common ring with any man that'll take you, or showing yourself naked to anyone that lies by night behind a bush, once the knot is tied, my lady, you may be sure of that, he told himself. Ah, and the way the Kennedys acted, looking down their long noses at him when he rode across their land even now, or when, as rarely happened, he was bidden to the Castle! That rhyme they had running about themselves . . . how did it go?

> No man need think for to ride there
> Unless he court—

Well, precious little chance *he'd* had of courting, never permitted to see the girl alone, hardly acquainted, almost, although they were near neighbors and he remembered her clearly enough as an out-at-elbows brat who ran wild with the stablemen. But now her harpy of a mother had such a mind to her that anyone would think she was a princess in a tower, when for all anyone knew the tower had been scaled already. If it had not been for the money—

"Sandy, what are you thinking about?"

The sudden sweetness of the voice startled him. His betrothed was looking up at him, eyes gleaming oddly between the thick lashes. It struck him that her coloring was unusual; green-eyed, and dark brows with the red hair, not disfigured as so many women of that type were by a bald-faced look and sandy eyelashes. Her skin was good, too, without freckling; the sun and air upon it now had brought a color into her cheeks. She was bonny, he admitted grudgingly. The arm that he had placed frigidly about her in the saddle tightened slightly; it seemed to him that there was more flesh on her bones. Unwittingly, the anger that he had had toward her softened; she had maybe meant no harm.

"Why do you hate me?" said the honeyed voice. Beneath her lowered lashes devils danced. Gordon swallowed; his voice when it came sounded thick.

"I do not." What more was there to say? He had the sudden feeling that he ought to say more and that riding here with his arm about her was not unpleasant. "I—" he began; but Jan forestalled him. She had raised her eyes and the sight of them, clear and limpid, put him out of all countenance.

"Then why do we always quarrel?" she said softly. "Is it to be thus when we are wed?"

"No—no," Gordon stammered. If only she would always be like this! He could not, try as he would, find words to express this to her. He moistened his lips with his tongue.

Jan watched him, her eyes wide and blank. It had suddenly come to her that he was like a stockfish. The wild leaping of her blood urged her on to down him, to destroy that irritating smugness so that it would never rise again; the madness of Midsummer possessed her.

I would have had the King for lover, she thought. With a swift gesture she shook back her hair, and laughed. The tight, closed sound bewildered him, and, seeing this, she paused; laying a hand near his, so that their fingers touched. She talked to him then in everyday words, but in no ordinary voice. Her body lay close against his; she had forgotten her former distaste in the urgency of her wager. Once at her hand's contact he withdrew his, quickly, as though he had burnt it.

At first Gordon tried desperately to save himself. All his life he had run to his mother for guidance; he tried to think of her now, but her image was not in his mind. He was aware that by subtle means a portion of his well-ordered existence was being reft from him with every beat of the horse's hooves. As a last concession to the being that had once been himself, he grasped at the thought that fluttered by; if she was wanton, as they said, was it not his duty to ascertain its degree? There was no man with a right to her body but himself.

He told himself that; and knew that it would make no difference. He was bereft and naked, without means to assert himself or command her; with nothing, except this queer hunger and thirst that drove him on, so that he was no longer himself or even anyone.

His voice when it came sounded weak as a goat's. In the mist that lay before him 'her face drifted like a drowned woman's. Only it was himself that drowned, and not her; flame-capped, wild-eyed, elusive, elfin and lost, she drifted by him, and he sank and followed. Her fingers, cool as snow, lay on his arm.

"I thought they were made of fire," he said, and heard her laugh.

"Can you wait a year, Sandy? It is a long time."

When they came out again from beyond the cairn and returned to where the horse had been left to grass, it was she who led the way. There was a faint smile on her lips; Gordon followed, crimson and ashamed. What had come over him?

"Jan—" he began uncertainly. She did not turn. "What is it?" she said, and climbed into the saddle.

She was up already, and without waiting for his aid! He was near tears; he stumbled to the horse's head, eyes fixed on the ground. Beside him, at the level of his cheek, her left foot swung. At that moment he could not have borne to touch her; he took, miserably, the bridle, and began to lead the horse.

By degrees, as they plodded on, remnants of his lost dignity came to him.

"It was necessary to prove that you were a virgin," he said primly. "If aught befalls, we'll have to marry sooner."

With a shock that drove the blood from his face, he heard her laughter. Amazed, he looked up at her, there in the saddle; she seemed like a devil, with blazing crescents for eyes. Her white teeth and laughing mouth mocked him; he could not believe that, five minutes back across the moor, he had possessed her.

"Who said I'd marry you?"

He stepped back, sobered by the words. Jan twitched the reins from him.

"I did not," she said, "and I do not now. Do you think I'd endure life at *your* pace, a fumbling fool who scarcely knows how to use a woman? Keep your memory for bedfellow—you'll have no more of me!"

A blow, sharp and sudden, made his hand fly to his cheek. With a scurry of turf, she was gone; he heard her laughter borne away on the wind, and saw her red hair tossing. The bleak waste of the moor and his own thoughts surrounded him. He stood for a while, lost and bewildered; then made his way slowly toward home.

II

"No!"

"But, Janet—"

"No, I said! And again no, and no, and no, and I would not marry him were I a dozen times with child and he as rich as Croesus. The man's a fish!"

Agnes Kennedy's gentle brow wrinkled in bewilderment. The summons that had brought her and David hurrying to Castle Kennedy for my lord's conference on this family matter today had set the place in an uproar; they had arrived to find my lord turgid with wrath, my lady vowing vengeance; the servants, scared and sniggering, whispering about the stairs. Everyone had heard about it, from here to Lesswalt, in a varying wealth of detail, but one thing being clear; the Lady Janet had been overset on the moor at Midsummer and got with child, and it was not the devil's but Sandy Gordon's. And now no amount of watching on the part of my lady her mother would undo the harm that had been done; and it was rumored that they would have had her to church with young Gordon with all speed, only that Flaming Janet would have none of it.

Agnes gazed helpless at the cause of the trouble now, thinking how this early home of David's had always seemed to her like a den of bears. She had never, she felt, been so thankful for their own quiet holding at Lesswalt, where they could have their children play about them and David slumber if he would by the fire at the day's end, disturbed by nothing more than the occasional ills of tenantry, or the sickness of a horse. "It looks," she ventured doubtfully, surveying the restless figure on the bed, "as if you must marry him, child. I can see no other way. Why will you not do so?"

"Because he has boils on his neck, and I find him dull of understanding, which makes a man very poor company in bed."

"Surely there has been a fondness between you," said Agnes gently, "or you would not have given him your body. This thing will be forgotten in time."

"There was *not* a fondness between us," Janet swore. She twisted round in the bed; her face was blotched and swollen and Agnes recoiled. "Child—" she began; Janet pushed up her shift and displayed weals, long and contused, on her body.

"Look at those, and see if any fondness would have held out as far. They didn't all use your soft words." Agnes gave a cry of distress. "Ah, leave that, for the dear Lord's sake!" Jan growled. "I would only have you know that nobody shall force me to it by either means—or any other."

Agnes hastily protested that there had been no thought of forcing her. "But reflect, dearest, a little—nobody will readily wed with you in all Galloway, once it is known you have been unchaste."

"No, not with a bigger tocher than my father will be induced to part with, now or later," said Jan, and grinned. She sat up in bed suddenly and hugged her knees. "Oh, Ag, there has been such a cry-and-do over the tocher! The Gordons won't return it, and Father is to take it to Court."

Agnes saw trouble piling up like clouds ahead, and quailed. "I do not understand these things," she murmured. "It is better left to the men."

"Indeed so, women being like cattle and having no thoughts of their own. *I* understand it well enough; old Lady Lochinvar has her hands on the four hundred merks, and will not part with it even for the privilege of not having me there likewise. Who would have thought she would be so loath to be quit of us? It all goes to show that honey, as they say, is no sweeter than gold."

Agnes stared at her. Her mouth was curved in a smile of enjoyment; how could she smile? "If it were I," the older woman thought, "I could not hold up my head for shame." The comparison that David had once

made came to her, of a brilliant exotic bird. How was one to understand
Jan? She turned to the tenets that she knew.

"Everyone will talk," she said hesitatingly. "You would not want to
have fingers pointing at you like any field wench—any slut."

Janet replied to the effect that she would appear in Court and like it.
"Talk?" she said. "Have I ever cared for that? Do you think anyone can
stop it now? Old Annabella won't be done out of her gossiping party
up north! She's talked—her Boyd relations have talked—the Douglases
have heard it and the Huntlys, and the Hays and the Errolls, and the
old tabbies that sit by the fire and God knows who." Suddenly her
bravado died and she slumped in the bed again. "Let them talk," she said.
"I do not design to wed."

Agnes smiled in spite of herself. "You'd not make an abbess, Jan."

Jan glared at her. Suddenly, she began to sob. Tears for her were
rare, even extreme physical pain failing to draw them from her, and
Agnes was touched. Going to the bed, she put her arms around the girl.
"Take comfort," she said shyly. "As you know, I have had children; it is
not, after the first—"

Jan rounded savagely on her. "*That!* My God, as if I cared for that!
I'll have this brat because I must, and there's an end of it! Do you suppose
I want to be like you, a brooding hen? Do you suppose—oh, dear God,
how can I go to Stirling now?"

"To Stirling?" Agnes followed the brittle weavings of that mind in
confusion. "Was Gordon to take you to Stirling?" she asked. "Was *that*
why—"

"You milk-and-water fool, do you suppose I'd sell myself like a cow?
Oh, Agnes, I had at last persuaded my father! He was to take me to
Stirling in November when he goes to render the teinds. You know how
mean he is and how hard I have to cozen him to make him do anything.
And I had done so . . . but now he is so angry he will have no more
dealings with me, and how can I go anywhere in November?"

Agnes was sorry but bewildered. "When the child comes you'll grow
fond of it, and cease to desire other pleasures."

Jan gave a piercing scream, and suddenly sat bolt upright. She looked
so fierce with her blotched face and tousled hair that Agnes retreated a
step, clasping her hands together for support in the wide lining of her
sleeves. She wished suddenly that David were here. What were they all
doing downstairs? Oh, to return to the peace of Lesswalt, and the crying
of sheep as they flocked at the end of the day!

"I've dosed myself with smut of rye," said Jan. "I've tried every damned thing and old wives' remedy under the sun, but nothing will loose it. That's how fond of it I am."

She writhed, remembering the day when her mother had found her with the little dark grains of rye smut in her hand. One made an infusion with them and on drinking it the child was loosed. It had not loosed it and her mother had come to her chamber and Helen's that night and stood waiting with a leather girth in her hands. She had said nothing at all but Jan knew that she knew. In the end it had been as always, with herself doubled over the bed's end and her shift flung over her head, while her mother thrashed her till the strength in her arm failed. And so often since then.

Ah, dear God, she'd kept to her purpose in spite of them, biting her lips till the blood came to keep from crying aloud. "I will not marry him," was all she had said at the end. She remembered her mother's dropped jaw and face highcolored with her late exertions; ah, my lady, she had thought, my will is as strong as yours, for I got it from you. I will not marry him. . . .

She had purpose, but it was uncertain where next it would lead. The answer was given her by Ag's white face. She had shocked her with the tale about the rye. She waited, brows raised quizzically.

"Child, child—you should know nothing of such things! Promise me—"

She came, in her agitation, and knelt by the bed. Jan regarded her curiously. To Ag, babies were precious, like jewels. She'd rather have a jewel any day than a baby. People differed, that was all. There had to be women like Ag. If not, she dared swear, there would be no more men. "Would that be a bad thing either?" she thought, with her tongue in her cheek. There was no one she could tell such remarks to.

Agnes was still talking. "Give me your word—no, your word, Jan— you'll not do such a thing again. These uses are very wicked. I am fearful when I think of what might have befallen."

"It can't be any worse than what has," said Jan cautiously. Suddenly she smiled. "Ag, if I give you my word as to this thing, can I come and stay with you at Lesswalt for a while?"

The voice was the one that had beguiled Sandy Gordon, but Agnes did not know this. Within herself, she saw the peace of their home ruined, alarums and storms composing their days for a length of time unspecified, but certainly till the child was born. Pity for the child wrestled in her, and pity also for the child on the bed she was no more, and so little knowledgeable of what was to come! Who was to say that she would not improve with motherhood, for all that she resented it so

strongly, and before that with affection and care? Agnes felt her own
soft heart betray her, and knew that she would yield.

"If you care to come to us—" she said gently. Her mind flinched from
the thought of what David would say about this.

Jan flung back the bedcovers. "That's good," she said. "Thank God
to be out of this correction-house! I'll have the women bundle together
my things."

She laughed at Agnes, sensing her discomfiture.

III

Lesswalt for a while satisfied her, with its newly won peace which for
her was novelty. She could not last remember when she had passed her
days without the sound of angry voices raised. Here, everything was
different—smaller (Lesswalt was, after all, no more than a farm holding), but in a degree more generous than at home. David might be lazy
and careless as a landlord, but there were not the endless squabbles over
accounts and the price of wine that she remembered, with her father
going over every item sharp-eyed, resembling, so they said, the new King
of England, Henry Tudor, in his shabby long-gown with the old fur collar, and ticking off on his dry fingers each penny spent, as Henry, after
the long Wars of the Roses, had had to do.

David kept open house, not extravagantly, but so that neighbors who
rode by might be certain of an ale draught and a cut at the day's end
from the dripping carcass of cow or sheep that turned for roasting always
by the fire. Lesswalt was not great hunting country and they could not
satisfy themselves with venison as she had heard was the way in houses
in the north; the gentle, rolling hill slopes kept the sheep or provided
them with an occasional hare. To be so near her father's house and yet
as if in a different country amazed her; often, visiting Lesswalt in earlier
days, she had sensed this difference, but never had it been so apparent
as now. Galloway was in her blood, but now there were two Galloways:
the one of hurt and violence, of the gray cairns on the moor, and this—
the silken air, the way the sky turned green before sunset, broken only
by the black winging of birds; kindness and soft voices, that had come,
it was said, first of all with Ninian, the saint who had landed in the
dark times at a point south of here, and built a church and spread his
faith north and eastward over the land.

To that famous shrine of St. Ninian many would come all the year,

even when His Grace did not visit it; and in that way she met again
her uncle, Walter Kennedy, whom she remembered from when she was
a child. She had been sitting one afternoon by the window that looked
out on to the courtyard, watching the sun on the weedy cobbles (David's
servants ate their heads off, doing a hand's turn only when they must,
and the outside of the house was neglected, no matter how Agnes might
polish and scrub within) and binding cream. She liked this task, taking
pride in the manner of changing the cream, swiftly and with an expert
strength of weaving fingers, to butter and whey suddenly, so that the
drops ran off one's hand. The cream was in a flat wooden bowl and she
slapped and wove it, lifting palmfuls from the smooth surface so that it
was whipped into figures of eight. At the same time she watched the
pigeons down in the yard, strutting and idling. They were like Court
gentlemen and the notion brought to her a half-remembered pain. How
far away that time seemed!

Then a voice from the door hailed her and she half-turned in her seat,
thinking it was David or her brother-in-law, Tom Kennedy of Bargany,
who often came. But on looking she saw that it was neither of these
but a tall fantastic figure, darkly attired but with an extravagance about
the lines of his dress which showed he came from abroad. She gave a
cry of delight and nearly upset the bowl.

"Walter Kennedy! Uncle Walter! I thought you were in France."

He possessed the hand which was not clotting cream, raised it in the
tips of his own fingers to his lips, and kissed it. All his actions had the
air of being carefully rehearsed beforehand and more than a little precious. He had grown older, she thought. It would not do to say so.

"I came here to pay my respects to the farmer's wife, and I find the
goddess Aphrodite, risen from the waves and sojourning here, so that
Phoebus shines the more brightly for her company."

"If Phoebus is shining it is the first time for three weeks, as David
would tell you if you had seen him. Sit down by me while I finish with
this cream. After that we'll go and find him."

"Adorable," Walter Kennedy murmured. He disposed himself on the
bench by her and, taking off his beribboned hat, began to fan himself
with it. She found his conversation amusing, being of a kind to which
she had been hitherto unused. In France, and Italy where he had lately
been, she understood that they talked thus in allegory, so that every
woman was a nymph or a goddess and every action initiated by some
virtue or vice. She wondered what he thought of her story; noting that
although her pregnancy was obvious now he made no mention of it. His

glance, worldly and noncommittal, rested on her; the thought that he found her attractive flattered her oddly, knowing that he must have known many women more sophisticated than she, who would respond with his own kind of talk. But now it seemed she was still Aphrodite, and that he had seen her already in the frescoes of Alessandro di Mariano dei Filipepi, the great painter of Florence, who had bound her hair not lately with pearls, as at the time when she rose in a sea shell out of the waves, but with a veil to symbolize motherhood, surrounding her with winds and Graces and the goddess Flora, but none of them so fair as she.

Anger rose in her; he had referred to it, then! He was no better than the scandalmongering old cats who came about here, eager to glance at her and carry the story home of how she looked, and spread it abroad. She looked steadily at him; the temptation came to her to fling the bowl of cream in his face.

"Now that you have gazed your fill, Walter Kennedy, you can go," she told him. "I need neither your pity nor your townsman's talk. You can carry back word to my father that I am well, and to my mother that nobody about here beats me. That that is what you came to do I know, and I am not one to delude with your fine speeches."

She worked at the cream furiously, tears pricking at the backs of her eyes. Today it would not turn, and she thought of the saying they had that ill-luck had touched it. "See, the butter's spoiled," she told him, "you have soured it. They will say very likely that I have sold myself to the devil and now he has got into the bowl."

Flinging up her head she found his eyes resting on her face, shrewd and not unkindly. "If I had thought you a dull woman, niece, would I have ridden out of my way to see you?" Walter replied. "I have no interest in their talk here."

"Then why have you come?" She was still suspicious.

"Why," he replied smoothly, "to give you the gossip of what is going on in the great world, so that when the time comes you will be fit to take your place in it. Do you imagine that you will spend all your life in Galloway?"

Color flamed in her cheeks; she could not believe her ears. "Why should you be so certain of it?" she asked him.

"I have known many women, but never one with bravery enough to flout every convention she had ever known. You will find yourself, but not here. You will not always sit above a courtyard clotting cream. You have taken a lover; what of that? Women need experience as men do. You will take no harm either bodily or mentally from this, for now you are free to live your own life, which you would not have been before."

She listened to him; the shadows grew and lengthened below on the cobbled stones. He did not refer to her as a subject again but talked mainly about himself; her mind listened, storing every fact away as once she had stored the things learned on that brief visit to Edinburgh for the tilting of the Black Knight. She was shrewd enough to recognize Walter as a timeserver, kindly enough but with no leisure to waste on one whom he assessed as of little value; his corresponding interest in herself healed her spirit as David and Agnes' gentleness could never do. Now Lesswalt was a resting place, not a home any longer; hearing of Paris and Mantua and Milan, the graystone walls seemed pitiful and small. Why, to stay here for the rest of one's life would be to stifle! She listened avidly to Walter's talk of the Scottish Court; of the rhyming feud, carried on over many years from many places, which he had with the little renegade friar poet, Wil Dunbar. Dunbar, Walter said, could write in mockery better than any man, burrowing under the skin and biting hard in tender places. No man was safe from his ridicule, least of all the King. Wil had held up His Grace to laughter as the Red Tod in an escapade at Dundee in the very first year he had known him. Often His Grace would reply with mocking rhymes, although not of the quality of Wil's. But then at a season of high festival or at Easter or Christmas, Wil would remember that he ought to be a priest, and would turn out bitter poetry that cried aloud his own self-reproach and the wickedness of the world he made himself live in. One never knew where to be with Wil.

Others he told her of. The Earl of Angus was back in favor at Court after what had been almost a civil war; His Grace, a year or two back, having ridden out with a force to dig ditches for siege about Tantallon, Bell-the-Cat's greatest stronghold, a strawberry-colored castle looking out on the North Sea. But then the Earl had capitulated, it was said, because his ally, Henry of England, proved to be less enthusiastic about invading Scotland than was expected. "Henry has enough ado conserving his own coffers after their late wars," said Walter. "It is like wringing blood from a stone to get silver or aid from him." And now King James and the Earl were on affectionate footing, and the King had sent the Earl a black velvet long-gown for Christmas gift and had later made him his Chancelor.

"The King trusts too easily," said Jan, her eyes narrowed. How like a great child Bell-the-Cat was, out to create a disturbance whenever he did not feel himself sufficiently important!

Walter replied that anyone could trust a cat without its claws. "His Grace stripped the Earl of every Border fief he had, and gave them to Patrick Hepburn, who has served him faithfully. There'll be no repetition of Lauder Brig in His Grace's lifetime. No, Angus is an old dog now; the Chancelorship should satisfy his ambition." And he went on to talk of wider issues beyond seas and how His Grace now, having quieted affairs at home, had turned to those abroad and was said to be pledging his support to the young man from Burgundy, called by his enemies Perkin Warbeck, but said by his friends to be the true heir to the throne of England, the younger of those two sons of Edward the Fourth who were supposed to have been murdered in the Tower.

"Henry Tudor has been no friend to His Grace, and would have kidnaped him into England, with Angus' aid, at the beginning of the reign," said Walter. "France, our ally, befriends this young man; Margaret of Burgundy is for him. Many English, they say, are crossing seas, after finding the Tudor more than they can stomach, or their purses afford. If all these come to lend His Grace support—"

"But if they do not?" said Jan.

He looked at her, with the weary patience of the old in diplomacy. "If they do not, then all will depend on His Grace's pleasure," he told her. "The King is no fool."

Ah, no, no fool, but a romantic boy, beset with the idea of aiding the wronged, willing to risk all in such a cause with the same abandon as he had once challenged a bonfire . . . So she saw him, the coolness that was hers assessing matters of which she knew little enough, having heard nothing except at third hand. She stared idly at the bowl of settled cream, seeing in its surface the face of the King.

She remembered the wars with England. All her very early childhood seemed to be bound up with the sound of marching feet, whether connected with the southern troubles or with the ever-present feud between Bargany and Cassilis, the two branches of the Kennedy family. These had forever fought for precedence, which was not to this day decided; only they had ended it for peace by marrying her half sister Katherine to the son of Bargany, and since then they had all got on well enough. Something of the same had happened in England, where they changed kings often, Lancaster and York and Lancaster again. There had been a lunatic, a lecher, and a hunchback on the throne, and somewhere in between the two murdered boys; and to show which side everyone was on there had been the fashion for wearing red or white roses. And at last they had ended it, or seemed to have done, by marrying the last meek heiress of York to the conquering hero of Lancaster, who had beaten the little hunchback at Bosworth with the aid of Scots troops and ascended the throne in his furred gown, at last, as Henry the Seventh.

And now it was to begin again.

"When do the musters commence?" she asked him. It was a natural question to put, knowing as she did that before any raid could take place there must be an assembly, from all quarters, of as many men as would fight. This was so even in the great Border raids, the King's nobles coming with their hundreds (Angus could raise, it was said, five hundred men in a night) and their arms.

But Walter shook his head and said that nothing was decided yet of musters. He seemed to regret having told her as much as he had, and murmured absently enough about the great reception that the King would give for the young man at Stirling, should he venture on to Scottish soil. "But it is by no means certain yet that he will do so," he told her.

Shortly afterward, he took his leave. She was uncertain whether to despise or admire him, and equally uncertain by whom, if any, he had been sent. A wild hope remained with her that it had been the King; even in the midst of his busy affairs, could he have remembered her?

IV

Walter Kennedy's visit had been brief enough, but it unsettled her so that she was never again able to fit into the routine of life at Lesswalt with ease.

She and David began to quarrel; his easygoing nature irritated her. "Can you not leave well alone?" he would say often, restive like a good-natured bear, and her own lack of gratitude toward him would make her ashamed for a while and then waspish again. She began to encourage the growth of his dislike toward her, seeming as if she took delight in making everything wrong; exciting the children so that they quarreled and cried, exhausting Ag's efforts at peacemaking; doing little enough about the house, spending much time embroidering a pair of sleeves of yellow silk, which Walter had sent her from the ships at Ayr. She found that she had an aptitude for stitchery and took some pleasure in the designs and colors, remembering the things she had heard about the whimsical fashions abroad where often they embroidered sleeves with crests, or with the words and music of a song. She fretted because she was short of money to buy the sewing silks and little glass beads she needed. Even Ag was shocked, saying she ought to be making garments for the child. But Jan had no interest in the child and said it could go through the world naked. Ag pursed her lips and brought out little clothes from her own babies' hoard. She put Jan's awkwardness down to the ills occasioned by pregnancy and nightly prayed that she would be better after the child was born. David was less hopeful.

"As soon as it may be, back she goes from here," he vowed. "Otherwise it's you will have Lochinvar's bairn to rear, and single-handed." He, he added, would be in a madhouse, or a monastery. He felt that he scarcely recognized his own home.

It was in this temper of things that the news reached them at last of the King's summons to spring assemblies of force at Lauder.

David grumbled, seeing in this the doom of his life as a peaceful farmer, although the fact of having preparations to make took his mind off Jan. Everywhere the place was filled with noise, of the sharpening of blunted metal and the buffing of worn leather. The men grinned because there was prospect of loot. None of them were very far away from the good reiving times. Over at Douglas my lord of Angus' men would be doing likewise, but with their swords the less rusty and their armor brighter, for my lord of Angus kept them always ready for the fight. And in the east His Grace the King would be seeing to his great guns, many of which had been made in France. They said there was one, Mons, which could shoot stones the size of three men's heads, which he would have brought down from Edinburgh Castle for the war. Edinburgh, someone had heard, was full now of Burgundians and renegade English, who did not pay their bills and debauched the women. But the young man who was the cause of it all seemed pleasant enough and rode out daily with the King.

Jan heard it all, watching from windows the turmoil below, or walking, as she still did, about the near fields and roads. The fact of being unable to take any part in the preparations filled her with sullen resentment. To be a man, and able to ride south to the foray with His Grace, and feel the swift onleaping of the horse's muscles in response to the pressure of one's own! It seemed to her that she would never know swiftness or ease or grace of movement again; her heavy body, full-bellied now so that even the folds of her cloak would not conceal it, hampered and tired her so that her steps dragged; it was all she could do to walk to the turn of the road, she, Flaming Janet, who had once been able to turn to her will a horse or a boat or her own wild strength and endurance. She swore that never again would any man bring her to this state; no, not even the King.

She did not help Ag with the fitting out of her lord for the muster, and she did not watch David as he rode off, not too unwillingly, to the gathering of his forces and those of others at Kilmarnock. It was some while yet till Lauder, and daily the roads were full of stragglers and parties riding by; it so happened that one of them paused on the road one day, nearby where she was standing, a chattering laughing party of young men and women whose laughter stopped abruptly at sight of her, and she saw that one of them was her sister Helen.

"We're going to Kilmarnock." Helen's voice was loud in self-excuse. Her eyes, surveying Jan, were hostile; they had never had fondness for one another. "My lord of Penkill is taking me with Adam and Jean." She stopped abruptly but the words were almost shaping on her lips. "What a mercy it is you are not in a state to come too!"

Jan arrived back at Lesswalt swearing and raving. "That little hellcat to make a public mockery of me!" She wheeled about on Agnes who seemed bewildered and lost in the deserted house where only children played. "Why in God's name do you not ride to Kilmarnock too? Does David keep company with other women, then?"

Tears rose in Ag's eyes. "David would have taken me," she said defensively. She was not prepared for the ugly look in Jan's, or the swift color that flamed in her face. Involuntarily, she stepped back.

"Then you can keep your Good Samaritan ways and soapsud vows to yourself, for by God I will go as I am, rather than detain you!"

She flung out of the hall, hearing Ag's scream behind her. Instantly the word went about the house that Flaming Janet had run mad. The servants gathered about the stairs, such of them as were left from the muster; some, hearing voices raised, withheld their own and listened, but the rest chattered. Her hour had come, the hour of the devil's own, that was certain; and what was their own poor lady to do? It was doubtful that even if Lesswalt himself had been here he could have prevented it.

"The child will be born in the litter," sobbed Ag. There was nothing for her but to go too. She gathered her courage in both hands and followed the swearing girl to where the bearers, old men who were unfit to accompany my lord to Kilmarnock, were getting the equipage out, quivering and uncertain under the lash of Janet's tongue. There was nobody in all that place who could gainsay her; was there anybody in the whole

of Scotland? The horses that were attached to the litter were badly
matched, one sick and newly out of foal; another was the one reserved
for Ag's use, and it was fresh for lack of exercise. Ag trembled in the
litter, knowing what the men, all of them, were saying; dreading what
David would say, when at last they reached Kilmarnock. She could not
believe that they would reach it without mishap.

Once started, she lay inside, tears running down her face. The figure
at the other end seemed to her a she devil; what could she find to say?
Every lurch of the litter sickened Agnes, fearing what might befall;
the closely drawn curtains shut them in, as if into a world of nightmare.
She heard Jan laugh.

"Take comfort, for God's sake. I'll hold till we get there. For the love
of heaven, Ag, dear Ag, anyone would think you were having the baby,
and not me! Wait till David sees us."

"What have I ever done but be kind to you?" Agnes wailed. Jan thrust
her head out to look at the passing roads. "All's quiet," she said. "Everyone has gone before us."

The roads lay flat and gray in the spring sunshine, backed by green
hills and unhedged fields in which at times sheep grazed peacefully. Comforted at last by Jan's persuasion, Ag allowed her own eyes to
close; denying to herself the feeling that still rose within her, one of terror
and dread. Within the breast of her own gown her beads lay, but she
could not bring herself to find them; it seemed, in some manner, as if
her hands for greater comfort must clasp one another, not moving at all
lest something terrible happen. She prayed that the Mother of God would
forgive her; she had no strength to ask any more. When the sound of
horsemen came suddenly about the turn, and after that the crash of
splintering wood and a shock, as though the world had come to a standstill and herself to trembling doom, she did not feel, for she had won
beyond, surprise. She did not even know whether or not it was her own
voice screaming.

Out of the darkness a face came, then voices. "Mother of God," someone was saying. "Our Lady of Pity, forgive me." It was Ag. Jan heard her
with impatience, beyond the tearing pain in her own body. "If I can
keep quiet, why can't she?" she muttered. Her thoughts seemed suddenly logical and clear.

She looked at the face that had appeared between the curtains and it
was that of a man-at-arms. "Whose man are you?"

Ag broke in with a wail as to what had happened. It was obvious what had happened, Jan thought, full of a swift impatience for fools. Someone had been riding fast and had crashed into their weary equipage, coming round the corner. Someone who had been making for Kilmarnock, or was it going to Kilmarnock? She felt another fierce pain rack her, and strained against it, biting her lips hard.

"Jan," she heard Ag say. "Jan." Hands were about her body. She didn't want hands, was not ready for them yet. She wrenched away. "I said I'd hold till we were out of the litter, but how was I to account for this?" she snapped. Somewhere, a voice was rumbling on about what had happened. She wanted to see the owner of the voice, find out who they had run amidst; why were the curtains drawn? She reached for the near curtain and drew it aside, hearing Ag's shocked rejoinder. "*Jan!*"

"Oh, leave be, will you?" Outside were more men-at-arms, engaged in argument. The sky seemed darkened with armed men, and men on horseback. Chief among them was a man on a great black horse, in full armor. The vizor was pushed up and she saw his full red lips above the concealed beard, and the blue eyes that surveyed her as before with a close-set, hostile gaze; but she would have known from the size of the figure that it was Bell-the-Cat, and from his standard. As so often before in untoward circumstances, laughter beset her. She heard the sound of it and the little, scrabbling sounds nearby of Ag's distress, which made her laugh the more.

The great Earl looked down. His Douglas temper had been frayed by the boredom of peace and of the necessity, after riding hard away from his son-in-law Kilmaurs' castle, of stopping at the junction of two roads for some collision, a landowner's wife in a litter. Why in God's name did women ride the roads in any case? The face he had seen on first scanning the opened curtains had been that of a young matron, comely enough, not one to set the blood rising; and seeing Lesswalt's lozenge on the staples he had cursed the necessity, which he knew would be his, of tursing the equipage into Kilmarnock. But now the curtains parted again and he saw a lovely petulant face, topped with flaming hair. Instantly the demands of chivalry made their impact on him and he alighted from his horse.

Bell-the-Cat's face was close to hers. Bell-the-Cat's little greedy eyes were running over what he could see of her body, having assessed the fact that she was near her time. Agnes was a faded figure in the background, wringing her hands. The men-at-arms waited expectantly. Jan felt the laughter and power strengthen in her again; here was a man like herself. She started to talk to him in the language that he would

understand, knowing that nothing she said would shatter him and that
he would waste no time in behaving like a fool. The knowledge that the
two of them were allies was with her as early as that, when she could
hardly think for pain. "Get me out of the litter," she told him. "I'm
Cassilis' daughter from Lesswalt."

Agnes was wailing about the litter. "My lord can ride faster," said Jan.
Her eyes traveled slowly upward over Angus' huge frame, making him
feel at once a man and her only protector. She had seen a gleam dawn
in his eyes and knew that he knew who Cassilis' daughter was; Flaming
Janet, Lochinvar's wench, who had dragged Angus' own wife's relations
through the law courts with regard to a tocher which they would not return, and refused to let them make of her an honest woman. Flaming
Janet, who'd had every matron in Carrick and Aberdeen in a ferment
talking of her; Flaming Janet, who had sold her body to the devil. And
Angus, whom many compared to the devil himself, would not deny that
challenge. But for now all she wanted was for him to get her to Kilmarnock, or into a bed. She did not know how soon the child would be born.

Angus stripped back the curtains of the litter and with his own hands
lifted her out. She had the swift sensation of complete safety in his arms'
great strength. He wouldn't let her fall, as a weak man would have done;
or hand her over, even, to a man-at-arms. "I can cope with this if need
be," he rumbled, and she laughed aloud and made the promise that she
had made to Ag.

"I can sit on its head till we get to Kilmarnock. How fast can you
ride?"

She saw his grin and Agnes' coif awry, and her worried face poking
from the litter. Then Ag too was bundled up on horseback behind a
Douglas man, and the fact of it set Jan laughing. She wreathed her
fingers in Bell-the-Cat's sewn surcoat for support, feeling the hardness
beneath it of the plated mail he wore. The steadiness of his arm about
her gave her strength.

"Why do you laugh?" said Bell-the-Cat.

She shut her eyes with the pain that came. "Because of my brother
David's face when he sees his wife tursed into Kilmarnock like a bundle
of washing, and myself in fair way to deliver in my lord of Angus'
saddle."

He grunted and dug spurs into the horse, which shot away from where
they had been. Jan gnawed her lip to keep from screaming. It seemed as
if the whole of her body were a chaos of pain, the only solid thing being that castiron arm, so that if it failed her she would burst into pieces.

But she knew that it would not fail her and that she would, somehow, survive this. What was it Walter had said?

She heard Angus' voice, coming out of the darkness that waxed and receded. "Hold hard for the length of time it takes to count a hundred," he told her. "I am taking you back to my daughter who is at Kilmaurs. You would never reach Kilmarnock."

Darkness again and voices, but Ag's wailings had gone. Dimly she saw against the light the coifs of women; the softness of her body and the blessed release from pain told her that she lay on a bed. At times the pain would come again, so that she could not have told whether it was night or day. Often she saw herself as she must have been when Angus carried her in, with the disconcerting habit she had always had of watching herself from somewhere outside. She was limp in Angus' arms and her hair flowed loose and bright over his surcoat; her hood had fallen off with the swiftness of the ride and her lips were bitten and sore. "This is Cassilis' daughter who has been taken in labor on the road. I have brought her here so that you can do what you may."

Angus. The Earl of Angus. She was Cassilis' daughter. No man need think for to ride there unless he court wi' Kennedie.

Laughter, alternating with tearing sobs, caught her. She gave birth to the child between paroxysms of this wild sobbing and laughter. It was a girl and when they told her of it, bringing it to her later placid and quietly plum-faced lying in a shawl, she turned her head away. Even then it looked like Gordon and the thought of him made her sick. Later she became aware of a large young woman with a kindly and broad-featured face, who moved quietly about the room and brought her gruel. This was Marion Douglas, one of Angus' many daughters, who had lately been married to Cuthbert Cunningham, Lord Kilmaurs.

V

Archibald Douglas, Angus, Bell-the-Cat, had started life with the triple advantages of high birth, a handsome face, and an unquenchable ambition. The first benefit had been mitigated owing to circumstances, the second remained unmarred (although he was by now almost fifty he was still considered by many to be the handsomest man in Scotland) and the third lay dormant, like an underscrub fire, ready to burst upward and spread, whenever opportunity afforded, into a conflagration that would with difficulty be brought under control.

His marriage, to a daughter of the Boyd family, had been achieved at a time when my lord Boyd was James III's governor and held in his hand all Scotland. The young sprig of the Red Douglas, as he was then, looked to rise; but soon came the revolt, unexpectedly enough to be an overnight coup d'état, of the gentle dark boy who had been in governing hands since he was nine and showed no signs of having a mind of his own till my lord Boyd was suddenly, and surprisingly, banished by royal command. From being on the edge of power, Angus found himself on the edge of the abyss; and retired, saddled with a wife who had no more attraction than usefulness for him, from any dream or hope of power for half a lifetime.

The Black Douglases went the way of the Boyds. Angus' kinsman, who had betrayed the King again and again and was a name with which to frighten children, was forced into a monastery and died there. Angus sulked and plotted from his great fortress of Tantallon where almost yearly his wife bore him sons. None of these had his great affection except Gavin, who would be a poet. Other times he would ride out and south to Hermitage on the Borders where, in the troubles that arose from time to time, he sent tentative feelers toward England. The King meantime was weakening, his delicate strength taxed and betrayed by his despicable brother Albany to the extent almost of driving him out of his mind; withdrawing himself, more and more, to the company of men who thought as he did, builders and jewelsetters, those who fingered fine stuffs for the love of them or who could put the soul of all music into the note of a lute.

To Angus came the grumblers, and the traitors and those whose hands itched for their swords. His great size and strength and ruthlessness made him a natural leader, and the taste of power was sweet to him. He rode out to war at last by the King's side and hanged the King's friends at Lauder before his eyes, making then a treaty with England and holding the King's person a prisoner in Edinburgh. That he did not make himself ruler then and there was due not to the fact of his own bashfulness but to the affection of the people of Edinburgh for their own Stewart blood; but Richard Crookback, the King of England's brother, came and rubbed shoulders with him. He, a true man and honest soldier, and Albany the rebel, who was neither, and Angus between them, combined a treaty; the end of it was that Berwick was lost to Scotland and Angus scorned as few men had been since Bruce's traitor son.

They would use him after that, but never trust him again. Henceforth his personal strength, his name, and the numbers he could raise, were employed in every revolt against the wretched James III. Angus it was who marched, with others, into Stirling Castle, seizing the fifteen-year-old boy who lay there and forcing him against his own will to set up against his father as King. Angus' signed name lulled the opposing side into false security when their strength was too great to oppose at Blackness. Angus thereafter took charge of the young royal prince, teaching him dicing and some said other things, causing the time to be passed pleasantly enough till it was time to take the marching road again; and then they took the road and it led to Sauchieburn, to the King's battle lost, and to the King's body murdered in a mill. And there were some who said that Angus' had been the hand there too.

He should have been too powerful to oppose. His allies, Drummond and my lords Grey and Lennox, and the dark Borderer, Hepburn of Hailes, who owed him allegiance, should have knelt to him in gratitude as they did in outward obedience to the new King. Yet it was noted that of the depleted treasure in the dead King's black kist in Edinburgh, Angus got his hands on none; that of the titles so richly reaped by all who had had part in the rebellion, notably Hepburn, he gained none; and that in the first Parliament of the young James IV, where Patrick Hepburn was made an earl and the murderers of the late King forgiven, Angus was not mentioned; and that a safe-conduct issued about then to allow him free passage through the realms of England did not mention that, besides the shrine of St. John of Amiens (the ostensible reason for his visit) he would also pause at Westminster.

He kept faith with nobody. What passed in Henry Tudor's closet at Westminster was a scheme for a harebrained plot to kidnap the Scottish King. Henry, shrewdly, committed himself to nothing; Angus was pressed for money. London was full then of refugees from the north, exactly as ten years previously Scotland had harbored fugitives from whichever side happened to be losing in the Wars of the Roses. Among them was a man it was safer for Angus not to meet. John Ramsay had been a boy at the time of the Lauder hangings, from which his youth had saved him and the fact that his mother had been noble. He himself believed that it had been the cries of the dead King.

They met again at Henry's Court. Angus was to remember the eyes, which were light in color and which he had last seen half-crazed with terror staring up at him, the hangman, by Lauder Bridge. Ramsay's voice ever since then had remained high, like a boy's; it was the only outward sign that fear had left with him. Ramsay, Angus thought, was unbalanced now, torn between misery at his poverty under the smallness of Henry's pension and a desire for revenge on the murderers of his King. Angus decided he was safer with Ramsay out of Scotland. All these men had been attainted by order of the first parliament. . . .

He came home. The King received him gladly but without any promise of rewards in the future. They diced several times and Angus found that his pupil was apter than himself. He had pulled strings to inveigle His Grace with the Countess' fourteen-year-old niece, pretty plump brown-eyed Marion Boyd, but although the affair had been so successful that Marion was now the mother of His Grace's son, my lord of Angus was still without appointment.

It was only after his discontent, leading to open rebellion, had led to the confiscation of his Border estates (including Hermitage which the King gave to Patrick Hepburn), that His Grace, as a sop to an old dog, made him Chancelor.

Jan knew a part of this but not all of it, and she learned other things, during her time at Kilmaurs, among them being that David would not have her return.

Kilmaurs himself told her of that, being more greatly inclined than his lady that she should stay on. She knew that Angus had spoken to him and the thought amused her. Kilmaurs was a tall lean weak-faced young man, with eyes like a rabbit and a straggle of beard, an effete edition of the Earl whom he strove to resemble. Everyone in that house seemed under the shadow of Bell-the-Cat. One lived from day to day expecting him to ride in; the meat was basted and the carcasses killed in abundance, as though to feed himself and his followers. Jan was unused to such liberality even at Lesswalt; she could understand that it would make very little difference to Kilmaurs having one more mouth to feed. Of her future situation she was not very sure. Agnes and David had been prevailed on to have her child and its wet nurse back again for the meantime at Lesswalt.

And then? she asked herself. Walter's prediction had been right and she was free. All that troubled her now was lack of money, and she had the notion that this might be come by in the employment of one means.

Bell-the-Cat had ridden in to visit her two days after the baby's birth. She had slept poorly the night before and was troubled by the weight of her breasts, which they had supported with a linen binder. She was glad ladies did not suckle their children themselves; Gordon's child aroused in her the same aversion that he himself had done. She had seen the stout countrywoman they had found carry off the child with a sense of relief; thank God that was over! Then she had slept for four hours and wakened to find eyes watching her, and the Earl standing by the bed.

She blinked; she did not know how long he had been there. The knowledge of her flushed face and tousled hair made her voice sharp; what right had he to stand there, as though he owned her? She made no doubt he had found out by now the rest of her story. Had he seen David in Kilmarnock?

But she made her voice civil as she spoke to him. "I owe my lord a debt."

Angus grinned shyly. "I have brought you a keg of wine," he said. "It's Gascony and I had it from a follower of Warbeck. Don't let everyone drink it. And I brought—" Her words were borne in upon him. "What debt?" he said.

"Why, that at the expense of some horseshoeing, you have saved my child from being born in a ditch. I am grateful to you for that, my lord." She noted that he spoke of Warbeck although he rode forth in his support as Richard of York. How like a child the man was!

She taxed him about Warbeck, and he laughed. "What is it to me if a Flemish popinjay sits on the throne of England, provided I do not have to bow the knee to him? For now it provides His Grace with an excuse for junketings at Court, and riding about Stirling streets exchanging ribbon tippets and white roses." He sat down on the edge of the bed with one leg swinging and looked at her. "God knows where it will end," he said, "for none of us can say."

"What junketings at Court?" said Jan.

Under the covers she moved slightly, easing her full breasts' pressure. Already she felt strong and able to face whatever came; putting, although they were so recent, other happenings behind her, planning to take up the thread again where she had dropped it that day of Beltane. She listened to Angus' voice rumbling on, tolerant with the ease of middle-age toward the feasting that the King would have at Stirling, the dancing to the tunes of fiddlers with the ladies in bright dresses standing in a long line, and the high lawn headdresses that were the fashion now from Burgundy dipping and swaying as they danced, like white moths' wings. She could dance too, if she were there, and had a new gown. She would dance too. . . .

She allowed her eyes to rest on Angus, seeing him dispassionately as the means to obtain her desire. In the coolness of her mind she surveyed the little lines on his face, the way the solid flesh sagged slightly beneath his eyes; the full mouth, too red and greedy for a man's, and the golden hair. The beauty and virility of his great body were apparent to her, and the shape of his hands. He was unlike any other man that she had ever met, but she knew him for what he was to women—a lecher, who would have neither pity nor scruple about casting aside an object which wearied him. And she had borne one man a child in scorn and loathing and she would not bear another. But now Angus was necessary to her. The green eyes traveled slowly upward to his face. "We understand each other," they told him.

Bell-the-Cat flushed and floundered, caught on a hook.

Lady Kilmaurs wept in private but had no option but to agree; she would take Jan under her protection till more suitable plans could be made for her, and she would present her at Court.

Her sister, Bess Douglas, who came in April for a while, had other views. "Father is an old fool," she said roundly. This heresy caused the blood to recede from Marion's face.

"Oh, no!" she said. Bess had never been afraid of the Earl. In her harsh features and with her abundant blonde hair, she resembled him, and she had no sense of humor. Perhaps that was why Lord Lyle's son had jilted her last year; Bess had had a tongue like a wasp and everyone was glad she stayed at home most of the year at Tantallon with the Countess, whose health was poor. But now she was here and would accompany them all to Stirling, where the situation would be quite difficult enough. Marion bent again to her sewing.

"Father is an old fool and Cuthbert a young one. Do not think I have noticed nothing of what goes on, or that I could not have told at a glance what sort the girl was as soon as she came here, and refused to admit her."

"One could not have refused to admit her, for she was in labor," said Marion practically. She folded her lips together to still their trembling. That it was true about Cuthbert she had tried to deny to herself, and she did not know how she was to go on. . . .

"Well, she should have been sent to the kitchens, to have her child there. The Huntlys told me she was more at home there than in the hall in her father's castle, and that she used to run wild with the grooms until her family tried to rid themselves of her to Lochinvar. If Father wants her as his mistress you should insist on a separate establishment. It is an insult to have her here when she is younger than we are. Oh, I don't doubt she knows more than we will ever do in a hundred years! Look at the damask Father gave her for shifts!"

Marion sighed. Perhaps if she were to take Jan to Court someone would offer for her there. In spite of what had happened, she could still feel pity for Jan. She was so beautiful, and had been so unfortunate. Why should not she make a good marriage?

"Ho! A likely thing, with no dowry," said Bess, when she was told. "There's got to be a good deal of gilt on the pill when somebody else has licked it."

Marion winced. Bess had a turn of phrase that often jarred on her.

VI

Jan's presentation took place in summer, at one of the many banquets which His Grace gave for the young man of York. The mellow nights at Stirling were heavy with the scent of Richard's white roses, which showed in every garden and at every lady's breast. For still there were smiles and optimism as the King rode out by day with the young man at his side, buying him gifts from street peddlers and showing him great affection. They would know by the year's end how many English would flock to Richard's standard when he and the King rode south; and although Their Graces of Spain, who were allies of Henry Tudor and greatly concerned with his near neighbors' affairs, had sent an ambassador to try and delay this happening, everyone knew that it would not be for long. And meanwhile the King was happy, as those who knew him well could swear; and this in itself was cause for joy in Stirling, which remembered many things.

Jan heard rumors of all this and saw the Flemings and Burgundians, the young man's followers, about the streets. She found them insolent, ogling her openly in a way that Scotsmen did not do. Besides the debts that Angus had mentioned, they were spreading also a new disease called the pox, which had been met with in England but never yet here. It was moreover less safe for townsmen to go abroad than it had been, for the new arms sent for equipment by the Duchess of Burgundy made the men eager to test the strength of their blades, particularly when they were drunk with wine. Often she would be wakened at night to the clash of arms.

For herself, she was better protected than she had ever been, and came to no harm. Angus' men-at-arms, and often the Earl himself, es-

corted her; stopping at the booths outside His Grace's new church of
the Grey Friars, or down by the harbor where the small ships, having
won upriver from Leith, discharged their bales. Jan had never seen stuffs
of such richness. She spent the days fingering lawn, fine as a dream for
shifts and headdresses, and lustrous velvets the color of jewels, come
all the way from Florence and Genoa and Veere. Angus took pleasure in
her pleasure, letting her buy what she would; often advising as to which
texture would become her, or color offset her vivid hair.

She found him traveled, with a breath of experience which in the
nature of things had been denied her; her avid intelligence drank thirst-
ily, remembering everything he said. It was glorious when a lord or a fat
dowager rode down the street with toes down-pointing from an old fashioned straight-saddle, to be told who they were and who their fore-
bears were, and every bawdy story about whatever had happened to
them, so that although one would of course meet them with dropped lids
it was possible to hurt oneself with laughter inside. It was good also to be
told of events which everyone in town knew and took for granted, although she with her country upbringing had heard nothing of them,
and would have made a fool of herself with some untoward remark, if
Angus had not schooled her.

One subject that she never discussed with him was the King. Of the
reason for this she was not herself very clear. She told herself that she
did not wish to be made known to His Grace, or to see him, till the night
of her presentation; that she wanted to astound him, both with her beauty
and the way it was offset by the gown she would wear, and with the
new grace and wit she had acquired since she last met him. Would he
know her again for the elf-locked creature that had come riding over
Galloway moors? Ah, if he did not, how she would tease him. . . .

Angus also she teased, differently and with reason. Without words
spoken between them she knew that he assumed that she was holding
out against him until his part of the bargain, her presentation, was accomplished. Of the future beyond that she took no thought. His Grace,
the time, good fortune; some of these, or all, would see to it; she danced
to no man's piping, and none should possess her that was not of her own
choosing.

She led Angus on, knowing how it whetted his appetite and made
him easier of persuasion to pay for a new hood, a string of beads, a gown.
The greed of ownership, which was later to show in her so strongly,
dated from those days; lovingly she fingered the rich stuffs and trinkets
he had bought, willing to tolerate him on account of them in every

respect but one. Her attitude to him at this time was that of a pretty, spoiled child; trusting and confiding in manner, as though he had been her grandfather. Puzzled and tormented and beguiled by turns, he denied her nothing that she asked for. The Douglases bit their lips, but could do little except gossip.

This they did. Jan found that her history, the fact that she was the mother of a bastard child, the manner of its begetting and the story of the lawsuits, preceded her wherever she went. At first she was angered, and later amused. Let the old women glance! They very likely envied her. She remembered Bell-the-Cat's tales of some of them and could hardly contain her laughter. Who would be a married woman, compelled to sit and embroider curtains in worsted, like Marion Kilmaurs? Or who would be a girl betrothed to wed to please her family, with no regard to her own inclinations or to anything except the money, which could be made in other ways? No, she had chosen the better part; and let them say if they liked that she was Angus' mistress. She herself knew that it was not so, and she would see to it that His Grace knew likewise. There were so many things that she would have to tell His Grace. . . .

Riding up the steep slope to the Castle on the night of her presentation, with the open flare of the men-at-arms' torches about and behind, Jan looked at Marion's profile and wondered what she was thinking. Although they shared the same lodging it was seldom now that they met, for when Jan rode out with Angus or Kilmaurs, Marion as often as not would bide in her room, by herself or with Bess Douglas, and sew her curtains. Tonight, though, Jan was aware of a dignity in Marion; what was it that made her feel ashamed? I've done her no wrong, she thought angrily. She jerked her head away and began to think of what was to come, and of her gown.

The thought of that gave her satisfaction. It was of green, of the same color that she had worn that day to the Baresse; the fancy pleased her. My lord had brought her a silver net for her hair, got from a shipmaster of the King's returned from Antwerp. What was the name of the master? Barton, Andrew Barton. What did that matter? The net had little moonstones sewn in its meshes against her hair. "You are not the moon, you are a sunbeam," Angus had told her, sliding his hands about her neck under the net's weight, thumbing her skin's smoothness as though she had been a filly for sale. She had let him kiss her cheek tonight for luck at the presentation. Remembrance of his beard's roughness against her face was curiously strong, and she passed a hand across her cheek as though there might be a mark there. But in the new French mirror that showed one's image clear, so unlike the old keeking glasses that she had used to buy from peddlers at fairs, she had seen herself to be without flaw and radiant, as Bell had said, like the sun.

Ah, she would be as fair as any Court lady there tonight, Bell had told her so. . . .

The horses clattered up the rise away from the town. The King's new entry gate that he was building at the Castle was not ready for them yet, and they still had to clamber up the old, narrow, winding Ballengeich Road instead of sweeping proudly under the great new arch with its gray towers. As she rode Jan saw the lights of the town shine out, one, two, four; it was not yet very heavy dusk. A candle at a townswoman's window, she thought, to light her to bed; but she would dance till morning.

They dismounted at the upper gate. By the entrance stood an Islesman, the torchlight flaring on his yellow shirt; the sad-old look in his flat dark eyes surveyed them impersonally. He would have come with John of Isla to attend the King. There was no Lord of the Isles any more, only a name; King James now was the King of Alba. He looked alien and lonely among the throng of chattering men and women.

On and on, through squares and passages; one courtyard, a garden, leading to the next. Everywhere was the flare of torches and the yellow shirts, and everywhere the crowd hurried, talking, laughing, scattering essences and bright colors against the dusk. Once the sound of music came from a high window; was that where she would find the King? Somewhere among the crowd she knew she would find him.

A door opening, the leather curtains swinging back on the night breeze. A room, so brilliantly lit with candles that the colors hurt the eyes. The sound of music she had heard came clearly; someone was playing a lute. She could see the player in a space by the window; a young man in a crimson gown. Outside the night was lavender, pressing against the glass.

"You are ready?" said Lady Kilmaurs to her. Jan saw that she was clasping her hands together to steady them. What has she done to be nervous about? Jan thought. I am as cool as water.

Two figures; four. One she had learned already was the young Duke of York. He was tall and inclined to plumpness, with long lint-white hair hanging straight to the shoulders, and by him, a fair woman, dressed like him in white—the Earl of Huntly's daughter, her own kinswoman, that he had married the time of Twelfth-night. Katherine Gordon looked at

Jan curiously as she advanced; about the room a little whisper ran. Jan heard it, smiling and holding her head proudly. This was her hour, and she was going to meet the King.

She saw him, resplendent in black and red and gold. A king of cards, she thought suddenly. The garter on one of his scarlet hose was fashioned in a little golden knot; she beheld it as she curtsied. Rising, she felt the grasp of the well-remembered hand, and on it the hard pressure of a ring. She looked up. He was as she remembered, only richer, grander; there was an air of calm about him and of happiness. He smiled; he was smiling at her, but not for her. There was a girl by his side with black hair and gray eyes. Jan did not think she was beautiful.

She remembered afterward being led away, but not what he had said to her, or what she had replied. Apparently her presentation had gone well; Angus came up to her, grinning like a bear. "Well," he said, "I've had various inquiries for you." And she saw the courtiers scanning her from the groups where they stood and a dowager asking who she was, and the whispered reply which made the dowager drop her eyes and shrug and turn away.

At the banquet which followed she drank too much wine and watched, from where she sat, the Chancelor at the high table and the Spanish Ambassador and the King. The girl with gray eyes, Margaret Drummond, sat by His Grace and the servingmen knelt to her after him, he and she dipping their fingers in the same bowl of rose water. Every now and again a jewel on her breast sparkled and caught the light; they said the King had given it to her. Jan watched her critically, trying to find what it was that attracted him. She has no color, she thought. Surreptitiously her hands smoothed her own gown.

Later there was dancing and many asked for her hand. She smiled and laughed and talked and danced gaily. She knew that she was tipsy and did not care. Out of the corner of her eye she saw Angus watching, seated in his chair, and laughed again; Bell was too old to dance. The world resolved itself into a ball of mixed and broken colors. Above it all she saw herself, dancing, dancing. It was as she had pictured it all when Angus described it to her and she had seen the high lawn headdresses dipping and swaying in rows like white moths' wings.

Once in a country dance the King came to her. Jan's smile was bright and her laughter shrill. "Are you very drunk?" he whispered. She saw the amusement in his eyes as it had been when Gordon led her away that day;

had he, like everyone else, heard the tale of what befell? She would have told him, but there was no time now, in the nightmare reel that was like, and yet unlike that other, with herself swinging and calling down the two long rows of dancers, and always back to him. But now there was no sound of one heart beating, no rhythm of the banefire drum. He was not hers now. He had never been hers.

She gleaned gossip, the time she danced with others. The King had seen Margaret Drummond last autumn in the house of Huntly when he had gone to the north. He had not told her at first who he was, and this with reason. Some years before, at the beginning of his reign, he had sentenced Margaret's brother to death for murder and sacrilege. It had been an atrocious crime and David Drummond deserved to die, but his sister, who had been a child then, loved him and swore never to forgive his executioner. It had required many months of stubborn wooing on James' part to break down her opposition and bring her here from the fastness of her Perthshire home.

Ah, what had she herself been at all those weary months but nourishing another man's child in her belly, waiting to rid it? If she had been here he might never have had eyes for Margaret Drummond, she could so quickly have enslaved him.

And can I not now? she thought fiercely. Can I not now?

She had never admitted defeat even when it stared her in the face.

She found herself once alone. She had had a partner, but he had gone for cooled wine; she did not care if he never found her again. She stood behind a pillar and leaned against it for support; beyond her vision the fiddles played, keeping time to the throbbing in her head. She had drunk too much wine and had laughed too loudly, and danced too wildly and the night would never end. There was nothing for her now but Angus' hands, to which all roads led. Somewhere about the hall he would be searching for her, lusty with wine. Jan placed a hand to her head. The noise of the fiddlers swam in the redness of the wine.

"You seem indisposed, mistress," a soft voice said.

The veiled contempt of it made her open her eyes. The owner of the voice revealed himself as a young man; it had been so soft she thought it was a woman's. He leaned his shoulder against the pillar by which she stood, the light showing up his clothes as threadbare. He wore plain dark dress in the fashion of England, relieved by a pair of sleeves of black, embroidered with green chevrons. His hair hung dark and lank. His eyes, surveying her, were light and not pleasant.

For some reason she did not wish to look at the eyes. She dropped her own, and the man laughed. "You do not know me," he said, "but I know you. You are Lord Kennedy's daughter from the house of Kilmaurs."

"I am not indisposed," she told him. It seemed of importance suddenly. A strangeness had come over her body, as though a draft had chilled it. It was like no other feeling she had ever known.

He was not young; and yet in years he might be so. Five-and-twenty? She was not sure. He had the look of one who is old through what has befallen him rather than through the growth of time.

That is what is so horrible, she thought, and realized that he was still talking.

"Who are you?" she asked him. He smiled slowly.

"Once Bothwell, now John Ramsay only. Will you dance with me?"

John Ramsay. Ramsay the Bastard, Johnny Ramsay. Where had she heard the name, whose variations had a familiar sound, here, among these walls, among the Court? Angus had not mentioned it to her . . . no. And she remembered.

Angus had almost killed this man once. Angus had held a noose about his throat, snarling with the pleasure of the kill, once at Lauder. All the other favorites of the late King had been hanged but Ramsay had escaped. He was only a boy, they said, and so they set him free. He had remained a boy still, all mind-growth frozen in the horror of that waking dream; the sight of the swinging bodies, the sound of high crying in his ears. He had clung to the King through all the wars that followed, and his loyalty led after Sauchieburn to his lands' forfeit, even the title of Bothwell being taken from him by the rebels who had seized the throne. The new King's conscience, it was said, would never let him rest until he brought John Ramsay back from exile. Why then should she regard this man, this unfortunate and loyal man, with dread?

She remembered that he had asked her to dance.

"No," she said. The thought of his soft, bitten hands touching hers made her sick. She turned suddenly and fled out of the hall, threading her way through the group of courtiers to the door. Behind her she heard his laughter.

Once she had found the outer air the hammering in her head ceased, and she stood for a while till common sense returned to her, sensing still the drowsy smell of melted wax which drifted from the hall.

It was brilliant moonlight. The clear-cut world contrasted with the one she had left so sharply that she welcomed it, walking on alone among the silvery squares and the lace-black shadows of the King's implanted trees. Lovers walked across the stones of the courtyard and murmured in the darkness of the arches, and she scowled and hurried on lest they see her and laugh. She was alone, as she would be; unless for Angus or the man with green chevrons. These were her lovers, and the King had gone.

She had come now to the ramparts of the Castle. The great dark shapes of the King's seven guns thrust blackly forward from the wall. She felt them, running her hand over the cold metal. She would be sober if she was cool.

She left the guns. A little way along there was the King's garden. One came to it by the high path along the ramparts, seeing below, by day, the little velvet lawn. Even here white roses grew, closed now against the night's coolness. She could see the pale shapes thrusting, patiently, like folded hands.

Someone stirred below and she saw that there were lovers there. The moon's light shone on a silver gown and on a thread of scarlet and gold. It was the King with his mistress, thinking themselves in sight only of the moon. She saw James' raised head for an instant, heard his voice as it deepened to comfort the girl. Neither of them had seen her.

She's afraid, thought Jan fiercely, the fool. Her hands clenched suddenly. If she, she, had been there with him! He was saying words now in a voice such as she had never heard, words no one had ever used, or would use, to her; with that queer protection, shutting out all the world, tenderness wrapped about them like a cloak. . . .

All the world. The world was watching them. She did not know when she had seen the watcher first or if she had always sensed someone was there. She did not know when she had first looked beyond the tree, above the town where lights shone. The moon was the only light here and it shone on a man's eyes, pale and evil so as to make her afraid. They had seen her and had not moved; and the man said no word at all.

She ran. She gathered her skirts swiftly in one hand and dropped silently from the wall like an animal, making no sound as she landed on the path below. Then she was stumbling and running and panic-stricken and lost, not pausing till she had put all space between them, the man and her, the world and her, the lovers who thought they were safe from the world. She heard her own breath tearing and sobbing in her throat, and her heart beat loudly. Among the Castle outbuildings she paused for breath, and then found the wall between one dark shape and another. Against the coolness of the wall she laid her cheek, and breathed in the damp smell of moss and stone and tried to shut out the horror of what she had seen.

They were not safe. King James and his love were not safe, there in the garden.

He thinks he can protect her, she thought. He thinks that if he hears a sound he will get up and cross the grass and find the reason, and if there is need he will use his sword. But there is nothing that can be ended there with swords, any more than the world will stop spinning if a man's hand thrusts it. Always they are watched and never safe, and she is afraid because he sees nothing. Ah, was it the wine in her that made her think these things? The evil eyes that watched from beyond the tree had not come there with wine.

It was then she knew who had followed her. Always wherever she went now he would follow her. He knew of her and how she had watched the King; John Ramsay, no longer Lord Bothwell. He would not leave her free to spread her story about the town. No, he would find her, with his eyes that stripped and assessed her; as though he saw her naked, but without desire.

That was why she was afraid of him. There was no warmth of feeling in him any more, in the frozen desert that was his mind only memory being left, hatred and the desire for revenge. If he had ever loved it was a dead man, a murdered man who had been tall and gentle with dark hair, a King who had been kind to him. And now no other kindness, not even love, could warm him again; he would step without pity on every obstacle that impeded his way to the goal, and would use any instrument that offered itself in the way of assisting that intent. He would use her, this man. He would use her for any ends at all.

He came walking slowly across the darkened stones and the thought crossed her mind that he was the devil come for her, and she grasped the ledge of the wall with both hands lest she should be seen crossing herself and he laugh at her for a fool.

But he did not laugh and the light shone on his face, so that his eyes lay in shadow. Seen thus his face had pathos and helplessness, like a young starved boy's. She wondered if the dead King had seen him so and taken pity on him, and if this King also remembered and had brought him, against all advice, back from his exile in England where he had been for many years.

These things she remembered afterward. For now she waited, until he should speak. Behind them the doors and the little dark alleyways were empty; here, at the back of the Castle, nobody would come on them for long. She knew a shudder of fear. Would he throw her down, over the ramparts, for what she had seen? Below, the rock fell sheer into the darkness, and they would say that she had been drunk with wine.

But his voice when it came was gentle, containing no threat. "They are still there," it told her. "They heard nothing."

"Why were you watching them?"

Her voice was dry; she hoped that it did not show she was afraid. John Ramsay laughed. "Why were you?" he asked her.

Suddenly he drew near so that she was pressed against the wall. Anyone watching would have taken them for lovers. He began to talk to her, softly and urgently; the words had a biting clarity even in the high soft voice. "They say," he told her, "that those two in the garden are more than lovers. They say—"

"What? That he has married her? I know, I heard it tonight. Why should it concern you?"

"Because it concerns others. Whether it has taken place or not—"

She sneered. "You are unsure, then?"

"—there will be no Drummond Queen on the throne. My lord is too powerful already."

Jan considered it. There had been Drummond queens before in Scotland. She had seen my lord Drummond tonight, talking to Bell. He was a shrewd thin man with a sallow high-boned face and white hair. Swiftly she accepted the broadening of her thoughts' field; it was not, then, a simple matter of man and maid. The issues involved intrigued but did not frighten her. She heard John Ramsay's next words without surprise.

"The King will marry Margaret of England."

"Henry Tudor's daughter? But the young man of York—"

"Will never be King in England."

She watched him, seeing the thin lips in the moonlight smiling faintly. She knew that he must be well enough versed in affairs to be sure of what he was saying, and contempt in her for him rose strongly. To feast here and dance on the King's bounty, to make ready, like every man, to ride south, all the time knowing that there would be no victory!

How many are like him? she wondered. She remembered the English knights that had come with Richard from abroad. Were they such that their own country would gladly receive them? No, they were timeservers, adventurers; living well now at the Scottish Court, glad enough of a place to lay their heads until it was time to move on. Henry Tudor, shrewd Henry, was king in England and would remain so. The White Rose had been conquered by the Red.

She listened to what Ramsay told her, briefly, of Henry's daughter. The analogy amused her; a little girl of five! Henry, it seemed, had offered on more than one occasion her hand to King James, who had refused.

"James is aswim in a sea of chivalry in which white roses are reflected together with the face of Margaret Drummond. He pictures Richard and his own cousin Kate on the English throne, all trouble ceasing on the Borders and peace abroad. That is a dream and it will not be so. England and Spain hold the coming power. Henry Tudor is a canny man with a clerk's mind and it will not be with swords and courage that wars are henceforth conducted, but with pens on paper. Henry will wed his son to Spain and his daughter to Scotland and have no concern with broken hearts."

The Spanish Ambassador had been here tonight. He was a little dark man with a face like a mole. Everyone was watching, she thought; from all over Europe, from France and Burgundy and England and the black lace shadows of the Alhambra at Granada. She felt like a very small cog in a great and relentless wheel. The wheel turned, turned. What would Ramsay do with her? What did he want to do?

"You want the King," he told her. The spoken fact dropped with cool brutality into the still air. Jan felt her knees weaken and her hands tremble. Yes, she thought, yes.

"Then do as I will tell you."

She stared at him, seeing in him a power beyond that possessed by men. She could guess nothing of the thoughts that went on behind his eyes, or what the outcome would be.

"I will take you back now," said Ramsay.

They walked back side by side, their arms hanging straight, hands not touching. Always they were to have this dislike of physical contact one with the other. She heard the wind rise in the little dark alleys; the moon was high in the sky and its brilliant shadows had gone. After death, she thought, it would be thus as she walked, no color anywhere, and alone; she hoped to God she would be alone, or else where would God be? If she were to walk then with John Ramsay it would be on the road to hell.

And then another shape came out of the darkness, a great long-robed figure, with the faint light glinting on a heavy shoulder chain. Angus and Ramsay faced one another; she heard the indrawn breaths.

What was it about the silence between those two? There was something there she did not understand. Dear God, had they met again since the crazed day at Lauder, with a man's high screaming in their ears and behind them the trussed bodies dipping, dipping, as the ropes jerked above the swirling water?

She covered her face with her hands; she could bear no more, she thought. If Bell killed Ramsay now, she would be glad; he might also kill her too. Nowhere about the Castle was there any sound; the music had stopped and everyone had gone. How long had they been there, back among the shadows of the outhouses?

But neither spoke. There was a low sound from Angus that was like a snarl. Then Ramsay was gone, quickly, a shadow; the sound of his feet died away. She was left facing Bell, and he with her; he took hold of her wrists.

"Angus," she said. "Angus." After that other he seemed suddenly wholesome. He looked down as though she had been a stranger.

"You tainted slut," he said to her. Raising a hand, he struck her across the mouth.

She stood where she was, the shock and pain coming dully, as though she had been drugged. "Take me home," she told him. "I have not been with any man."

The hair of his head and beard seemed to bristle, she thought; he was like a boar lowered for the kill. "Have you not?" he said. "*That* was no man. But I've searched everywhere."

"You knew him," she said. "He was afraid of you."

"Ay, for I nearly hanged him."

He moistened his lips with his tongue, thinking how no one knew of that later encounter in London, with Ramsay swearing on the naked steel to be avenged on the late King's murderers. That one of them was himself had mattered nothing, then; the hatred fastened on His Grace, the heir to the bounty; God help His Grace if Ramsay had his way! "He should never have been let back over the Border, but His Grace would have him brought; for love of his own father who loved that rat, so that His Grace imagines he has wronged him. But Hepburn has his title now and lands, and he can do no harm."

Yet he himself could fear Ramsay a little, knowing that he was aware of that visit to Henry Tudor, all those years back, when he should have been at Amiens. And yet . . . it was likely the King knew! His own day was done for treading lightly, he was too old. . . .

Thoughts of his age brought him back to her and he remembered his desire for her, shouldered out just now by hatred for Ramsay but returned, as strong as ever. She was like no other woman he had ever known and she had fleeced and tormented him. Tonight she'd pay. "You know what I would have of you," he muttered, and moved furtively; she felt his breath, heavy with wine, on her hair. "Jan, Jan, it has been over long . . . you know well, my red vixen, my comely one, my torment . . . you promised me, tonight, that I should not wait longer. I am not used to wait so long . . ."

She lay against him, everything in her crying out to resist, but that would anger him; the thrusting, lecherous hands made free of her body. "Not here," she whispered, trying not to add, you fool! "When we are home. . . ."

"Ay, and at home you'll deny me, as you have always done. No. . . ."

"Would you take me against my will?" she almost screamed. She saw him glance round; he was afraid, she saw, with a little touch of scorn, for his Chancelorship. "When once we are out of here," he said coldly. "Fetch your cloak."

She left him, hurrying on to where the Islesman guard waited; once with her cloak wrapped about her, she felt warmer and more secure. Once she could gain Kilmaurs' house there were those she could waken, who would protect her. She was resolved that he should not have her body. Ramsay would lead her to the King.

On the way home Angus talked with bravado, the words ringing loudly in the deserted street. She made herself play with him to keep him in humor; leaning up against him in the saddle and twining her fingers among the beryls that studded his great chain. "You'll not get that from me by any whore's trick," he told her. His narrow eyes glinted possessively, dwelling for a moment on the gold. "That I drew from the neck of Cochrane, the dead King's mammet, at Lauder before I hanged him; that, and his hunting horn, that had a like stone in the end."

He laughed. The theme coincided with his mood and downed the late fears of Ramsay. He told her, taking delight in it, the story of the Lauder hangings. "The King loved a fiddler and a mouthing poet and a piper and a tailor and a mason. I hanged them, seven of them, all in a row like sprats. The King himself was kneeling to me to spare them, but I would not; only Ramsay I spared." He paused, wondering at himself; why had he spared Ramsay? Then the importance that he had been rose in him again, making him forget it. "I could have hanged the King himself," he said, "had I had a mind. And, mark you this, in the end—"

She stopped him; fear of what he would say next made her voice sharp.

"You would have been hanged yourself, and may be yet," she told him. After her late experience the street seemed full of watching eyes.

"Not I," he told her. "The King's murderer is the King, none other."

Steady, steady, the clipping of the horse's hooves; grayly the dawn showed, now, a little, between the watching houses. Say nothing, her mind told her, but wait. Everything will be known if you wait.

"He turses a great iron chain about his waist in penance," Angus grumbled. "*That* is proof enough—" He turned suspicious eyes on her. "What interest have you in it?"

She shrugged, and smiled easily on him; making him tell her again of how, since the Lauder hangings, he had been known as Bell-the-Cat. "There was no other man would hang the bell about the cat's neck but I!"

"Bell-the-Cat," she murmured, as they reached home. "Bell." Her tone was half caressing, but when he carried her into the hall of Kilmaurs' lodging she whimpered, and turned her head away.

"I am tired," she told him. The hall was dark. The men-at-arms who guarded him had long since gone about their business, everyone having their own this night of the King's feasting. He left the clatter of grooms to lead away the horse, carrying her himself upstairs to her chamber. Her weight in his arms was queerly light and she had no more resistance than a child. Angus did not stumble as he mounted the narrow stairs.

In the chamber a taper burned and her woman, who was also Marion's, was absent. Angus laid her down on the bed and stood over her, seeing that she was already asleep. Her breath came evenly and her face, with the tears still wet upon it, showed wan in the faint light. The tumbled hair lay darkly on the pillow; her silver net, that he had bought her, had one of its lattices torn. Oddly, pity rose in him.

Poor young bitch, he thought. The feeling drove out lust in his mind. He moved uncertainly, moistening his lips again with his tongue. To take her now would be easy, he thought; why did not he? Something, an emotion to which he could give no name, struggled in him for recognition; he, the Red Douglas, who had always known and taken what he desired, giving no more thought to it thereafter.

If he had ever loved, this was his love; this wanton child, a girl younger than his own children. He did not know it, even by its name, as such; later, as he could tell even now, he would curse himself for a fool. In his mind at this moment came no thought of his own youth, or of the way he had put aside all thought of love for political advantage; if the chance came now, he would do the same again. He had never known love, except for himself; and now in self-denial came nearer to it than ever before, or after. But there was no one to tell him so; for Jan, asleep behind weary eyelids, the world was dark and blank.

The Earl took the taper and snuffed it. He was bewildered by the turmoil that his own actions had aroused in him. Quietly, he turned and stumbled from the room, pausing to call her woman on the way. Jan slept on, warm in the dark folds of her cloak. Outside, the silver night abated, and the colors turned to dawn.

VII

The King was to march toward England in mid-September. During the rest of that summer there was dancing, hawking, feasting and merrymaking at the King's palaces of Stirling and at Falkland, where Richard of York for a time had residence. Everywhere the Court moved, Jan went too, under the protection less now of Angus than Kilmaurs. She was like the fair tumblers who walked with reckless bravery along the surface of a rope stretched tight and high in the air, deeming the money worth risk. She lived every moment of these days to the full; the misery of her presentation night was forgotten. Radiant and beautiful among that court of many fair women, she had her own circle, her escorts and those who sang her praise. Walter Kennedy gave her his patronage, letting her be seen in his company among the young poets of Stirling or the capital, when they moved there; songs, in the stilted manner of the day, were written about her grace at the dance or her fearless riding, which had won praise even from the King one day in the green Woods of Keir.

But these songs were forgotten by reason of their shallow roots, another being sung long after which had arisen before her coming, that late spring. On Tay's bank after the snows had melted the King had watched Margaret Drummond, and the song he made held phrases whose wistful unsatisfied beauty wrung the heart when greater poems were forgotten and other songs unsung. Every now and again a minstrel or a player in a corner would strike the notes of that elusive, haunting strain; always, she would think that the first hot resentment of hers on hearing it had died, but always it came to her as strongly as ever. For now she knew that the King's passion was more than a passing fancy and would endure; it did not need John Ramsay to tell there was nothing for her to achieve.

He still kept his hold over her; she wondered why he troubled. Their place of assignation was in the Grey Friars' Church when the Court was at Stirling; it was almost the only place where she could meet him unexplained. She would be kneeling with her beads between her fingers, hearing the sounds of women muttering prayers, and Marion's coif with its broad wings of lawn between her and the altar, with lit candles guttering in the heated air and the smell of incense mingling with the scent of flowers. Then often Ramsay would slip in beside her and kneel also, and under cover of the muttered responses to the prayers he would whisper gossip, and, sometimes, instructions to her; she began to remember him most clearly by the wooden beads slipping through his hands.

"Drummond is with child," he whispered. "She took a bout of sickness at the Spanish Ambassador's departing, and was unable to accompany His Grace and them all on the boat." Or again, "The King has sent Drummond spices, sugar and mace and cloves and saffron, from the ships at Leith." Or once, "The King will ride foremost of all in the train of guncarts and gear at his departing; the whole of Edinburgh will be there, and Drummond on her balcony to wave him farewell."

Always Drummond, fanning her hatred; even interspersed with other things. He it was who offered to procure Jan a balcony stand in Edinburgh for the King's departing. Everyone of note would be there, he said, and she would do well to persuade Kilmaurs to bring his wife and her household from Stirling to the capital before it was too late to find houseroom. Jan felt a stab of anger override the suggestion's usefulness; she disliked his reference to her influence over Kilmaurs.

Where his own influence lay it was hard to tell. His appearance, as on that first time she had seen him, was that of a man hard put to it to pay for bread; but he dined at the King's table free. He lived, she knew, always in the cheapest of lodgings, having no dependents except a white cat. Yet for a man so devoid of friends he had one who was worth many; the King loved him, as his father had done, and well as she had studied the King she could find no logic to account for it. Johnny, the King called Ramsay, speaking always gently to him as though he were a boy; having him always near his side. After the notoriety of his late exile had died down His Grace would, she dared say, load him with titles and land again to replace those he had lost. And Ramsay would accept all this and still not love the King.

The streets of Edinburgh were full on the day the King left. Above on balconies the ladies crowded, in a stirabout of mingling colors with round hoods pinned securely against the autumn wind. The white roses were almost over now but here and there they showed, threaded in a

gown or tied to a pillar, as though this had been a festival. Jan wore them,
standing at the front of Todrick's balcony. Todrick was a merchant with
a house in the High Street and had, oddly, married the King's cousin, the
girl-bastard of Lady Daisy whom Jan had missed seeing that day at the
Baresse. By this means John Ramsay had known of him and approached
him for the place for her; Ramsay himself would not occupy it for he
rode with the King.

The balcony was warm with the scent of close-pressing bodies. Jan
leaned out, fastening her fingers about the twined pillar for support;
below, the heads seethed and folk jostled one another. From every window tapestries were hung, their colors blending with the colors in the
crowds. They deck their houses as though it were a wedding, she thought,
not a war.

Jan's hand strayed to the bosom of her gown. On the opposite balcony,
her women about her, Margaret Drummond stood. Jan scowled, pretend-
ing not to see her. Today she could pit her beauty against any other
possessed if the King chanced to look that way; Drummond's skin was
sallow now and the blue cloak she wore neither enhanced her color nor
served greatly for concealment. She's plain today, Jan decided spitefully.
Everyone knows by now that she's pregnant. Why make a show of herself
standing there, when she would have been better to stay at home?

"They are coming," someone said.

Far away a cheer arose, coming down the street like a wave. With it
the sound of hoof beats grew.

His Grace came first, on a black charger; his coat armor was of crimson
taffeta, with blazoning of gold. Beside him rode the young Duke of York
on a white horse. A fairy boy, thought Janet scornfully. It was hard to
imagine that flawless silver armor begrimed with the smirr of battle, but
no doubt James would do the fighting as he had paid for the armor.
Above, the banner of York waved, red and blue and gold.

They passed below the balcony. Janet leaned over and threw her rose.
It struck the King squarely on the chest. He looked up, caught it, and
laughed, the teeth flashing below his vizor; said something aside to York,
and then rode on. Later, he searched from side to side of the street. Janet
stood still, eyes shining, hands clasped to the place on her breast.

"He missed her," she thought. A dancing devil that was her mind
turned and tumbled. "He missed her. He missed her, my pregnant-lady-
on-the-balcony. He missed her because I made him look at me. I made
him look at me."

Angus saw her, riding by on his powerful chestnut; the memory of her as she appeared then was to haunt his mind for long. He rode on sullenly, vizor lowered, thinking how she had had no farewell gift for him on the eve of his going to war. He and Kilmaurs, riding close together so that their knees touched against their horses' flanks, would not turn their heads to meet each other's eyes. That was what she'd done to them, Flaming Janet, and he made little doubt Cuthbert had had as much earnest given as he. Bitterly he recalled his folly in not possessing her. Unless he perished by force of Henry Tudor's cannon, in which case she'd be less likely to regret him, he swore he'd have her yet.

Ramsay saw her, surveying with a little mocking smile the picture she made on the balcony. "Let the flower bloom," he had told her, "the petals are almost fallen." She'd stared at him with the hard look in her green eyes that showed she pretended not to understand. But she understood well enough, which was why he made use of her; women of intelligence and beauty without scruple were rare. Yes, he had her in his hand, but not as that old lecher with the golden beard would have had her; his, to shape or mar, a sensitive instrument on which to play, but with toughness, he thought, enough in its strings to withstand this Scots winter. And then? Why, then, when he returned, riding by James' side (for that the Duke of York would be displaced he knew, having to hand all the intelligence from Henry) why, then, Flaming Janet should cool her heat, and in the service of better heads than hers.

At first when Ramsay had come from England he had sworn to kill the King. The charm of James and his generosity, coupled with his feelings for Ramsay himself, had destroyed that urge in his mind. Now instead there had grown resentment, both that a man should disarm him with kindness and that the King should be so happy. He had not been such a boy, Ramsay thought, at the time of his father's murder as not to know what was being done.

No, the King had no right to happiness, in love or any other. Against Ramsay's breast a medal lay, the size of a great crown piece. Concealed beneath the linen of his shirt he would at times cease to feel it, but never forget it, or the gentle face portrayed there, oval-shaped under a hat with a high crown. That that dead King would have been the last to show petty spite did not deter him; the reality of his idol had been lost in the lean years' misery, being now no more than a shadow in his own unbalanced dreams. So Ramsay hated Margaret Drummond because she was the instrument of the King's happiness; rejoiced at the anguish plain in her eyes for all to see, now that the King had ridden off without waving farewell. That women set store by such things he knew, and cared little. He rode on, eyes watching straight ahead, thin mouth smiling. He was already forming the words in his mind of the dispatch he would write to Henry Tudor concerning this march south.

VIII

The five young women who sat sewing did so in silence, nothing being heard from outside but the patter of heavy rain. It darkened the golden color of King James' palace towers, seen beyond the window of the house in the long street of Linlithgow where they sat. Hills and sky and streets were cast in a leaden gray, as though the gloom occasioned since His Grace's return with his army several weeks ago had spread to include the weather and the very air of the room.

Jan raised her head and looked coolly round, making no attempt to break the close-lipped Douglas silence. The bright sleeve she was sewing lay smoothly in her hands; idly, she stroked at it with the needle. Little Eliza Douglas, who had been lately married to Bell-the-Cat's second son, had ventured some while ago a remark about the prettiness of it; but the others had descended on her with swooping beaks and she had been made to feel almost an outsider.

Poor little Eliza sat stitching drably at some garment by the side of the fire. An occasional flicker lit up her face when the rain spat down the chimney and showed it pertly pretty. She was an heiress, and for some time now the Douglases had been fighting over her tocher like dogs over a bone; the outcome was still not decided. If they lost the tocher Eliza would fare badly. All was fair in love and war but gilding sweetened everything.

The green glance shifted to Elizabeth Drummond, the wife of George, the Master of Angus; a harassed matron with a large and growing family, over which she brooded as continually as a hen. Nothing that she said at any time was regarded by anyone, but being Margaret Drummond's sister she had acquired a vicarious importance. The dull light from outside filtered through the lattice on to her faded face, and the small nervous movement with which every now and again she would push back the straggle of fair hair which always strayed from under her cap. Everything about her was dull and dun, Jan thought; Ag would be like her in five years' time if she bore David as many children as Elizabeth had borne George. One of them, a small girl, played on the floor about the women's feet; a placid silent fair child, with Bell's narrow eyes set disconcertingly in her head and liable to accost one suddenly with their straight, non-committal gaze. They did so now and Jan was reminded of the time long ago when she had stared out Bell-the-Cat. The memory of that tilting and what befell aroused in her hysterical laughter; anything, anything, to break the silence of the room!

"Ailie," said Elizabeth gently. "Ailie, your mammet."

"My aunt has been crying again," the child announced. "Why?"

Everyone broke into immediate talk except Marion, who stitched calmly in spite of her swollen eyes, and Jan. Jan and Alison Douglas were worthy of one another's steel and should have met in a mutual generation where they could have dispensed with age. As it was, Jan regarded her sleeve. Bell's granddaughter had stared *her* out and won. She listened to the chatter which resumed about everyday things.

"I could not avoid bringing her," said Elizabeth breathlessly. She dabbed the mammet up and down in front of the child's eyes, bringing no other reward than a contemptuous stare. "She is not fond of dolls and says she prefers horses. Archie and she plague the life out of each other and I am always glad when he has gone back to St. Andrews."

Eliza Douglas asked timidly how Margaret Drummond was. "Oh, well!" said Elizabeth, adding that Margaret was going home to Drummond Castle soon to await the birth of her child. "I walked in the garden with them yesterday at the Palace, the King with her. They were saying what a pity it is that the cherry blossom will not be out; she will miss it when she goes to Drummond, but the King says she shall have the cherries to eat when she comes back again."

I wonder how long I can stand this, Janet thought. I wonder how long it will be now before I shall be forced to admit I have failed, and take myself back to Galloway.

They would rejoice to get their claws in her, she thought, all of them in the room. The spinster Bess Douglas was staring at her with hooded eyes. As soon as she had gone the heads would fly together, drab crows tearing at the remembrance of her flesh, leaving her no shred to cover her.

Always, women would hate her. It did not matter that she had done nothing more than ogle Kilmaurs. That she had had to do for money, for she was short and Bell no longer gave her any. Bell, always watching her, often in his cups; he and Kilmaurs ready to fly at one another for her cause. . . .

What was she to do? There was no one.

The King and Margaret Drummond walking up and down Linlithgow paths, too early for the snow of blossom, cared nothing for her; why should they? They would be watching the swans on the calm water and thinking what to call their child, not even remembering Richard of York, who was out of favor now. Richard like herself out of favor, Richard like herself no longer welcome to live on another man's bounty. They said he purposed crossing seas since the failure of the Northumbrian war and that his wife would go with him. Should she go with Kate Gordon as waiting maid; and see the spires of Burgundy?

"Or an Irish bog, maybe," she thought wryly. There was no saying where that might end. This was a time of waiting, as though the whole of England and France and Europe waited like Drummond for a new birth. And she, she, she could do nothing.

A frigid voice; the servant at the door. "A young lord below," it said, "to see the lady."

Jan rose. "With your permission," she said to Marion. Before the door closed she heard the crows' parliament begin. She picked up her skirts and descended the stairs; the woman trailed grimly after.

"This way." The voice was like iron. Heavens, did even the servants hate her? At the turn of the stairs she met Kilmaurs. He stood watching her, hat in hand, flat against the wall; his tongue passed, nervously, over his lips. The servant stood, dour and solidly waiting; when Jan moved she would move. "This way," she might have said again.

"Holy saints, am I a criminal?"

The thought fired her, and she determined to give them something to talk about. Flaunting her body, she smiled at Kilmaurs, dropping her eyelids as she passed. There, let the flat-faced Boyd woman take that back to her mistress! She felt the rabbit's eyes follow her, ensnared.

But therein lay danger. She could not continue in this for long. As always in a time of need, there was sent to her a way to circumvent it. When she opened the door of the lower room it was to see Ramsay standing there. The rain dripped from his cloak.

She stared at him. Of late he had avoided her, and she had taken this to mean that her usefulness was finished. Swiftly with the sight of him came anger that he should have come here; did he follow her openly now? She stayed by the door, her fingers resting on the latch; the servant, satisfied, had gone away, and she could hear the footsteps dying away down the flagged passage into the distance.

"What do you want?" she asked him. "There's press of work upstairs."

"With Lady Kilmaurs? My congratulations."

The soft voice mocked her, as always. Why did she have the feeling that he knew of everything that passed in her mind?

There was a chair in the center of the room. She went and sat down on it, disposing her skirts unhurriedly. If he had anything of importance to say, she thought, it could wait. Finally she sat back, hands gripping the carved arms of the chair, and regarded him.

"Well?" she said.

Ramsay smiled. "It is some time since we met," he said. He had taken his hat and now shook it, thoughtfully; the wet sprayed out from the dripping plume on to the floor. "When there was nothing to say to you, I said nothing," he told her. "You cannot say I ever buoyed you up with false hopes."

"You?" she said. She began to laugh. Ramsay watched her, waiting, arms folded, till she had finished. It was as though his determination to reach one goal had made him impervious to any insult. He met the look in the green eyes squarely. "Shall we admit that we both have our limitations?" he said.

"I'll admit nothing, till I know what you've come for. I do not care to have you hanging about here."

Ramsay flicked at the feather in his hat. "It may not be necessary for us to have converse again," he said coldly.

"Thank God for that! Why so?"

"Because of—circumstances becoming the more favorable."

There was a pause. She sat and watched him, her eyes bright and wary like those of a bird. He came and bent over her suddenly and began to issue instructions, in the crisp yet soft-voiced manner she remembered; she could not endure his nearness to her and shrank in the chair.

"I do not come to you for the pleasure of it, but of necessity," he told her. "If you would serve yourself, do as I say now. There is an exile from England of the name of George Nevill. He came here in the service of Richard of York."

Jan nodded. She knew Nevill, a big loud-mouthed dark man who was often about the King.

"Drummond goes home at the month's end. She will not return immediately. If the game is played to the full she need not return at all. My lords are at one in opposing Drummond and in fostering the English marriage."

She moved; his intensity scared her vaguely. "What do you want me to do?" she said again.

"Hear me now," said Ramsay. "Some days after Drummond's departing, Nevill will give a supper party at his lodging."

"At which I am to be a guest? I hold myself honored."

"You, I and some four others; and the King."

Jan was silent. Into her mind had come the remembrance of His Grace the many times she had seen him. Did they think that with Drummond gone only a few days he would be the easier of access? She doubted it; the quarry would not be snared.

She said as much to Ramsay. He smiled, one finger stroking always at the sodden plume. "There are ways of overcoming a man's judgment," he said, "with good company and with wine, James has had—some long spell of domesticity, and every man, unless he be a saint, is human, Jan."

"Unless he be a saint? A devil!"

She rounded on him, hearing his laughter. "If you'll not play, there are others will serve my purpose," he told her. "Do you suppose that in this net that reaches widely there is no one caught but yourself? Think of the alternative, my dear; how long can you withhold Kilmaurs? And after that, what will be the outcome?"

She was silent, thinking how he reminded her of a white slug, a crawling thing; making its way between curtains, over walls; finding out what should not be known. Or was it as the ignorant supposed and there were men who found, by divers evil spells and customs, what passed in others' minds?

"It is nigh on twenty years since the Earl of Mar was tried, and he a warlock," she told him. "Do you also make wax images and stick pins in them and utter spells? The filth that blows about the roads is cleaner than you. Why should I do what you ask?"

Characteristically, he made no reply to her, now that he was sure she would do so. Briefly, he told her in a few words the hour and the night and the manner in which she was to reach Nevill's lodging; "and for the rest," he told her, "leave it to me."

Then he bowed curtly and left her.

After he had gone she found that she was shaking, not now with her fear of him but with the knowledge of what she had consented to. It was like a denial of any power she had ever possessed; a denial, almost, of her own identity.

At Nevill's lodging on the night arranged those met who were to bear His Grace company to dine, and as always when the King ate among

friends the talk about the table held a good deal of laughter and wit
flowed with the wine.

Nevill's man had piled logs in the hearth against the chill spring night
and now, with the flames drawing high, the room grew warm. Janet could
feel the heavy perfume of the musk she wore rising to assail her, and that
and the wine she had drunk made her, in the heat, feel sick. They had
all dined well and, she thought, drunk too well, except Ramsay; who was
sparing and nibbling in food and drink like a rat, as though his years of
poverty had caused his capacity to narrow. And His Grace, of course,
drank always so little that never had any man seen him the worse for
wine.

Jan had come late. She knew of the impression she created, as Ramsay
had intended her to create it; this was a different air from the Douglas
house, and the women here were such as Marion and Bess would have
no traffic with. She looked at them, lolling about the table; Nevill's mistress, in grape-purple satin, her face flushed now and laughing to show
her black teeth. The English all had black teeth because of the sweeten-
ing they put in their wine. Nevill had his arm about her and was sweating and laughing too. It meant a great deal to Nevill to have the King
here tonight. He was, Jan had decided early, a fool who knew nothing.
His great laugh bayed out, congesting his short bull neck and suffusing
his eyes at something the King was saying. "That Twelfth-night? Ah!
Ah! And Will to dance in mockery before the King of Bean so that his
priest's belly danced too under his gown. And later we all ran out masked
to the house of—who was it, Your Grace? Who was it?—and kissed his
wife and—"

Laughter. More laughter. The King's face was alight with it. How he
gave himself up to gladness, loving company, feeling safe among friends!
It did not matter that Nevill was a nameless exile without a penny to
bless himself with, so that the bill for this supper would very likely come
back to the chief guest. James leaned now, glass raised, back in his chair,
with one hand flung over the carved arm; the doublet he wore was of
black and crimson, a jewel flashing as he moved. To watch, she thought,
was to betray her love for him; this boy, whose pale high-boned face and
red hair were so little changed from that first time she had ever seen him.
Always he would be a boy to her, the world and all its laughter in
homage at his feet.

She lowered her eyes. Who was she and what was she, that she sat
here? Around the table the flushed faces and jeweled chains winked; the
feeling she had had once in darkness of walking with Ramsay along hell's

road was with her, strongly; this was hell, the porter-gate to feasting with the damned. Now the wine rose strongly in her, reminding her of that other night; Ramsay's soft voice was in her ears, plying her with more wine, bringing, with an unobtrusive flick of the hand, the servant near when her glass was empty. He would have bribed the servant, Nevill's servant, to do what had to be done.

Did Ramsay relish his own power, then, feeling his fingers tauten the strings, knowing that with a jerk given, a signal, they would all dance? She turned, suddenly, and looked at him, as though in the full knowledge of her mind his outward appearance would change with what lay within, giving him horns and a tail like the pictures she had seen in old monk-books of the devil. But still his profile, pale and fine-drawn by contrast with the grossness of Nevill's, betrayed nothing, and watching it she felt less fear because from here one could not see his eyes.

A pale girl out of Falkirk, and a young man, Spens, made up the party. Jan could see Spens sprawling, mouth loose and heavy with wine, across his chair by the far end of the table. A lock of sleek fair hair fell over his eyes. He was a tenant of Angus, a young laird from Kilspindy, and since his coming to Court for the first time this year he had made enemies with his fool's tongue and with the quickness of his sword. There was neither good nor harm in him, Angus had said. He was a dull dog and would not have been bidden here at all except that the man intended could not come.

Staring at Spens' square-featured and still boyish face, she heard the talk continue. It seemed to her that she had never been silent for so long in company as now, never so deserted by such wit as she possessed, never less herself, for what that might be worth, as tonight. Her gown was limegreen and of the stuff called sarcenet that first, it was said, had come from the East with the Crusaders. Its swirling lightness made her movements graceful and unstudied like the fairywomen in tales, or the nymphs and goddesses in the frescoes of Walter's Florentine. A ribbon of silver bound it under the breasts and the neck was cut low, displaying her white flesh; the sleeves puffed and slashed cunningly after the manner of Italy and the overskirt looped to show an underskirt of silver. It was a gown Angus had paid for and she had never worn, and now that she had done so she felt it showed her for what she was, or would have to be—a whore, who might as well have come naked, and worse than that, for honest whores took a man only in possession of his will. No, she could not do this thing, and she would find, in some manner, the way to circumvent it . . . ah, but she must do it or what would become of her?

Spens smiled aimlessly, his moist glance dwelling on the low-cut neck of her gown. "How is it with you?" said Ramsay to her; his voice sounded close in her ear. "Don't drink the hippocras."

He turned away, smiling, and began to say something to his neighbor on the other side. George Nevill and the King were discussing George's cook.

"You're fortunate," said the King. "I never could obtain—"

"Neither a Frenchman nor a Savoyard, but one of Your Grace's own—"

"What, a Scot? And to have knowledge of spices? I will take him from you, George, and he shall come to Linlithgow."

"Does Your Grace deprive me of my only possession?"

"No, by no means, you shall dine every day with me. . . ."

Jan began to see the faces blurred, as often with objects seen very close at hand. The servant was coming to the table again; he bore a flagon with a beaked silver lip and, bending assiduously over His Grace, began to fill his glass. The talk at the table swelled and died and began again, and His Grace held his glass up to the light so that the candles sparkled through it and began to talk of the curious, clear, beautiful, interweaving strands of milk-glass that one found in the ware of Venice, and of how although the French traders had spent half their country's gold in trying to filch the secret there was still nothing to be got from France but worthless imitation.

"And Murano, the sacred island, remains inviolate."

Nevill's mistress crammed a fruit into her mouth. No one here cared for rare glass or would have aught to say besides that it remained less durable than horn or silver for flinging over one's shoulder after having drunk deep. Nevill laughed uncertainly and said that he had nothing so fine but indeed, he had heard, there was much to be got in loot by the troops of French King Charles, bringing back cups and gems and studded gold all stuffed in the capacity of their lined leg-drawers when they came back over the Alps from Italy. "One should be there," he said sententiously, "though it is said the Italians put up no fight."

A little frown came between the King's eyes. "We must content ourselves then with the flavor of the wine." He raised his glass, bowing gravely to Nevill.

"Don't drink, Your Grace. The wine's drugged."

There was a sudden lull. George Nevill gave an exclamation, and half rose in his seat. James paused, the glass suspended halfway to his mouth. A moment, and then one eyebrow flew up incredulously; he smiled, with closed lips, at Janet's flushed face.

"You malign our host—madame."

He raised the glass to his lips. Janet could never clearly remember what next happened. A force compelling her which was herself, yet not herself, made her limbs move; swiftly, above the hum of comment, there came to her ears the tinkle of breaking glass. Then, in a sudden clearness, the sea of astonished faces; herself, leaning across the table; the wine spilt on the cloth, and on the King's gown, spreading darkly like blood; her own hand, grazed, as she found later, and bleeding freely; and shining fragments of glass everywhere; and a man swearing.

She began to laugh hysterically and the voices swelled to a roar and drowned her. There was a sound of benches being pushed back; herself seized, and set in a chair. "The drunken bitch," a man said. Jan heard it and sat and laughed on with a hand over her eyes, so that she saw nothing at all.

Then a gentle voice, a soft voice, speaking for her. She could not hear the words and did not wish to hear them, and she turned her head toward where Ramsay was and screamed out a torrent of words; what they were she did not know, only the force beyond herself was still compelling her so that she had to scream aloud.

And then someone came and stood over her and slapped her face, once, twice, again, hard, so that the sudden shock was like cold water and she stopped the noise she had been making and began to cry, quietly, like a child, with her face between her hands.

"She will do now," said the King. "No, John, I'll take her home."

She was walking swiftly down the street and someone had put her cloak round her shoulders, and the orange flare of the torch the servant carried streamed back the way they had come with the wind and the speed of their going. Everything was cooled and swift-moving and washed by the night air and wind, and her own hair blew about her, shedding the scent of musk that she recalled, but cleanly, as though it were only in that room that the evil made everything stale.

Their cloaks, her own and the King's, were swirled about them. The King's face in the flaring light was etched against the darkness like a coin.

"You thought I was drunk. It was truth I was telling you."

"Honest, then," said James Stewart.

She gave a hard laugh. "Make no mistake as to that—Your Grace. I'll confound myself in the morning. I'm only generous when I'm full of wine. Ask anyone who knows me."

"Why were you there tonight?" he said. He made no response to her bravado.

Tears rose unbidden, making a burning in her throat. "Why will you have me as different from those other women?" she said. "Do you not know of me and what I am?"

"No," he said. "Tell me."

"Any dowager'll do that. Do you never listen?"

He smiled into the darkness, his face at once mischievous and withdrawn. "I am of that following of the new thought that believes only what it has seen, and discards nothing as valueless until it has been proved so, and strives in every way to find the secret that has the name of life," he told her. "It is nothing to me whether you have been wanton or whether you have not, and your reasons may be your own and these I know not. I remember only a fire on Galloway moor and the best of company."

"Ah. . . ." Did he not know of the conspiracy against him?

Suddenly he became grave and turned to her so that the shadow of the hat he wore concealed his eyes, showing only the firm mouth to her, and the bearded chin. "Whoever was with you in this night's ploy I know not, but it would not in the end have served, as I think you knew. I will ask you no more but that you do not lend yourself to such a scheme again."

"Your Grace is—trusting."

"Some say too much so," he said wryly. She wondered how much he guessed of Ramsay. Surely, surely, if he suspected even a tenth, he would not keep the man about him!

"Do you believe me incapable of doctoring my own wine?" she said, to tease him. He answered quickly; did she believe him incapable of containing himself in a roomful of whores? And then they laughed together and she felt gladness overwhelm her, making her blood like wine.

They were approaching Kilmaurs' house and its windows were dark. The thought of warning him against Ramsay came to her and then left her; he would not, this King, hear a word against any man, or hearing would not believe. What did Margaret Drummond suffer, knowing without proof of the dark forces assembled against her, and able to show nothing of it to her lover who trusted every man?

The thought of Margaret Drummond stayed with her, marring her pleasure in the King's company, and making his trust in her worthless. He had entered Kilmaurs' hall with her and they had candles lit; and cloaked still, for the room was cold, they stood facing one another in the faint light. She stood looking up at him, hands hanging straight by her sides, as she had done that day two years ago. The memory of that came back to him, shutting out the time between; it was so long since he had thought of any woman but one that he was like a man who blinks at a sudden lamp's brightness so that he cannot see his way.

But meantime he was rather touched than otherwise at her loyalty and the fact that she made no attempt to ensnare him.

"You are an unfortunate child, are you not?" he said. "Go home, and I'll arrange a marriage for you."

She was silent. He frowned.

"What is your desire, then?" he said. "I owe you a debt; I admit it freely."

"My desire?" She stood very still. "Do Your Grace grant me that, I'll die content."

Suddenly, irrationally, amusement welled up in him. She was like a child, standing there in the candlelight. He could see the pale oval of her face and throat, rising from the dark cloak that might have been a man's. It came to him that there would be no harm in what would content her; it would be no more than kissing a child. He bent, and brushed her lips.

There was no accounting for the thing that happened.

It was often said, less then than later, that Janet Kennedy was a witch. He, who credited nothing beyond the senses and natural things, with the exception of the faith which was to him a part of himself, was beleaguered now; the transformation from child to woman without words spoken or muscle moved, to something more than woman, an elfin enchantment, a flame-pillar, was before him; he could neither explain it away nor, as at that time of Beltane, resist it; it was suddenly as though, with his mouth on hers, a fire burned within him. He remembered, before his senses left him, other things; and flung her back, so that she staggered against the wall.

She had an instant's memory of him, face white as paper, an arm flung across his mouth where her lips had been. She thought that she would never forget the reproach in his eyes. He brushed past her silently and went out by the door; the candles flickered with the draught of his going.

She waited, crouching as she had been where she fell back against the wall. Her breath was coming in small high gasps. Presently she began to cry, noiselessly and with intensity, while her hands clasped and unclasped themselves against the wall's unyielding strength. She groped her way to the chair, still crying; and sat there, she could not have told how long, while the tears dried on her face.

Below at the foot of the stairs, Spens had watched the King go. He was still hazy and uncertain from the strength of the wine, and when the torch had burned out he had not had it relit. His Grace, in any event, had said no word.

His Grace would not be waiting till morning.

He groped his way upstairs. He knew the room from which the King had come. It had come to him with a compulsion that would not be denied that he must go and offer his services to the lady with the red hair. That she was Janet Kennedy he knew, and often he had seen her with my lord of Angus and others riding abroad. But never had she seemed as she had done tonight, with the fair flesh glowing and beckoning within her gown's thin folds like fruit among its leaves; and never had he seemed to himself so bold as now, with the splendor of the hippocras that he had drunk in Nevill's house, so that his heart was as a lion in him. He could defend her against all comers, he thought, even the Earl of Angus himself; no man was better qualified than he for her service. All night this thought had grown within him, ever since he had watched Lady Jan across Nevill's table, drinking wine. Now it was so strong it moved his limbs for him, guiding his hand to the latch.

Jan heard the latch click and for a wild moment thought that the King had returned, but when she saw Spens she gave no gesture of surprise; if Angus, anyone, had come in at that moment she would have received him. She listened to the mouthed words dully, no longer seeing Spens' face. This is the end of my life, she was thinking. This is the end, and I am back where I began; and tomorrow I go back to Galloway.

The light shone on Spens' sleek hair. Anyone, she thought, to drive away loneliness. Last time, and this; was she any better than a whore, all told? She had been honest, and her honesty had brought her nothing; if at this hour she had held James drugged in her arms, she would have been better off.

Well, there would be no more honesty, and no more relenting of heart. For one like herself there was no course open but the one; to take the moment, such as it was: the experience, for what it offered. To watch for tomorrow was to look into darkness; should she not have known that?

Women without scruple were rare, John Ramsay had told her. Perhaps there was a curse in her stars.

A babble of words brought her back to Spens and her glance swept

idly over him. He might have been anyone, but she saw that the light
shone cleanly on his hair and that his body was not gross yet or old.
He knelt on the floor in an attitude of total subjection; his hands scrab-
bled at the silver pirning on her gown.

Her lip curled. "You can stay," she said. She turned swiftly and blew
out the light.

Next day, she rode back into Galloway.

Part Three

MARSH LIGHT

1497–1499

I

HELEN KENNEDY was frightened.

She stayed crouched down between the brown cow's place and the wall. In the straw, the eyes of the new calf regarded her. Its coat that had been matted yesterday had dried out now to a roughened tan-and-white fluff.

In the bowl four eggs lay. She had gone round the places where the birds sat, thrusting deftly under each one in the way which she could do because they knew her. She had always been good with hens and animals and could bring the brown eggs out and place them without getting her hands pecked. That was one thing she had always been able to do, whereas Jan—

Helen clutched the wooden bowl to her, meeting the calf's stare angrily. Why must she think of Jan here, the only place where she was free of her? Jan couldn't cozen the swiftly pecking birds the way she had cozened Adam.

In the peace of the byre Helen saw Adam, his rough black hair cut short for greater ease under a casque and the way his white teeth showed when he grinned, the eyeteeth longer and pointed like a cat's. She had been glad when they had betrothed her to Adam, whom she had known all her life; it would be, she thought, like going from one home to another to Penkill, which was not very far away and where Jean, who had always been her friend, would be her sister.

But now everything was spoiled and the black horse, Suleyman, which had Arab blood in him, was for Jan's use and not hers, to ride down into Whithorn.

Helen pouted, in the way she had used to do when she was a child. What right had Jan to interfere and behave toward Adam as if . . . as if . . .

One hand stole slowly up to her throat. Jan and Adam—Adam and Jan. It had been, she knew, out of revenge for that other day, the day she, Helen, had been coming home past the wood, and happened upon them, Jan and the man Spens, who came here often, riding all the way in haste from the east coast till his horse got in a lather. Their mother had tried to get their father to stop it but my lord said leave her be. . . . And there Spens and Jan had been, that day, and she had heard before she saw them the greedy sound of their kisses, and Spens' flushed face as Jan twisted away from him and round to face her, that showed he had been drinking again before he came to her. And then the devil-may-care look in Jan's eyes, the same that had frightened even their mother so that she no longer dared to lay a hand on Jan as she had used to do.

Was Jan a witch, then? Many said she was . . . and stole out by night to pick herbs, especially at the right time of the moon. Helen, who slept in the same chamber, could swear that sometimes Jan did go out, although she had never followed her, being afraid.

But if she told Adam of these things he would only laugh, or think she was jealous.

She remained staring into the bowl where the eggs lay, seeing the faint speckling on the surface of one with an odd, clear intensity, to be remembered afterward. Often the old women who knew of such things would foretell the future by the casting of an egg into a bowl, seeing the shapes that the white made when it floated on the water, but she had never had hers cast and now she was afraid to do so. Everything now seemed to be colored with fear from the time she woke to the time she lay down at night. It had not been so before.

It is the same for all of us, she thought dully. What had happened to everyone in Castle Kennedy? Before Jan had come back from town it was pleasant, things going on in the way they had always been used, only with fewer scenes and more peace now that her mother and Jan were not always at loggerheads about every least thing. Of course there was the child, Janet, who had come over from Lesswalt at Yule, and every so often Lochinvar sent money for her maintenance; but she was a quiet little thing with brown hair who gave no trouble, and nobody would have known she was Jan's. And then suddenly Jan had come riding home, with a pack of splendid gowns and no money, and no suitors for her hand in spite of all the grand tales from town, and the hope they had had that at least the Earl of Angus would set her up as his mistress. And since then everything had changed and grown queer and unpleasant, with that man Spens who rode often down and the other, who was shortly to be their neighbor because of land given him at Kirkandrew by the King. But Jan, it seemed, shuddered at sight of John Ramsay, and he had not come back more than twice on a visit to their father, after drinking with him the customary flagon of ale and talking, in his high soft voice, of the plans for the new house he meant to have built nearby.

Helen had never found out why Jan was afraid of Ramsay, and she was too much in fear herself to try. It wasn't that Jan had done anything fresh to make her afraid. She hadn't even said anything beyond answering when she was spoken to and an occasional sharp word to the child. And she had taken to the spinning tasks their mother set her without a word, also—and now by the hour would sit and spin, spin, while no one could tell what thoughts were going on behind her green eyes. Helen began to hate the sound of the wheel, having whenever she heard it a picture of Jan sitting there.

No, she had said nothing, and it was Helen herself who had burst out with angry reproaches, ashamed after what had befallen that day in the wood. It hadn't been the first time, as she knew also and told Jan. But Jan had only laughed in the shrill way she had, leaning against the doorpost with both hands on her hips as though she could be there all day.

"Your nest egg is safe, little bird; leave tocherless sparrows to their own concerns."

Helen replied primly that it was her concern, as how would she feel if Adam heard of it?

"Will not Adam eat of the forbidden fruit, then?" said Jan. Her eyes glinted mysteriously and Helen was uncertain whether she was laughing or not. She thought the remark in poor taste and said so. "We're not *your* kind!"

"No, poor mammet, you're not." The tone was full of pity.

Helen bridled. "You do not make me envious with your tales of Court," she said. "Where has it led you? Nobody will wed with you, there any more than here; and even the Earl of Angus wearied of you and did not offer for a settlement, as Father expected. And now there is nothing for you but to make a show of yourself with common men, for tell me not Spens is any more, though even he—"

"Wearied of me?" said Jan.

She advanced toward Helen. "Do you spread that abroad with your tattletale tongue, or aught else, my weasel in its burrow," she told her, "I'll give you proof that no man ever wearied of me, and that there is none who will not dance to my bidding if I choose—not even your Adam Boyd!"

And so Helen was frightened.

"I am no great hand with a lute," said Adam Boyd.

Jan watched him as he knelt there, one lock of rough dark hair falling over his eyes, and his square-ended fingers tinkering earnestly at the pegs that bordered the lute. The notes at last fell thinly on the warm air; in the corner, near the fire, a dog dozed. Outside it was raining and pleasanter to stay here, doing nothing, with one's feet up on the long-saddle that fenced the hearth, while Adam tinkered with the lute.

Her eyes rested on Adam but did not see him. He was a pleasant lad and she found him restful company. His adoration would never grow tedious as did Spens'. She frowned a little and wished that she could dismiss Spens from her mind; his tainted breath and unsteady hands were beginning to make her afraid. At first she had tolerated his riding down here to see her because of the news he brought, at a time when he was almost her only harbinger of news.

She shifted a little, casting off the memory of this last year, herself bogged down, as it seemed, for ever in a dreary round of bake and mend and spin. Seeing no one, hearing nothing, going nowhere, shunned by most; the prodigal returned, unwelcome, without either honor or a husband. She could see her life drag out year after thankless year in a gray Galloway marsh, until she grew dull and old.

Had it been any wonder she had been grateful to see Spens? To have him come to her, after his frenzied ride across half Scotland, eager only to see her again, to cover her face and breast and arms with kisses, to possess her . . . and he was young, and from the gay world she remembered, and she had given herself to him again. And now with the passing of time they had become necessary to one another as the damned are necessary, their bodies' urges having no other satisfaction but in the fulfilment of a need, although he had bored her long ago. She could watch their damnation from the outward place wherefrom she had always watched herself; seeing him killed slowly, body and soul deteriorating in the desperate need which she herself had created and fanned so that in the end he would be hardly a man at all; and she would go on draining the life out of him and ripening in the accretion of strength experience brought her; a succuba, who fed on men.

Idly, her shoulders moved within her hair's warmth. She had washed it yesterday with birchbark and the fragrance still lingered. Why did I trouble, she thought wryly, when there is no one to see? The consciousness of her body was strongly with her; firm-fleshed, smooth as fruit, clear and with warmth in the hollows. She had never been so fair as now, nor would be again; she had put on flesh this past year and every vestige of coltishness and angularity was gone. She could feel when she rode abroad the desire of men reach out like clutching fingers, their blood warmer for the sight of her, and the sun darken when she had passed. The power in her made women afraid.

"Did I ask for this?" she thought wearily. She listened to Adam, strumming at his lute. That boy could kneel there hour by hour and take no harm for all of her, only she would torment Helen who was a little fool.

No, what she wanted was not here, was very far from here, and she could do nothing except wait, and waiting every year grow older. She turned over in her mind the last news Spens had brought her; poor Spens, clutching at every least thing to keep the boredom from her eyes.

"Drummond has borne the King a daughter." No, that had been Ramsay's voice. Ramsay was here at Kirkandrew and she dared not think of him. . . .

"The Countess of Angus is dead."

Poor Countess, no more important dead than alive, immured all those years at Tantallon. She had done her duty and then lived too long so that everyone was wearied of waiting, and her lord had not made any pretence of being a sorrowing widower but had ridden off at once with the King to a justice ayre in the north.

"The King will ride down to Whithorn when he returns from the north."

And that had brought joy and an upspringing of hope such as she had not known for long; and the gray days, the dreary days, were lit at last by a lamp so small it still seemed like a star.

She too would ride down to Whithorn when the King returned from the north, and whether he would or not he should remember their last meeting.

Adam Boyd remembered the King's visit that year chiefly by reason of three things: the childish behavior of Helen, his betrothed; the skittish behavior of the Arab colt; and the dazzling, exasperating, unlooked-for magnificence that was Jan.

He could not remember when it was that he had decided the colt should be for Jan. All his life had been bound up with horses and he understood them like women and on watching the vital, black-bodied, vicious beautiful thing—at first untameable with its wild mane flying, until at last he got its body between his knees and his fists with a good grip that kept its head where he would have it, and the shining, responsive muscles alert to his will—it seemed not only a pity but unnatural and wrong that anyone else should ride it when the King was coming to Whithorn, except Jan.

Jan thought so, too. She had made no demur about accepting. He had forgotten Helen, and that had lain on his conscience so that when she spoke of it to him, the day they were to ride, he answered sharply, and that was a thing he had never done before and would not, come to think of it, have done then, if he had been himself and the enchantment had not happened to him. He should have said something soft to Helen, told her the colt was too wild for her, maybe, kissed her or—oh, God knew! But he remembered then he had promised it to her long ago when he should have broken it in, and he felt sorry. By then, though, it was too late and Helen had burst out crying and run back into the house, saying she would not go with them.

So he and Jan and the grooms had gone alone.

He would never forget her as she was that day, cantering over the green knolls to Whithorn. She wore a green habit that she had got from her grand days at Court, the hat with a curled feather in it that hung down by the shoulders, and streamed when the wind caught it with the speed of their going. The little stubs whin and alder and hazel that were all they had of trees flashed by as they went and shouted, he could have sworn, for joy; he, Adam Boyd, and the swiftest rider in Galloway, racing each other over the hills to meet the King. And often at something they said Flaming Janet would fling back her head and laugh, so that the laughter was borne back on the wind like the sound of elf-bells, and he remembered the tale of Thomas of Ercildoune who rode swifter than the wind at the tail of the Fairy Queen. Ah, he'd give seven years of life to remember this day, though luck never befell him again! And the jangling of little bells from all the King's riders sounded over the countryside as they drew near, like flocks of birds homing. The long road down to Whithorn had never seemed shorter to Adam, and they clattered into its decked street too soon for him and stopped, breathless, with foam on the black colt's bridle, and watched while a group of men rode out from under the gray arch of the Priory and into the cobbled square.

There were others there watching her, envious women and curious men; he felt their eyes follow her, poised there on the black horse; forgetting, almost, to watch for the King, as though she had been a stranger. Why did they all stare so? The knights' wives, dim and demure on clustered palfreys, watched her with hate in their hearts, eyes gleaming beneath broad hats, tongues whispering. Why, there was no woman like her in all Galloway; she was alive, a flame; the dead women, the cobweb-women, whispered with words that would brush off her shoulders like dust, for she cared nothing. . . .

She turned and saw him and he heard her laughter.

"Fear nothing," she whispered. "If I played the fiddle they would all have to dance." And at thought of it he fell to laughing again. But then the whisper changed into a shout and he saw the King was coming, and out from under the gray arch rode the Prior in his furred violet robe, and the King by him on a white horse, followed by many noblemen mounted and the monks running on foot to wish them Godspeed. The crowds that waited about the streets cheered and laughed and cried, and shouted blessings on His Grace and wished he might ride soon again to Galloway.

"Come," said Jan to Adam, and bewildered he saw the black horse canter forward across the square, and Jan with her curled feather tossing urge him on the crowds withdrawing like a tide at ebb when a rider comes down the sands. Suleyman rose on his hind legs and neighed and pawed the air. A woman screamed, but Jan was cool as glass, holding in the saddle like a man and gripping hard, so that swiftly the colt was calmed again and trotted forward, with the little bells jingling on his reins.

Then Jan was the center of a laughing admiring crowd from Court and their mounts on all sides pressed in and he could not get near her.

Among the first to claim her was His Grace, who leaned over in the saddle and took her hands and raised them to his lips; his eyes were half-laughing and half-rueful, Adam thought, as though there were some word between them that had passed unspoken. But he heard the King speak, and that was before Jan remembered *him* and brought him up to be presented, and to kiss His Grace's hand so that he too would have a clear memory of those shadow-brilliant eyes, and that deep voice.

"It is no scathe to a fair woman to say she can handle her mount like a man."

A fair woman! Now that the knights' wives had heard *that*, there would be the devil to pay this night in all Galloway. And there was one other who heard the King's words and that Adam also saw, and he was a big nobleman in a gray long-gown, his carriage very magnificent and

his beard silver-fair and full. His blue eyes dwelt on Jan narrowly and
had done so since she rode across the square; some look in the eyes did
not please Adam and he was inclined to square up to the nobleman and
tell him to take his glance elsewhere. But little enough would be noticed, no man in that place having eyes for anyone but the magnificent
woman placed superbly, and rightly, on his Arab black, as though she
belonged there.

How glad he was that he had not remembered Helen!

II

That was in summer. By the time winter came again much had befallen, some of it beyond her power to foretell, all of it beyond her to
prevent or alter.

His Grace rode north again. His time was divided, unlike a common
man's, between one place and the next; he had no settled home. Stirling
his father had loved beyond all other palaces, and had shut himself away
there, unknowing at last of the things which went on against him, up
and down the kingdom. Stirling had been this King's place also in his
boyhood, and from there they had taken him and made him king. He
would never settle there again or in rich Edinburgh, not even in the
new palace of the Holyrood house that he planned to build on the site
of an old abbey beyond the town. He would never settle anywhere, becoming as the time passed as restless as a bird of passage; riding four
times a year up beyond the Mounth, the great northern range which
divided Highlands from Lowlands, and visiting the fierce wild places
where chiefs did homage to him, newly their overlord as he was after
John of the Isles; and then to Inverness and Aberdeen, and down through
Perthshire which was the home of Margaret Drummond and which he
would never pass by without a memory of her. For memory would soon
be all that either he or she would have left of loving; the forces, wide-
rooted and inexorable, which were drawing them apart would soon display their full power. Jan, withdrawn again into waiting, heard of what
passed from Spens or else John Ramsay, whom His Grace had made my
lord of Trarinyean. Other women, Ramsay told her spitefully, had succeeded where she had failed. The King and Drummond were apart and
then together again. The ambassador from England, William Warham,
came to St. Andrews officially on a visit, unofficially to send out feelers
regarding the English marriage. Richard of York was a disgraced ridicu-

lous prisoner in the Cheapside stocks and then the Tower. Everything was changing.

Jan herself felt it, even where the gray winds blew. They were not so far from towns as to have no word of change. And long before that her own horizon had altered and broadened in a manner unthought of. Adam Boyd had been right when he remembered the gaze of a nobleman with narrow blue eyes.

She had been watching at a window one day when the riders came. Seeing them, she was reminded strangely of that other time, and the half-remembered Douglas horsemen, seen against the skyline when she was almost too small to understand. That was before she could make out the standard, or the identity of the men who rode. Then she saw that one man was her father, the little dried-up lord slumped on his horse; and the other my lord of Angus, and that the Douglas men and the Kennedy men rode stirrups touching, and there was talk and laughter. And although there was nothing amiss in my lord's riding so, he and the Earl being no longer at feud, there was that in her mind which made her eyes narrow, and her breath draw sharply and her hands clutch at her skirts.

Gordon's child was with her and she put it away, handing it to the nurse who came. She watched it go without affection, seeing the squarish back of the little brown head below the cap Ag Kennedy had made for it, and the way the hair hung flatly, without spring or curl. It was as though she must be reminded of Lochinvar at every turn, every hour, no matter where she went or what she did, unable to be free of him.

She raised hands to her own hair, feeling it disheveled. She had been working in the dairy and had only now come up, pausing for a minute to watch, doing nothing, from the window. "The devil rewards those who have time to watch for him," she thought grimly, and began to take the pins out of her hair. It fell to her shoulders in a heavy tumbled mass and she ran her hands through it, glad of relief from the weight of it coiled about her head. A sound from the door disturbed her, and turning she saw Helen standing there; she had no idea how long she must have stood there, watching and saying nothing.

"Well?" she said sharply. "What is it?"

"Our mother wants you downstairs," said Helen. There was no flicker on the closed young face. She still stood, waiting, in the doorway.

"How in God's name can I go down with my hair like this? Go and call the woman—no, help me, yourself, with my hair! Fetch a comb. . . ."

Helen went passively and fetched the comb and tired Jan's hair. She did not speak again. That done, Jan seized up her skirts and went to the stairway, giving herself no pause.

One day a Douglas rider had come here, she remembered. He had worn the Earl's red and green livery with the new device he affected of a salamander. Her father had said nothing to her of why he had come.

Dear God, if they'd deceived her. . . . Did they take her for a fool?

They were all there when she reached the turn of the stairs, all waiting below in the hall. My lord, my lady—still in old-fashioned riding points, the skirts kilted so as to sit astride, for she had been going round the farms today to collect the teinds—and Angus, watched her come. Lady Kennedy stayed becomingly beside her lord, and her expression, Jan said later, was that of a cat who has swallowed cream. Jan halted, wary as an animal; she could turn, but where to run to? Into her mind flashed an understanding of everything that must have passed; she even had time for anger, standing there on the stairs. All things had come to this, then; how long had they known? What was the price agreed on among you? she longed to ask.

But no, she must pretend to gratified surprise, descending the stairs slowly. The Earl had moved to the foot of them and stood there, waiting for her hand.

Damn their duplicity, she would pretend nothing!

Her eyes blazed. Lord Kennedy's little dry voice came, somewhere, from the well of the hall. He said the words she had known he would say. He'd sold his damaged goods, then, for no tocher. A bargain struck!

"The Earl of Angus has done us the honor to demand your hand in marriage."

"By God, the old lecher!" thought Jan, as the narrow eyes blazed at her and the well-remembered fingers crushed her gown.

Lady Kennedy's triumph stayed with her for some weeks.

She had known the Earl of Angus herself in the days when he was young and golden and had jilted, for reasons rather social than personal, one of the Huntly girls for poor Bess Boyd, to whom he had looked for high placing. My lady had not seen Bess since her eclipse, but everyone said she had taken her life very hard. My lady on the other hand, though not endowed with easy living, had made the best of things; and her first husband, the Earl of Erroll, having died, she had come down into Galloway to marry John Kennedy and all in all had not regretted her departure from the north. At times, though, when she heard news of her girlhood friend Elizabeth Hay who had married Huntly, and the gay times they had when the King rode north, she would be envious; for Galloway was remote and quiet in spite of the popularity of St. Ninian, and Kennedy himself would rarely entertain, being far too mean.

But now, with Janet's unexpected windfall of a powerful suitor, there would be comings and goings such as my lady remembered and—she admitted it—loved; and for Jan, the black sheep of whom everyone had long despaired! It was all very well for my lord to carp and say there was no fool like an old fool, and the Angus marriage meant nothing now that all power was vested in the King's own hands. My lady saw the situation in a sea of widened horizons; Janet, as the Countess of Angus, with lands of her own at Braidwood and Crawford-Douglas that the Earl would give her, castles to the east and west to live in, a high place at Court—Janet would have at her beck and call every great name in the kingdom! Janet would entertain the King! There was very little Janet would not be able to do for her own family, were she so minded. Why, the younger girls need never despair of husbands!

Meanwhile, she kept her daughter by her. There would be no repetition of Galloway moor.

"The Angus family are not for the marriage," said David.

He leaned his hands on his leather-clad knees and stared forward in the way he had, showing the way his hair was thinning on top and the flesh of his forehead thrown into worried folds. Jan tossed her red head and said it was to be expected. "What do you suppose they say of me among themselves?" she asked him. "They don't relish the thought of me for stepmother!"

She thought of Bell's family, more of whom she had lately met when her father took her to buy gown-stuff for the marriage from the ships at Ayr. Chief among them she remembered Gavin Douglas, who had entered the Church and spent half his time at his clerical duties and the other half writing verse. He was a fastidious young man with brown curling hair and a profile like a Greek god, but although she had heard Walter praise his work she did not look on him with any warmth. It was obvious that *she* would never be the model for his Floras and Venuses in beribboned chariots with their hair shining in the sun, she thought, remembering the way he had looked down his classic nose. The rest were as bad; George, the eldest son, who spent most of his time on the Borders, as harassed by the reivers there as his Drummond wife by her large, increasing and badly spoiled brood. And the others had been warned against her in advance and had not made her welcome. At any rate, she thought angrily, soon I'll be as good as they!

Their antagonism did, in fact, more to reconcile her to the marriage than anything else; opposition had always fired her. Nevertheless she was pleased enough when, one day, my lord flung in in a pet, and said that the wedding date would have to be postponed because the lands Bell-the-Cat had promised to Janet were no longer his to bestow.

"What!" screamed my lady. "Did he think to deceive us?" But my lord reassured her; only, he said, a precautionary measure had been taken, the Earl last year having made over most things he possessed in deed of gift to George, to avoid taxation. But this piece of news chafed my lady sorely, as she said he might have foreseen. "For when in all the world will George Douglas be induced to part with Crawford and Braidwood?"

Lord Kennedy admitted he might be induced to do so for money. "Well, neither yours nor mine!" retorted his spouse. That, in fact, was the rub; and my lord of Angus was like a goaded bear, eager for his wedding but not, as the event would have it, unduly anxious to part with his gold.

They talked and quarreled and fought round it, and Jan watched with her heavy-lidded smile, saying nothing. She knew well enough her dame would be a match for the Earl.

She kept her own counsel these days about many things, including Spens. She had seen him soon after news of the betrothal leaked out; he had come to her, white with shock, as she was busied about the dairy.

She was angry with him for coming and also afraid. "You can't be seen here as you used," she told him. "Can't you see how things are altered now?"

"That old man—Jan, Jan, that Belial, who devours women—"

"He won't devour me. Now do as I tell you, and go." But he would not and flung himself at her feet, there on the stone floor of the dairy among the churns, clasping her about the knees and begging her, praying her, that she would not go on with this thing; said he would kill himself and her; raved and threatened.

She had been afraid someone would come upon them, seeing his puffed changed face and shaking hands; half-sickened, between fear and pity, she had promised that they should meet again, if only to say farewell. And so they had met, once, in the inn near Bargany, evading with difficulty the eyes that watched, always, everywhere, now that she was Angus' betrothed, in the same manner as they had once watched when she was to marry Lochinvar. And it had been easy to say with truth to

Spens that she could not meet him again. He had threatened then to tell
Angus of their relations, but she knew he would never dare.

"He would kill you," she told Spens contemptuously.

Preparations for the wedding grew apace in spite of the delay. The
Castle was filled with the chatter of women snipping at cloth and dropping pins about the floor; my lady would wear russet for the ceremony,
Helen's gown was to be yellow and Jan's blue. The Earl of Angus ordered
himself a cloak of miniver; he rode over as often as time would allow,
alternately sullen and possessive, and eager like a boy. Below in the
kitchens, the walls were hung with carcasses salted after the kill and the
floors stacked with kegs of wine and butter and oil; there were dried
fruits and honey from last summer, mace and cloves and cinnamon from
the ships; salt pork, fish in vinegar, grain in great stacks and malt for the
brewing of ale, to be doubled this year owing to the increased demands
upon it. That they could use all, and more, my lady had no doubt; it
was a feast fit for a king, she said. My lord heard her drily, counting the
cost.

He had been much with His Grace in Dunbarton, rendering due
aid for ships. Jan heard avidly the tales of His Grace brought home; how
he would watch a boat building from the first laying of its keel and
often work with the parts himself, jesting with the workmen and sharing
their bread and ale, knowing them all by name, running his long fingers
over the wood's surface or striking with precision and strength the nails
and rivets in their places; wood was scarce and dear and Lord Kennedy's
masts welcome, and Jan heard her leathery little father's talk of friendship with the King, and envied him.

Often in those days she would find his glance resting on her with a
weighing, secret look; he never confided in her and she did not know
what to read from the expression in his eyes. He had surprised her with
his lack of stint over preparations for the wedding; it did not seem to
her, however, that he was in great haste to see her wed. She wondered
if he and the Earl had fallen out again; the difficulty over Braidwood
and Crawford-Douglas was not even yet smoothed over. She felt relief,
and yet apprehension, at the thought that there might even yet be no
marriage; she was in no haste to marry Bell, but if she did not, what was
to become of her?

And then one day my lord announced his intention of showing the
King hospitality when next he rode down to the shrine of St. Ninian.

She had waited for the noise of bridle bells, and chatter and laughter and the sound of hooves, clattering up the long road from the sea. She had watched the sky change with the passing of day to a delicate late green, the color of birds' eggs. Now it seemed that the water and sky were one and the little clouds floating islands, or the islands clouds. A bird winging across the sky was like a ship's sail, and she pictured the boat that brought her father and the King to Galloway. The two men leaned over the boat's edge watching the gliding past of the green water, and there was color on the decks and singing.

She waited till my lady called for her to hurry down, to be ready in the hall when the King should come. Pausing on the stairs as she had done that day of her betrothal, she saw them; a spell hung over them all, of waiting silence. Helen stood with lips parted and hands hanging by her sides; she had always the air these days of passive waiting. My lady's full lips smiled in her high-colored face; she, the center of all, the seat of welcome, with her sons and daughters by her like a flock of geese, should curtsy to His Grace before any. The servants fidgeted at the back of the hall.

"They are coming," someone said. This was as it should be, in the house of the greatest lord in Galloway! Jan stood still, hearing the sound of horsemen. About the doors the men waited with lit flares, ready to fire the daubed wall-torches before the twilight changed to dark. Presently her father led the King into his hall and Jan felt herself swept forward, one of many and not, as it had once been, herself and James Stewart only. It was almost a year since she had seen him. She curtsied low, sweeping in an accustomed manner the full folds of her gown before her. As so many times, the hand grasped hers; she heard the well-remembered voice.

He had altered. His features were unchanged but it was a face carved now of brittle alabaster. She had the impression of this new brittleness as he smiled and addressed her, rallying her about her horsemanship at Whithorn when he had last ridden down. About the company there were more smiles and satisfaction; that tale had spread already over the green knolls north.

The King laughed much; he bore her company at supper, tucking her arm in his to lead her to the high table. The meat and the species and confectionery meant for the Angus wedding were brought; the talk flowed headily, everything everyone said being turned to brilliant nonsense. Jan felt herself glow and sparkle with the praise and wine; she played her part, as the King his. Dropping her eyelids was part of the game; she saw the changed eyes appraising her, as a buyer will do a thoroughbred or a strange rich jewel. She fluttered and laughed and flirted and offered and withdrew again. She saw herself, lolling at ease in my lord's high seat.

After the wine had flowed tongues were freer, and she saw about the table veiled winks and smiles; my lord and my lady smiled always, lips moist in the light of candles with the growing heat and the wine. Everything was resolving into separate points of light; the candles dipped and swayed, the jewel the King wore flashing as the light caught it; had she seen that before? James was in crimson, the doublet parti-colored with black sleeves; a paradox in a man with red hair, that no color so well as red became him. The cap he wore had a rolled brim and in one side was a heron's quill. She took in small, remembered details; the fine stitching of the shirt he wore, the way the nails on the expressive hands were very slightly broader at the tips than the roots, and a long scar, threadlike, across one palm. He saw her look; the arched brows flew up in inquiry.

"I would know of your scar. Your Grace will forgive me."

Was she a fool to ask such a question here? He laughed again; it was better to forget scars, he told her. Swiftly he slid by it to some sparkling ribald tale of Dunbar and Walter Kennedy at Court. "You must come again soon," he told her.

I might be no one, she thought. Only a shell.

Later, in her room, she laughed, to keep from crying. The excitement and the wine rose high in her and she lay and shook with laughter on the bed; her hair, loosened at last from the coif, tumbled in masses on the pillow. Helen turned, peevishly, half in her sleep. "Be quiet," she muttered, "it's near morning." Jan jerked for reply at the curtain so that the moon flooded over the bed. "Sleep if you can," she said. "I cannot."

Helen said nothing more and turned over again and closed her eyes. She was thinking of Adam Boyd this evening and how he would neither look at her or speak. Jan slipped out of bed and shook her hair back and went to the window. Leaning with her elbows on the sill she could see the loch, mirrored like glass under the sky. The night breeze, warm with coming summer, stirred her hair. She thought of James.

If she were to go down now there would be no one to prevent her, remembering my lord's smile. If she were to go . . . and if not? "Am I a fool?" she thought fiercely. "There have been other women since Margaret Drummond."

A memory came to her from that time she had ridden to the Clyde, seeing the masts thickly clustered on the broad river and the gulls that perched everywhere, on masts and roofs and stones. The King was in the Isles then and she had seen with quickened heart a barge slide upriver, a lion bearing a sword on its sail, thinking he might have returned. But he had not and in the barge was a woman with a crimson headdress, of shape much pointed and dagged as they wore them now in England. In the moment it took the barge to pass her, Jan had caught sight of her face; it was Margaret Drummond. She remembered the hard clenching of her own hands on the reins; unbidden, uncontrollable, at sight of her. And yet she had seen how the face was changed, like that of a woman in fear; the tight fine drawing of the flesh over the bones, and the quick nervous side glance of the gray eyes which showed she had seen and made no sign. . . . And the King's face tonight had had the same fine-drawn look, as though someone had died that he had loved, as though the barge had held a ghost that day, as though . . .

"They have parted and quarreled and kissed again," Ramsay told her. "Soon it will end, because it must."

Meantime there had been other women. She must remember that. And why not I? she thought. Why not I? She could go to him and he would not refuse her.

She leaned further out, feeling the chill hard damp of the stone strike her body through the thin shift. The thread of it was loosened and it had slipped down, leaving one shoulder bare; her blowing hair in the night wind lifted free of throat and breast. One passing below would have seen her so, hands gripping the stone of the sill; a woman in a portrait, with loose hair and the window like a frame about her.

Below was the marsh. In the moon's light a thousand little points gleamed, cast up from the gathering dews of neither night nor very early day. They were like swords, she thought, in an elfin army; bared for war, lifted shoulder-high by a thousand thousand tiny malevolent horsemen, shaking-still. The world outside was not as humans know it, an eerie half-light world where sounds were dulled, even the night wind blowing over the sedges.

And yet there was someone there. Down in the dark was a horseman, still and waiting in the gray enchantment of the thousand little swords. He sat his horse motionless, guarding the night, watching the Castle where no lights gleamed. She heard her own breath draw in softly; she was looking down into the white and hopeless face of Spens.

Presently she turned to Helen again and saw she was asleep. There was a bedgown flung over a chest by the wall and she went and put it on.

Then she fetched a comb and combed her hair, hearing the crackling sound of the heavy tresses. Her hair was like a live thing, she thought. She heard her heart thudding strangely. When she reached the King would he know she was afraid? But she must smile and make him laugh again and beguile him. He would want nothing of the fears that came in the night hours; he would have had enough of that, and of fear in a woman.

"Well, my lord, you'd best look to it."

The moon, which had flooded over Helen's coverlet, did not penetrate my lord and lady's couch, heavily swathed as it was like a catafalque. Within, the voice of my lady went on. This was her council chamber, where nearly all matters at issue were settled. There is almost nothing a man will not do for the sake of being allowed to sleep.

"It's late," my lord grunted.

"Heaven and earth, did I say tonight? But I know Angus, and you must make him sign. Otherwise there will be little recompense should he slip through your fingers. We have been laughingstocks once."

"You'll not hurry George Douglas," said my lord. "Angus is hot enough. He'll pay the money, so long as he's made wait. And time is not against us."

He smiled in the dark. "Well, not so much as a handfasting—" began his wife indignantly. "Be quiet," she said suddenly. "Someone's about."

She shifted restlessly and sat up in bed. Kennedy's voice droned on. "If you have an eye to her and keep her by you, there is nothing to fear," he said. "Give ourselves to the end of the year for wedding or no wedding. He will wait, and if those lands do not come there will be other lands. We must set our price high." He talked on, one ear pricked for the sound of footsteps. He could feel his wife's impatience at his noise.

"Go you and see. It's someone. It may be *her!*"

He scoffed. "More likely a man gone to the privy." He grumbled on about women's fancies. In the end he rose, flung his gown about him and his feet into slippers and made for the door.

"See who it is." He heard the voice behind him. Into his mind came a sullen resentment at her carping. A sense of triumph was with him that he had kept his own half-acknowledged, ambition to himself and, so doing, had left her unsuspicious. He'd keep his thumb on other plans; stop her meddling. She was like a hen with the Angus marriage and her connections and dreams of settlement.

He opened the door, hearing the faint creaking of its hinge. "Can they not use oil?" he muttered irritably. The corridor was full of gray-white light. Shafts of it fell from the windows and lay in scattered oblongs on the floor. At the end, where the stairs turned down, he saw a figure move. It was Janet. He could see the pale folds of her shift dragging and the half-scared look she turned back over her shoulder. Their eyes met; she had seen him.

Lord Kennedy came back into the room and shut the door. "There's no one there," he said, managing to keep the satisfaction out of his voice. "No one at all."

The King had found the moonlight not enough to read by and so lit a candle, setting it on a table by his bed. Often he would read thus until dawn, when sleep evaded him.

He focused his eyes on the page, seeing the text. Opposite, the myriad faces of the Apostles stared up at him, smirking each one with the same mouth, the same eyes and smile. They had been painted by hand by a monk of Wadstena and brought to Scotland by his mother when she was a bride. For that reason and because it was small, he carried the book about with him.

"If, O Trinity, on a lie I rest, lead me into truth's way. Cover me not with clay alone, but with the waves of judgment, not so as Thy wrath overwhelms me. Nothing else is there to hide me but red fire—"

Fire, earth and water, he thought; the elements which made up all. The flame of the candle rose high and still and to one side the wax guttered. Was there so much more fire in some that when the flame was out there remained nothing but black ashes? The things in his mind would not let him rest, and the candlelight hurt his eyes.

He wished that he could sleep. "Nothing else to hide me—" For long now he had been unable to hide, from anyone or anything. Long enough now since he had been a king only, his every move watched, his thoughts read and anticipated as they lay behind his eyes. They had seen that he and Margaret could no longer shut out the world and they had taken her away. The world had come pressing in and it had forced them apart.

He stared at the flame, seeing in it his love's face. But she had not been made of fire. There was nothing for them now in this world but to part, any contact being liable only to hurt her more than she had been hurt already, branded with the heat of the flame when she had been made of coolness and gentle things. The peace she had brought him drained her. . . .

What was she doing, this very night? Did she sleep quietly, dark hair shadowing the pillow as he remembered, down-drawn like a nun's veil, with their child by her? The great trees about her father's Perthshire castle guarded her like a procession of kings.

"But this king could not," he thought. He, two men, a king and a man, with two loves, herself and Scotland.

Ah, there was nothing now to fill his hours, pass them away till the English bride should come, a child, who meant nothing!

He remembered the woman tonight. The desirability of her flesh had roused him as once before, in Kilmaurs' house, the time she had tempted him. That had been before Margaret's child was born and he had thought he could hold her against all men . . . and himself against all women. Earlier tonight he had hoped that the woman would come. Now, with the darkness and the quiet and memory, only the flame in the silence, he hoped that she would not; he prayed so to God.

His shoulders lifted. Such women would be his lot from now on; anodynes, all of them, able to make a man forget his pain in lust and the drowsiness that followed its fulfillment. That would be all that was left for him, himself, as a man.

He raised his head; the draught had stirred the curtains. He turned back to the book again. He had expected her; Kennedy, with his gifts of masts and wood and his sudden hospitality, weighing the fall of Drummond ambitions in terms of the rise of his own. Kennedy, with his little mean eyes. . . .

"Of earth and fire didst thou make the world. Of earth and fire are all men made; and so will it be found at the end."

The door opened softly. She was standing there with her back against it, hair hanging loose over her shoulders. For an instant, sick with anger, he wondered how it would be if he were to send her packing. But Kennedy was his servant and the night was long.

Jan saw his eyes, surveying her unreadably. "I must smile," she thought, remembering her fear upstairs. What would he say if she were to tell him that she had come, at last, because the world outside made her afraid?

She smiled, seeing the faces on the painted page.

"If there is aught else that Your Grace requires for your comfort—"

The King closed the book slowly and looked at the woman who had come. The shadow cast by the candle upthrust between her breasts, showing them matured and experienced. Resentment against her, against all women like her, against the world that made of them his need, was with him. He would not use her gently, as was his way with his women. Idly, he snapped his fingers, beckoning her to come to him.

She came slowly; her lips had parted and he was afraid she would speak again. She slipped her arms out of the sleeves of the gown she had about her, leaving it by the bed. The last clear memory he had was of her body's curve through the thin transparency of the shift, and the candle shining beyond it as she leaned over and snuffed the wick. She did not speak again.

When he slept at last it was toward morning. Jan slid her arms from under his head's weight and silently gathered her things together and put them on. Tears pricked at the backs of her eyes; the hangings in the room showed gray as ghosts. She hurried out of the room and upstairs, while about the Castle sounds stirred that meant a household waking.

Some weeks later, she found to her great joy that she was with child. She said nothing of it, at first less in dislike of concealment than of her father's watching eyes. She could not have explained in words her unwillingness that he should go straight to the King.

III

Bess Douglas the spinster had less to occupy her, in the nature of things, than her sister. For some time after her rejection by Robert Lyle she had kept close at Tantallon, but after the Countess' death she began to go oftener abroad. Some day, her father said, he would arrange another marriage for her, but when this would be he was not decided, and he was at present much too busy arranging his own. Meanwhile Bess put in the time at Bonshaw, where her mother's kin resided; at Kilmaurs and the Herries house, with her sisters; with George and William when they had houseroom; and at Penkill, where her cousins were and where she had been bidden that year for Yule. Before that she had been with George on the Borders, and it was refreshing to come from that place where of all others talk was most rife about the old Earl's folly, to Penkill, where young Adam Boyd was betrothed into the Kennedy family which was causing all the uproar.

Bess pursed her lips over the latest happenings at home. George had at last yielded over the question of Braidwood, his large family and heavy commitments making it impossible for him to refuse payment. As a result the wedding date was fixed, and a document, with swinging seals, had been drawn up, and presented to Janet Kennedy *"pro singulari affectione et amore* . . . the lands to be the property of the said Janet all the days of her life" and after her death to the heirs which she would bear the Earl. "He'll have to make haste," Bess had said sourly, "or other men'll father them."

She did not know what had caused her to make that statement. If pressed in a court of law, she admitted, she would have had no grounds. But she remembered clearly the unhappiness caused to Marion a year or two back, and the money Kilmaurs and the Earl had lavished on Janet then. She did not know where she herself would bide after the wedding; she did not relish the idea of having to be at Tantallon. "With that woman!" she said to Elizabeth Drummond, adding that it was unlikely any of them, except Gavin, would attend the wedding. "He is a son of the Church," she had said, in response to Elizabeth's inquiry. But George's wife had hardly heard her, being occupied with the pranks of young Archibald Douglas, who was home from the University for the holidays.

Although fixed in her resolve not to meet Janet if it could be avoided, she met Janet's sister without complaint. Helen was also spending Yule with the Boyds, but Bess could not help noticing a lack of warmth in the approach of the young couple. Adam Boyd she thought uncouth. There had been once when she came on him without warning, when there had been company and his presence was sought. She had found him in the stable, kneeling in the straw by a black Arab colt, grooming it. When she spoke to him and caressed the horse, he answered rudely, and Bess, who had sharp imagination, saw between him and the dark wild colt a likeness; but speaking of it afterward to Helen Kennedy she was surprised when the girl burst into tears. Helen had always seemed to her a placid, rather dull creature, and it had seemed safe enough to speak to her of Boyd. But now it appeared that the same trouble was at work, the witch who had beguiled Kilmaurs. Adam, it seemed, had eyes for no other, ever since one day Janet Kennedy had ridden on the black colt down into Whithorn.

"And since then he behaves as though it were a sacred relic," sobbed Helen, "and will let no one ride it but himself. And he says Jan is the Elfin Queen and will not hear a word against her. If he knew what I do, he'd not be so hot after her; but how can I persuade him when he will not listen?"

Bess earnestly begged Helen to repose all confidence in herself.

Helen often wondered, long years afterward, what would have befallen if she had not told that tale.

At the time, she had been possessed with hatred for Jan. It seemed to her that she always hated Jan. Right from the time she could first remember, Jan had been there, finer and swifter and more vivid and beautiful than she. Walter Kennedy had brought a dog and a bird once; the bird he gave to David and the dog to Jan. There was nothing for her, Helen, at all; and later everything else was so. Stern elder brothers yielded to Jan and young grooms fell in love with her. It was as though everyone, when she was there, became bewitched. Jan would do mad things, crazy things; behind her back they would talk, but to her face they could do nothing, nothing, only stare into her eyes and watch her move or speak. There was nothing Helen could see that would account for it; feature by feature, she would inspect her own face, seeing her skin white and smooth, her eyes clear, her lips full-curving. She had brown hair, but it was thick and shining, with golden lights when she had washed it. She was too fat but she would outgrow that, her mother said, when she was older. She was in every way as good as Jan, and she had kept herself chaste and did not follow men. She would make a good wife to Adam, if he would let her.

Ah, he had seen Jan often in the old days, and made less fuss of her then! He'd seen her once when she was far gone with Gordon's child, a clumsy sight on the road between Lesswalt and Kilmarnock. Helen had reminded Adam of that meeting one day when his talk of Jan grew too much to be borne, and it was then that he looked at her for the first time as though she were a stranger, and now he did so always. They weren't Adam and Nel any more, who had used to play together as children; they were two polite strangers who seldom spoke and never kissed, and although the wedding date grew nearer it did not seem that either of them could believe it would take place. All comfort she had had in Adam was destroyed; always now in his eyes she would see reflected green eyes, and hear a wistful longing in his voice.

If only Jan had wed the Earl swiftly and gone away, or stayed in Edinburgh! But although Angus rode down often and followed Jan, as everyone else did, with narrowed hungry eyes, their mother was always there, talking of Braidwood; there seemed no conceivable way on earth to speed the wedding on.

Helen had found relief in the knowledge that the Douglas family disliked and feared Jan as much as she. At first she had been wary of them, finding their harsh faces and commanding height a matter for fear. But then one day she had been winding wool with Bess Douglas and found that she was not unkind, only rather soured and lonely, and that she had a betrothed who had forsaken her for something the same reason as Adam was now doing to herself.

"He mustn't, he mustn't!" Helen had cried in sharp fear. The bringing of the thought out into the light of day made it abominable.

"How are you going to prevent him?" said Bess calmly. And then she told the tale of the stable and the colt and from then on Helen had told her of Jan.

She told herself afterward that she could not possibly have known what Bess would do. For afterward, when the thing had befallen, it seemed to her that she did not hate Jan at all; she would have done anything to save her. But it was too late and now, for all her life, there would be that look in Adam's eyes when he surveyed her; a wondering, a suspicion, gradually grown between them like a wall.

There was comfort for her; she would be a good wife, as she had said, and look after her house well and bring up her children. But they would not be Adam's children. In the year after that wedding that was to have taken place, she married Robert Graham, the laird of Knock-dolian, older than she. She was happy enough; Robert would never look at her as Adam had looked, with the shaggy brows she loved down-drawn like an animal's; his eyes dark so that she couldn't read them, not friendly as they had used to be, or trusting any more. And the words he had spoken were enough to confirm that suspicion, although he would not hurt her willingly, she knew; he would never hurt her. But she was so bitter with the loss of him as he had been that she never answered him, then or in later years, only remembering. "The joy's gone out of loving," he told her, and she knew that he was thinking of the day when Jan had ridden down to Whithorn, like the Queen of Elfland clad in green. "It isn't the same, Nel, for you and me. I'm sorry." And he turned away. There was nothing she could do, only remember; and begin again her hatred of Jan. Jan was far away by that time and should have done no harm; but Adam would remember as she herself remembered his words, and his voice.

It was true enough, she thought. The joy had gone out of loving; where her heart had been there lay a stone.

After Helen had gone downstairs Bess sat motionless for a while, her mind active.

Helen's tale had shocked but had not overwhelmed her. Here was proof

of her suspicions; she was clear about what she would do. The triumph
of the situation brought a flush to her face; she looked almost handsome.
Her movements were purposeful as she went about the room, collecting
pen and ink and paper.

She had deliberated whether to ride straight to the Earl or write to
him. In the end, not out of cowardice, she decided on the latter. It would
be better to keep the affair impersonal; the whole matter must resolve
without fuss. In her clear, unemotional mind was no room for irregu-
larity. George, everyone, would be grateful to her for ridding the Earl
of that woman. Anger burned in her at thought of the deceit offered to
her father, and pity for his making such a fool of himself.

"Even the night the King stayed, she slipped out and went to him."
The young voice, quivering with long outrage, sounded in her ears
again. And "him" was Spens, whom Bess remembered as a common man,
her father's tenant laird. Spens, hanging about below the Castle in the
marsh where Helen had seen him; and other nights, God knew how
many, or where. Spens, who drank like a fish and had once said of her
father, "All is not good that be upcome!"—and this although the Red
Douglases had been names in the land for three centuries. But, Bess admitted, it would have been bad enough had it been any man but Spens.

She sat down with the writing materials and took the pen and wrote
unhurriedly, seeing at the end her clear decisive handwriting and the
way "Elizabeth" finished evenly, the spidery uprights balancing on a
short horizontal stroke. Having read the letter she sanded it, sealed the
containing sheet, called for her servant and bade him ride east with all
speed. "You will give it into the Earl's own hands," she told him. "There
is no answer."

Going down into the great hall after the man had ridden off, she reflected that her father would certainly be angry. But she had no qualms
about what she had done. It was time that it ended, she thought, and he
has never made me afraid. She faced the future equably.

IV

Bell-the-Cat received the letter seated in his own great hall. Of recent
years he would be found there at late day, when the air began to chill
outside and the sky darken. Beyond the windows the gray sea threatened the cliffs below; he knew the sound from earliest childhood and
no longer heeded it except to miss it when he was not there. Often now

that he had grown older he took time to watch it, the gray sea; never
having been tempted, like the King, to ride its waves, and find the unknown lands that lay beyond; a man was happier at home. This was his
domain, of all that he had once owned, and here he hoped to die; in the
rose-red castle, where as now the bright eyes of his hawks gleamed in
the high rafters, and the soft ruffling noise their feathers made disturbed
the sleeping dogs so little that they no longer raised their heads to
snuff the air, and then subside again.

Ah, they were all growing old, he and the dogs and Tantallon. Outside
the world was changing, but he'd not change; remembering, even if only
by the King's great trench beyond the far wall, the time he had challenged Scotland itself to war. The good days were dead, but he remembered them; he could sit here remembering by the fire.

A woman sat by him, the firelight gleaming on her vivid hair. That
she was in his mind only did not disturb him; soon now, in reality, she
would be there. The fair flesh of her throat rose like a pillar and the
curves of her breast beckoned. Often thus he had had her with him, over
the years; borne along by his saddle on the wind with hair blowing, a
witch with a body of white fire, coming to him in the night hours, so
that he in his mind possessed her. Ah, she'd made him wait, to the limits
of all endurance; all other women seeming gray and stale, the image in
his mind preferable. "It is not a right thing," he muttered, "to live only
in the mind."

Nine days . . . and still the cup might slip.

Angus moved restlessly. Why was he so filled with his own unease?
Soon now, the waiting over, things would be as they should have been,
long since; and would have, but for mischance. He wondered if any man
had such a series of mischances; when had he ever been at peace? Bess,
his wife, hardly seen of late years, a dragging reproach to him, nothing,
even when they were young, bridging the gap between himself and
her. Last night he had tried to picture her face and could not, and in
the end he had gone to a room upstairs where a chest lay and opened it,
and finding a little box with metal hasps had unlocked it with a small
flat key. Inside were trinkets, some of them bought when she was a
bride; head jewels, in the older style, long chains of brilliants and
wrought gold, rings and brooches. The rings had been too small for his
fingers when he tried them on. They'd do, he thought, for Jan. His eyes
gleamed as he saw her there in the firelight, weighed down and shining
with his jewels. He'd have her here by the fireside with him night after

night, his rose of Sharon, that no other man should see . . . and, himself, grow old in peace.

The dog growled. Angus turned his head toward the door. Presently his servant, a young man, one of his bastards, came; a letter, he said, from Lady Bess. Angus grunted and signed to Bess's own man to come and took the letter from him unwillingly. He had been content enough, left alone with his thoughts.

He slit the missive. Smoothing it out, the spidery precise signature stared up at him; Elizabeth. Bess, his spinster daughter. There should be no spinsters; every woman ought to go to bed with a man or else become a nun. He'd have to see about Bess; she was getting sour. After all this was over. . . .

Spens. The other name danced before him. What of Spens? An impertinent vassal; he'd never liked him, since that time in the King's hall when he had spoken of him, Angus, saying all was not good that be upcome. In the old days he would have trodden him underfoot for that and kicked him out of the way like dog's flesh, but now—

The Earl let out an oath.

Swiftly the servant, Robert Douglas, waiting at the door, laid a hand on his sword. It was a gesture commanded by the blood that was in him, inbred rather than conscious; he was too young to remember the wars. He turned, seeing the Earl where he had risen. The veins on his face and neck stood out and he was like a great murderous animal, there by the fire. A stream of filth met the servant's ears; Angus took the letter and held it in the fire, watching till it burned. He turned then and roared instructions, sending the servant running. From where he ran on his various errands he could hear that great voice still roaring; it pierced the thickness of rose-red stone, sounding from turret to cellar. From everywhere in the Castle came the tread of hurrying feet, the word cast back curtly in the time it took to fasten on a sword. The women would speak of it when they were gone but meantime it was a thing well understood; the Red Douglas was hot for blood, the old lion was young again, and a thing would be this night that had not been for many years. The salamander, with the bleeding heart, would ride forth on his banners, and the clash of swords ring out in the King's Scotland, as it had not done since the Red Douglas went the way of the Black and he had thought, James Stewart, that he had made a tame old bear. But grim jaws set in purpose now and strong hands wrought with speed, buckling the harness on the horse as firmly as armor on a Douglas man. The bear was old, but he was game; there would be sport to see.

That night the devil and all his men rode out from Tantallon Castle.

He found Spens hawking in the early day. He had no memory of the methods used to find him. The servants who were with Spens drew back, clearing a path for Angus in full armor to ride down on his great gray horse. His own men were behind him; he had little concern for that. This was his prey, for no other man's sword; he rode for it, baring his teeth like an animal at the chalk-white face.

Spens waited, handing his hawk to someone. On all sides the watchers withdrew a little, up the slope of the valley where they had been. The ground underfoot was full of sodden leaves. Some of the men crossed themselves. The Douglases made a ring of steel, guarding the valley so that no man might ride out or in until the thing was accomplished. There were no women to make outcry; the silence was complete.

Spens unsheathed his sword. He was not attired for fighting and the .plume in his hat hung downward, foolishly. The sword Angus carried was the weight of a man; it was a legend in the Douglas country that no one but himself could wield it. It glinted now, ice-sharp, in the early sun. Spens saw it and curiously, at the same time, his hawk, watching from the servant's shoulder with impersonal bright eyes. A little wind stirred the leaves.

Then Angus rushed at him, the gray hooves thundering close. The great sword whirled in the air, an arc of light gleaming about its axis. Spens moved to parry, hearing the Earl's harsh breaths. He had a sense of unreality and felt no fear. The watchers waited, hearing the clash of swords.

Spens' horse reared, terrified, on its haunches. The blow, which had been intended to strike the head from the shoulders, missed, cleaving instead the thigh; bone and flesh severed as though they had been butter. The horse screamed as the sword caught it, rearing again; Spens slumped over in the saddle, the blood spurting from the stump and spattering the onlookers and the beast's flanks. The horse, maddened with terror, made off, dragging its burden; the Douglas men-at-arms opened the circle to let the watchers go. Their lord sat with lips drawn back, and when the thing had gone by he sheathed his sword.

Back in the wood Spens' battered body, disfigured with blood and mire, jolted on among the flying hooves, still dragged by the stirrup.

Angus rode westward, not slackening speed, and those whom he passed by knew him for the devil, and hid themselves. Even his men dared not

speak; they lashed their horses into foam to follow. They rode down into
Galloway, to find Janet Kennedy. If she had been in her father's castle,
they would have burned it down; but they found her on the road with
two grooms only, between Lesswalt and Bargany. They jerked her horse's
head round and made for the north.

V

She had not gone quietly.

That winter Agnes Kennedy had died at Lesswalt and Jan, who had
been guarding herself because of the child, did what she could in riding
back and forth. She knew David would have little enough time for grief
and she was sad to think that Ag, poor Ag, was dead; the only woman
who had ever loved her, and who had treated her with kindness and
without much reward. She was determined to do what she could for
David and for Ag's children. For the present it was little enough, beyond
seeing that the household ran itself. She took the journey ungrudgingly,
often in rain or snow. She had never known harm from the weather.

Wil Kennedy was with her this day whom she remembered from
Beltane, and a young groom who was his kinsman, a boy from beyond
Luce. She took little heed of them, preferring her own thoughts; these
held an odd fatality, unlike herself. She wondered if it were her state
that brought to her this waiting calm, content to watch the days run
ahead. In eight days, unless something befell, she would marry Angus;
and she had done nothing except to watch the time draw nearer.

The roads were quiet, with a promise of frost after the night's rain.
The snow on the high hills lingered; it would be colder in the north.
Here in Galloway it was quiet, warmer than elsewhere and with the
gentle air she knew.

"There are horsemen riding," said the little groom. Wil answered nothing. He was taciturn now, with a plump wife who served in the dairy.
Jan did not think that he remembered his old passion for herself. Recalling that time, amusement rose in her; it seemed so long ago!

The horsemen slowed about the bend and then came riding, solidly
like an advancing wall, toward her. Their vizors were down and they
carried no banner. Queerly she had a vision of silver men, machines
such as the Florentines made, sent to do a god's bidding by the winding of engines. A god's bidding, or a devil's. Their leader was in the center and she noted his great height; then the riders spread out fanwise,

closing the road and her approach. She heard a frightened gasp from the little groom.

"My lady, my lady—" The leader rode up. He laid a hand on her bridle and she knew now that it was Angus. His eyes surveyed her through the vizor's slits and she saw how they glittered strangely. "Were you thinking to meet your lover?" he said. "He'll not come again."

Jan struck out blindly with her whip. She brought it down again and again, but could not reach his wrists through the armor. She tried to wrench the reins away from his hands' grip; he laughed, with a sound that chilled her. Seizing the whip, he laid it about her horse's sides, so that the beast reared and then made off, with the Earl still in charge of the reins. She could feel the wind tearing through her hair as they rode; it had all happened in seconds.

"Are you mad?" she screamed. He did not turn or answer.

She remembered tales she had heard of the Douglases, scarcely credible to normal men. These came to her as she rode, seeing them about her. The men had drawn up on all sides so that she could not escape; they carried short axes slung from saddlebows, and in each man's hand was a spear. These things were real enough, but she still saw them in a dream. "Your lover will not come again." The King was dead and Angus had killed the King.

A cold wind blew, holding a promise of snow. The speed at which they rode jolted her. They would all die, then, James and herself and the child; Angus would kill her. She wondered how soon he had planned to do so, and how. She had no fear of dying, but the blood in her cried out at the thought of dying tamely. She would fight with her bare hands and with her tongue.

"You'll hang for this." She heard him laugh again; the beaked vizor jutted ahead. She fell silent, and they rode on; turning sharply off the main path and making for the moors. Jan fought down the panic that rose; on the roads, in her father's country, anyone she met would hear her, see her, ride and tell them at home where she had gone. But now there would be no one met with here, till they came to Douglas land; a shepherd, maybe, some clod who would do nothing for fear. She began to swear softly, till he bade her be silent.

Over to the left was the Beltane path. Would he take her by *that* road? But someone was riding along it, unhurried, with two men behind. She could see their dark shapes against the slope of the hill.

"Say naught," said Angus. "Do you hear me?"

He caught her wrist in one hand and squeezed; she bit back the tears
that rose. The rider plodded along slowly; it was John Ramsay, returning
to Kirkandrew. He did not raise his head or turn as they rode by. The
speed of their going left him soon behind.

The spy, Ramsay, the abominable, paid spy . . . coward, she thought;
he'd say nothing. Angus released her arm, and laughed again, not pleasantly. Jan stared ahead of her, sick with pain. The throbbing in her arm
blotted out all else for a while.

They rode on, it might have been for three hours or four. He kept her
away from the main roads, going by moorland paths and grass. She had
long lost any idea of where they were, knowing only by the setting sun
that they must be going north. It grew very cold, the land rising as they
went on, and the air toward the close of day was heavy with frost. She
set her teeth, gripping the reins with numb fingers; she had been in the
saddle since morning and was stiff with weariness, hungry and half
frozen. They must, she thought, be over the shire border now. It was his
country, then. There would be few here ready to give evidence against
him, no matter what he might do.

By degrees she forgot her fear of him in the greater one that she
would lose her hold on the reins and fall. When they passed by a hostelry
she screamed that he might stop and buy warm ale for her. He gave a
curt order then and the horses clinked and jostled to a standstill; she slid
down from the saddle stiffly scarcely aware of her limbs or her body.
In the distance was a track, red with mud, winding away into the distance, to be lost in the gathering dark and the blur of cold that had
come down.

Angus would not allow her to go into the inn. They brought the ale
outside and she drank it gratefully, holding onto the stirrup and seeing,
against the red sky, the dark Douglas figures grouped. He helped her
into the saddle again and they made off at the same speed as before.
Presently the sun set and the world was a dim grayness. She was not
conscious any longer of cold; only her will kept her in the saddle.

He did not speak again till they were in sight of a castle. She could see
it hazily in front of her, a great gaunt bulk in the half-light. Beyond it
the hills lay and the night sky. It was a desolate valley, with no sign of
any house nearby, or any human thing. She shuddered, even before she
heard his voice telling her that this was Douglas, the Castle Dangerous
of legend, which had never been taken except by trickery, and from
which no one could win out.

She vowed that she would win out.

He had left her at first. She was taken upstairs into a stone room, with some furniture, a bed and hangings, and a window in the far wall. In the grate a fire burned and she went thankfully and sat by it, feeling the warmth gradually returning to her chilled limbs. The terror she had been in receded, leaving her with a curious hard courage. Time passed and he did not come.

Presently the door opened and a servant brought food. She made herself eat a part of it, and drank down the wine. The food made her feel better and there came, in her mind, knowledge that she had not eaten since early day. The swiftness of the thing that had happened to her left her with no time to plan; she sat back, putting the dishes away from her, and tried to collect her senses.

She hadn't miscarried. That fact was always first with her, knowing now that it was all useless, that the King was dead. She found she could not picture him as dead and that her grief had no sharp quality, leaving her bewildered. She felt the resolve growing in her to save the child, having it for a memory of him. If matters moved so, Angus might think it was his.

She watched herself, half aghast at her cool planning. From the instant the resolve grew in her, she had known she would live this through. He wouldn't kill her—now. What happened then was unimportant, unless he branded her. She jerked her mind away from that. One must be ready to meet trouble when it came, not before. She was ready.

She poured out more wine from the flagon that had been provided and ate a little meat. Now that her blood was warmed and the child safe she could manage Angus. He wasn't a devil, only an old man. It was like Helen and the goblins under the stones.

Waiting, she felt the minutes pass. Outside, the darkness deepened, making the fire brighter. The lamp they had lit above the door burned and sputtered in its oil.

The door opened and Angus came in. She saw at once that he had been drinking. He walked with a curious unsteady motion and in one hand was a bullhide whip. She knew a small pulse of terror, and watched him, forcing herself to keep her eyes on his. If she let them stray to the whip, she thought, he would use it. For oneself to keep steady was the only way. He's drunk, she thought, and I'm not. Her wits set to work swiftly. She could see him coming nearer, advancing across the floor.

"Angus," she said. Her own voice sounded steady and she was pleased. He paused, at sound of it; passing his tongue over his moistened lips and

staring at her. His eyes were sullen, like a betrayed animal's; she could
hear his heavy breathing. He had taken off his armor and attired himself in a furred gown.

"You're a bitch," he said. "I can school bitches."

His fingers tightened on the whip. Jan rose. It took as much courage
as anything in her life to rise and go toward him. Step by step, moving
steadily, she came to him; her glance never let his go. She could see the
narrow eyes flicker and blink at her; all his life, he would be thinking,
women had tried to run and hide. This was a new thing for the Red
Douglas. A smile curled the corners of her mouth.

She used every attraction she knew in that instant. It was only that,
although to her it seemed many minutes. It was as though her sheer will
could make her hair flame, her flesh gleam more whitely so that his
desire overcame anger, her very presence transform him into a thing of
no purpose except the one that had burned in him for long—overriding
hurt and blind fury and the lust to kill and maim, and to bruise her
flesh so that no man would ever want it again.

And now all that had gone and he was back where he had been. . . .

"Jan." He could hear his own voice huskily. He was trembling.

Suddenly he seized her. He could hear her laughter. The reason for it
stabbed in vain at his dulled recollection; he could understand nothing
any more. The color of her hair blinded him, making a mist before his
eyes; in it he found her body, more fair and deeply enchanting than he
had ever known in dreams; she was here, herself, with her red mouth
and her warmth and the sound of her laughter, not resented now as her
hands dragged his head down and the whip clattered to the floor.

He was young again.

He had forgotten everything, even ambition. For the moment he did
not think of the future or the past. Soon he would tell her about the
killing of Spens, in the manner of a small boy showing off the birds he
has taken. She bewildered him afresh with her joy at the news and the
way she lay back among the covers and laughed, and still shaking and
joyous with laughter pulled his head down again so that it lay against
her breast. He was physically her master and she showed that she had
pleasure in it, taking pride in the strength of his great arms and the way
they would not let her escape. He watched her now, seeing her skin's
fairness against the tanned leather and furred golden hair of his own;
had she cared nothing for Spens, then? The discovery pleased and puzzled him. He left it, turning to pleasure in other ways. Why had he

waited? "We might have been as happy long ago, if I'd carried you off before," he told her. He felt her kinship with him and that also gave him pleasure; rogues, both of them. A spirit burned in them that some called greed and others ambition disguised under a variety of names; he didn't know. For himself, he had left ambition for the first time since all those years ago he had married Bess Boyd for her family's sake and lost. It seemed now as if the gods recompensed him for that, making him young and golden again. It seemed as though she loved him.

VI

The waiting-woman padded about with a lighted taper; the candles needed renewing and were thick and misshapen with yesterday's gobbets of wax. There was, in his houses, a more than usual mixture of luxury and discomfort; foul rushes lay on the floor, which the draft lifted; but the head of the stuffed white bearskin over the couch on which she lay had ruby-glass for eyes. They glinted in the firelight knowingly.

The late Countess' robe was lined with beaver fur. She drew it closely about her, sliding each hand into the opposite sleeve. The woman went away, and she curled up on the couch again, and waited. Her arm, the one he had hurt the other day, throbbed faintly; she pushed back the sleeve and examined it, noting the swollen discolored flesh. Her eyes, under the long lids, gleamed.

She wondered if they had acted yet at home. Her father had been out of Galloway and the hue and cry for her would be later than if he had been at the Castle. She knew her mother would make less haste, seeing in this a consummation of the marriage. The snow would prevent communication for a day or two in any case. It had fallen three days ago and taken some of the chill out of the air, and would lie deeply on the southern hills.

Her thoughts drifted on. There was a light draft from the window. The curtain flapped loosely there and one could hear the wind outside, singing over the hills. Jan shivered, and turned again to the fire. The drafts made the floor cold.

There was a pewter dish on the couch by her side; on it lay sweetmeats, variously colored to resemble fruits and frosted over with sugar. She chose a pear and began to nibble it. Soon the boy would come.

Her eyes narrowed at the resemblance of him standing there, the little groom from Luce. She had not credited that so much intelligence lay behind his narrow eyes. That he would keep his counsel she knew, in the same way that he had ingratiated himself with the guards and made it possible for her to receive a message from Ramsay's man.

She surveyed her own hasty judgment of Ramsay, riding past them that day on the moor. He'd had too much sense to get himself killed; she should have realized that, and that he would go to the King with his tale. Angus in his fool's paradise had no thought of the repercussions that would come, or of the inevitable fact of his discovery when they had found the body of Spens. He lived still in a dead world, wherein the Douglases rode as lords of Scotland. But James had changed all that.

She wondered how soon she could draw Angus away from here. Ramsay had sent word only of his going to the King; but she knew well enough that none dared act with her still in Angus' hands, here, in Douglas. It was impregnable except by siege and, even with that, Bell would kill her before they got her out. She knew him well enough for that, after all that had happened. No, she must wait for the boy. . . .

The pear was very good, with a subtle flavor compounded. A small clove stuck in the end gave the air of a real fruit. She licked her fingers delicately, and got up to fasten the blind. Its flapping irritated her.

Angus' wife must have been the size of a ship; the gown trailed after her, dragging along the floor. She picked her way across, holding it up with one hand; the notion came to her that Angus must buy her clothes. He had torn the gown she had almost to ribbons, that day. She thought of it, leaning on the sill; remembering how she had seen yesterday the little groom from Luce standing below. He had not taken hardly to his imprisonment, being on the best of terms with his guards. She wondered how Wil fared.

The light had almost gone when the boy came. She could see the curve of the hills nearly black against the sky, and the snow lying gray and thick in the half-dark. She thought she would always associate grayness with Douglas, remembering the first she had seen of it, riding down. There had been a time in Bruce's day when the English garrison was in church, and the Good Lord James whose name frightened Englishmen had ridden in with his handful of Scots and made a bonfire of the Castle stores and the surprised English bodies, setting them ablaze with the name of the Douglas Larder. But no one would take Douglas by surprise when its owners were in church again. She remembered the little chapel, the shadows thrown by the branched candles up over the painted walls, and the tombs where dead Douglases lay, watching and hearing.

"No," she said aloud. There were things she would deny had happened. She turned at a sound at the door and there was the little groom with fresh candles.

Angus came in as she talked to the groom. "What do you there?" he said suspiciously. He dismissed the lad with a jerk of the head and he went, his eyes holding beady innocence. Jan knew that he would convey the message as she had related it; she was ready, as she had been that first day.

Bell strode over and laid his hands on her shoulders, looking over the darkened sky line to where there was nothing to be seen but the hills. "I said what were you doing there?" he repeated. "I do not care to have you show yourself thus."

"He is my groom, and he brought fresh candles. And you have left me nothing else to wear."

"You'll order my servants," he said curtly. He jerked the blind into place and carried her back to the fire. She watched the glow of his hair and beard in the firelight, thinking how all things resolved in the end to her bidding. She would work upon him with regard to the subject of clothes.

Later, he put her from him, and went to fetch the box that he had brought. It was of leather, in the form of a little chest, with the clasps and hoops of iron closed. He unlocked it as he had done in Tantallon; she gasped at the glitter of jewels.

"I had these brought here," he said. "George's wife shan't have them." He pulled her toward him again and dragged out, as they came, the chains and sapphires and brilliants winking in the firelight. He crammed the rings on her fingers, twisted the chains in her hair and about her body. He was laughing. "They are yours," he said. Fumbling, he hung drop pearls in her ears, and paused with his hands behind her head, grinning, and surveying his handiwork.

"What think you of me for a lady's maid?" he said. To his astonishment her eyes were full of tears. "Why, why—" he mumbled. He could not understand. Were gems not to her liking, then? He never remembered having seen her tears.

But she blinked them away and answered him almost roughly. "How the devil can I wear jewels naked? You've destroyed what I had; take me into Ayr and get me some more."

He grunted, suspicion asserting itself; but she cozened him. "Are you so afraid that you will bide in Douglas Castle all the days of your life?" she teased.

"Ay, with you."

"I can't pass my time in your late wife's bedgown. It isn't seemly and it doesn't fit. What can befall us now, when we—"

Angus hedged. He would send John Douglas, he told her, to Dumbarton for bales of stuff. She pouted, and moved away from him on the couch. The chains he had hung about her glittered and the gems flashed like some barbaric Sheba. He thought he had never seen her look so beautiful. In the end the logic of what she had said and the desire he had to please her won him over. He was beyond anything at that moment except the sight that she made with the jewels.

Jan yielded herself again and smiled, remembering how she had sent word to Ramsay that she would bring the Earl to Ayr.

She saw him taken.

They had made their way to the coast town not in secret, but with the train and clatter of men-at-arms as though he were the King. He had sent a man ahead to prepare lodgings; everything was done leisurely, openhanded and without haste. He might have been an innocent man for all that was heard of rumor concerning him; no breath had reached them of the whereabouts of the King. They rattled into Ayr streets, seeing the tall ships in the harbor. The town was full of foreign speech, dark little Italians from Turin set up in booths, selling bales; gangrel women with trays of strung sea shells, ribbons and paint for the face; Irish savages from the north glens; sailors with rings in their ears. Angus was pleased enough to let her spend at will, riding about with her always and remembering other times. Gradually as the days passed he grew less wary, discarding the heavy train of men for a handful as nothing befell. He took pleasure in watching her comb the booths, seizing on a trinket or a curch she coveted with eagerness as though it would be taken from her; she had always this greed in grasping things. He paid agreeably, knowing he would receive in kind; the open affection she showed pleased him. He knew they made a striking couple, he with his great height and flaxen coloring, and she with her head of flame. The half-foreign, bizarre town was a background for them, with its blue sea and the colored bales.

The lodging they had looked out on the town, its windows facing away from the sea. The rooms were small and the stuffs Jan had bought cluttered them, leaving the place in a wilderness of colors and keeping the sewing women busied with gowns. Later he would take her to Court, he told her; she would be fine enough to cut a picture there. Her reactions to things bewildered him; he never knew whether she would laugh or frown. She turned away then, speaking of the woman at the booth whom they had seen that day; she was to go there tomorrow again for lawn for shifts. "A pretty penny," Angus grumbled. He did not really mind. The shambles in the house diverted him and he had become used to the page, the groom, she had about her, a sly Galloway lad with narrow dark eyes. The other he had sent back to her father's house when the snow melted.

The Kennedys had not ridden north. Tacitly he assumed that they supported the situation. My lord, he knew, had not been for him, but my lady had. Later, he'd square with them; but in the meantime the days were pleasant, and the nights more so; that, in the end, was all a man need care for. He was pleased with Jan, approving the change in her which he attributed to his conquest of herself; she was comely, good-humored, complaisant but never dull. The wild fire he thought was gone; it had intrigued him, but he did not regret it. He began to look on her as a husband might have done; the memory of his black ride south was far behind him.

Their last night he remembered it, but dimly as with a matter long past; and having fulfilled himself with her had turned over on his side to sleep. The sea wind outside was rattling at the casement windows, straining the leather hasps as though they would break; he heard its wild fury and pictured its lashing of the waves, rocking the King's ships where they lay in harbor. The storm heightened and he wondered if Jan were asleep; she had turned away like a child, head hidden in the shadow of her arm. For the first time the difference in their ages came to him; did he weary her? As if in answer he heard her voice in the darkness.

"Bell."

"What is it?" he said, and turned toward her. The scudding clouds beyond the window cast a fitful light on her face; he saw with bewilderment that she was crying. "Is it the storm?" he asked her. Awkwardly, he reached out; he was touched by her use of the name she had for him, the old name, significant of his blackest crime, turned to fond folly, made brief and ridiculous.

"Bell. Oh, Bell, take me again. Love me again. Who is to say what will befall either of us?"

He felt bemused and humble, taking her again in his arms. She was a witch, he thought, beyond all human reckoning; who would have thought that she would want him, now, as he wanted her? And what had she meant by that saying? "No matter what befalls, we can pleasure one another," he mumbled; his mouth was against her hair. It seemed to him that never had he had such pleasure as tonight, when she gave herself willingly to him. He was to remember it for long, seeing it later as a farewell gift, and remembering her tears against his shoulder.

The next day she went again to the woman of Turin. The little groom had brought her word that all was now in readiness. She knew what she was to do and the woman would aid her. She stooped in entering the little shop, dark under a roof of stretched ship's canvas and stacked behind the counter with bales.

Angus was behind her and she left him blotting out the light, while she went behind the counter with her tale of shifts. The woman brought the fine lawn and held it out, murmuring over it and engaging the Earl in approbation. Her broad-nosed face had sallow skin and a texture to it like an orange, and in her ears she wore a pair of gold rings.

The bales rose high, hiding Jan as she rounded the back of the booth, with a variety of jutted shapes and colors. "I will come and measure," the woman called, and she answered, saying she was ready. Angus grunted something, and the woman came round, edging past the stacked bales and bearing in her hand a rod for measurement. She talked idly of yards and fingers. Meanwhile there was a cloak laid at the back of the shop, and Jan put it on. The woman pulled its dark hood over her face; the strings drew tightly. She had a sense of unreality as the hands thrust her out through the back of the tent; the voice still talked on. Once outside, the sounds of the fruit criers, the bawling about the market, came loud; she threaded her way, quickly, between the booths, and when she came past the other the man was there.

"Hurry," he told her. "They are not here yet."

She wondered how long it would take Angus to know she was gone, and whether he would have time to kill the woman. But hurrying down the eternal huddle of mud-colored houses that leaned over alleys with steps going up and down, she saw them come; the King's men, as the Douglas men had ridden, quietly and with purpose marked, toward the place which she had left. The clatter of hooves sounded in the street, drowning the cries of fruit vendors.

"It is arranged," said Ramsay.

She saw his cool light eyes survey her, and felt suddenly sick and faint. "When?" she said. She put back the hood of the dark cloak, loosened its strings and smoothed her hair. The smell of garbage and of cabbage water came to her from the yard below the stairs.

"Tomorrow. Tonight, if you will. I am commanded to bring you to His Grace direct."

"You waste little time," she said, staring at him.

"His Grace wastes little." Ramsay pointed beyond the window. She rose and joined him, looking down on to the street. The crowds that gathered there were watching something, backed by the permanency of high roofs and the masts that rose beyond. The noise swelled in the streets.

"They're coming," said Ramsay, and unfastened the casement. She wondered at the triumph he showed in this, seen by the way the pale eyes gleamed; then she remembered Lauder. Was this sufficient revenge? They were leading an old man down the street. He was still mounted but with his hands tied, and she could see from his hatless state he must have fought; he was disheveled. She shuddered, and tried to turn away. "Watch," said Ramsay.

"*You* didn't go to take him. You were afraid." She flung the taunt despairingly, to shut other things out. Ramsay gave his soft laugh, watching her. "Is it Angus you wanted," he said, "or the King?"

"What will they do to him?" she was trembling all over. Last night, she'd lain in Bell's arms; he had been strong as a god, every muscle in his body firm, and he had loved her. Once he had saved her when she was in trouble and pain. Once he'd—ah, dear God, what was the use of remembering now? The King's men led him away and his own had left him, and he looked no longer a warrior but old and tired. It mattered little enough now what he had done, to her or another. With every facet of her will active for him, as once it had been against him, she was determined that, if it could be avoided by any effort of hers, he should not hang.

She heard Ramsay's voice beside her. It was curiously gentle, like a child's. "He grudged Rob Cochrane a silken rope, saying he was not noble. It is like enough the King will allow him a block, for the sake of his own black blood."

She would have turned on him then, but Angus looked up as he passed below, and saw them. The look he cast her she would never forget, if she lived to be an old woman. When they had led him past she sank down by the sill in spite of Ramsay's presence, and wept bitterly.

"The lady, Your Grace."

The room held a hearth with polished tiles. In them she saw her own reflection, a tiny advancing figure with a high headdress like a nun's.

The change in her appearance surprised herself; she had always thought of Janet Kennedy as a girl with wild flying hair. The woman in the high coif curtsied, spread skirts sinking; the high coif bending like a nodding flower. The man's dark figure neared, stood, bent and raised it; he led her to a chair.

This was James Stewart and he was the father of her child. She remembered the care she had been at to save the child, and the thought of that gave her courage. She listened to his shrewd questioning, keeping her head.

"I have proof that it is Your Grace's child in my dates, which are certain. It is true that my word may not be of value and I ask nothing. I pray that when the child is born it may resemble Your Grace. That should still all tongues."

"I do not disbelieve you," he said.

To her surprise he came and kissed her hands, raising them slowly one after the other. The respect he showed bewildered her; had he forgotten that night? He saw her eyes watching him and met them with his own; she saw again how he had changed.

"I will protect you."

Suddenly he began to talk, bewildering her with his words' intensity and the way they belied his appearance, which was expressionless. It might have been another man of whom he spoke. She listened, grasping the arms of the chair.

"That night you came to me I took you in lust, for which I ask your pardon. It was caused by my grief, which in itself was caused by the loss of the only woman I would desire to be my wife. I will not speak her name again, except to tell you that when I rode away and left you that next day it was to go to her, in her father's house, and ask her forgiveness; for I realized what I am. She returned to me—"

The long fingers tightened imperceptibly. "She returned," said James Stewart, as though he recited a tale. Jan watched him, hiding her thoughts; he was almost unaware, she saw, of her presence in the room. "For a while we were together, but it befell again as always."

"As always?" she said harshly. "If you love her, and she you, what befell?"

She closed her eyes, regretting that she had spoken. This was not her part. Whatever became of them now she would be remembered, Margaret Drummond; her place held high above all other mistresses, higher when she came than the wife's. But she herself, among others, must pretend nothing of love; what would she know of it, who had sold herself?

"I can no longer see her," said James Stewart.

She stared at him. "By her wish, or yours?" The thing nagged at her.

"By neither. By circumstance, and the fact that I am a king."

"And so she bides in Perthshire, and you here. Is that the way of it?"

He nodded; he did not seem to resent her questioning. "I have not her strength," he said, "that can endure solitude."

Impatience flamed in her; must they talk all night of that nun? He had turned away from her to the window and she saw the bearded altered face; the flesh below the cheeks had tautened and was no longer boyish, showing the contour of the high-set bones. The drawn look he had tugged at her heart; to make him laugh again, she thought, would be worth much grief. She could, if he'd let her.

"There have been so many women," he said. "They weary me."

"I'd not weary Your Grace." She heard her own voice speaking.

He looked at her quizzically and she felt her cheeks flame. "Look not at me as though I were a paid whore!" she flashed. "Do you think I could not have married Angus? What's one more woman to Your Grace, or one more bastard? But give me the chance other women have had, and I'll swear I make the hours less gray."

"I brood too much," he said. She remembered the tale about the chain. Dear God, he had enough behind him to make him wish to be merry now!

She went to him. "Don't kill my Earl," she said. "He was good to me."

He looked at her in amazement. "He's a murderer; a ravisher. He caused much trouble before. Can I have women abducted, harmless men done to death at their pursuits? No, he'll hang."

"Spens wasn't harmless. He menaced me often, after I had bidden him go." She did not care how much she blackened Spens.

"There was provocation," she said, and told him of it. In her mind was the knowledge that he would never now look on her as anything but a whore. But she had to save Bell's skin, and grudged nothing.

"I was bored," she told him. "Dear St. Ninian, how bored I was, down there again in Galloway! If the devil with all his horns on had come to bid me dance, I would have done so and then bidden him lie with me."

"You shall not be bored again," he promised her. Suddenly he smiled, and his face was transfigured. "I will save old Angus, then, as you wish it." He quizzed her. "There was no marriage ceremony between you, there in Douglas? If so your evidence is valueless, and he will hang."

She smiled at him. "Is a marriage by force valid?" she asked him. It was true that a wife's evidence was valueless regarding her husband. She shrugged and laughed and amused him, glossing over the subject of marriage.

He left it, gravely assuming her good faith in a way he had. He assured her again of his protection.

When one has climbed a mountain there should be satisfaction in reaching the top.

There were many who envied her. Seeing them from her height, she understood their viewing of her; seeing her in the coveted place, counting the gifts she acquired, and these were many. She had always had a high regard for material things, her greed often overcoming her conscience. So it was now when James denied her nothing. She collected more in the way of household plenishings than her mother in the course of two rich marriages had ever possessed in her life; and all this before she had a house to put them in. But soon His Grace rectified that, and the brass candlesticks and objects in gilt and silver, the liveries for her servants' servants, the petticoats for herself; the sewing silks and altarcloths and linen and the hangings and gowns found a home, and were conveyed there.

The great sweeping baggage train with the King and the lady at the end rode north, astounding all who met with it by its richness and the number of carts, and the beauty of the lady, by then near her time, who rode in a litter with His Grace and many lords in attendance. "You shall have Darnaway," the King had said to her, and straightway set about perfecting his plans; giving her a home, far removed from the Galloway moors and from all who knew her, up in Morayshire where the air was sharp and the ground thick with His Grace's pines for timber.

They laughed together and it was a promise that he should come to her when he rode north for timber, and also when he made a pilgrimage to the shrine of St. Duthac by Tain. "Last time you came it was on a pilgrimage to St. Ninian," she teased him. She knew that he had also other reasons; that when the English bride came it was as well to have herself some way removed from Edinburgh. But of that she said nothing, having learned when to hold her peace.

The child when it was born was a boy and his christening was a gala affair. Jan sat in bed at the upsetting feast holding court in a flower-decked room, flushed with the adulation of thronging courtiers and with wine, and with the King's generosity. For Darnaway with its castle and farms and fisheries he had made over to her *pro cordiale amore*, a few days before the document *pro paternali amore* was signed creating her son Earl of Moray. Also he had heard her request for David, finding him a second wife from the semi-royal branch of Boyds who were descended from James the Third's sister, and creating him Earl of Cassilis on the death of my lord. And the lands also that Angus was to have given her, which the King had confiscated, he recompensed; giving her in their stead Bothwell Castle, with its title to use as her own.

So she was the Lady of Bothwell, and she noted the flicker in Ramsay's eyes when he heard. Ramsay had been my lord of Bothwell once, till his honors were taken from him in exile and an earldom created for Patrick Hepburn. But, she found, that need worry her little; she had small need for Ramsay in these days, or he for her.

Angus abode for three years in fortresses in Arran and Dumbarton. On his release he found a wife, a young girl, a daughter of Stirling of Keir. She was a mouselike creature, Jan remembered; and wondered how they would fare. The sword with which he had killed Spens with a single blow through the thigh would be preserved, for future generations to gaze at, hanging on the wall at Tantallon. Jan tossed her head and laughed when it was spoken of. She laughed at almost everything now.

The only way was to laugh, she had found; few men were not bored by tears. She had not bored James; had given, she thought, good value for his purchase of her. He was a courteous and undemanding lover; she tried to shut out the memory of Beltane. She knew that he was fond of her; he was fond also of his horse. That he was capable of jealousy, and of pride in her possession, she knew; did not the terms of the Darnaway deed specify that she was to remain without husband or other man? But that meant little, and there was a woman who was never mentioned between them, whom he had never loaded with gifts, and never now saw. She tried to shut out the remembrance of the woman from her mind, and at times succeeded. One's body had needs; she had never denied that. At times with a kind of brilliant and sophisticated lovemaking he could almost convince her that it was Beltane; if she had not remembered that, or if Bell and she had not belonged, surprisingly, to one another; or if she had never heard the deepened voice that night at Stirling in the time of white roses, she might have been satisfied.

That the white rose had withered now she knew. It was on the twenty-third of November, 1499, that Henry Tudor hanged King James' friend on the gallows at Tyburn; and whether Warbeck, or Richard of

York, or a madman, was never known. And it was less than three years later that the betrothal embassy was to set out, plighting the troth of Margaret Tudor as Queen of Scots in St. Paul's; but before that many things befell.

Part Four

THE LADY OF BOTHWELL

1500–1509

I

"YOUR DEAL, Your Grace."

She leaned back on the cushions idly. There was a buzz of talk in the room, and the air was warm; here, in the King's palace of Falkland, which they would all leave tomorrow to ride again north. She turned her head so as to survey the room, impressing it on her remembrance; the small exquisite room, carved and faceted like a jewel as all the rooms were here. Falkland was agreeable by reason of its little size, she thought; no room for pomp here, only the sound of a horn in the woods as the King rode home from hunting, or the cry of an owl in a tower, or the notes of a song. It was hers, Falkland; nowhere any memory of that other. There were tales of death and treachery here as in all royal palaces but she had never found in it any cause for other than joy; it was her home, as Darnaway and Bothwell were, and she always knew a little leap of pleasure at sight of the approaching towers. And tomorrow they would leave. She sighed a little. The King would ride north with her and for a little while there would be music and feasting at Darnaway. Then he would go and she would be alone, with nothing but the dark pines for company and the time to put in until he came again. The child was there with his nurse but he was too young for interest yet, and she would sit by night and listen to the wind in the trees, and wonder how long it would be till the King again rode north.

Well, there were things to remember. She smiled, recalling her farewell to Galloway, made in a pilgrimage of thanksgiving to St. Ninian at Whithorn after the boy was born. The King had been with her and she had ridden a white mule sent from Spain, its harness of red Spanish leather in which little gilt bells were set. They had jangled out as she rode down and to their tune had followed all the countryside, and the knights' wives and others who had envied her before had not dared show their envy now, for she was the King's mistress and the mother of his son, as good as any queen who had ridden that way, the last of them being His Grace's own mother after *he* was born, in a gown of gray and a coif of black velvet, with twelve maids dressed likewise. Ah, that had been a royal farewell to Galloway; she would never go back, the gray moors and the gray skies and she had parted company.

Here was her life now, and her friends were here. She raised a hand to one and another; they responded eagerly, forgetting, she thought, how they had slighted her when she was at Stirling, a waif without power. There wasn't a dowager now but would receive her with pleasure; Jan smiled on them all and imitated them behind their backs.

She saw Ramsay, over in a corner playing cards. He's fallen on rich earth too, she thought sardonically. He was a well-known figure now, the Laird of Trarinyean; no stouter, but dressed more richly and with an air of sleek well-being, like a stray cat that has fallen on good times. She had almost forgotten the discomfort his presence gave her; only when the pale eyes raised themselves would she remember, and ask herself in an irritated way what the devil ailed Ramsay now. . . . Perhaps it was the thought of the plague, which he had left behind in Glasgow; he was mortally afraid of infection, and carried always about him a bunch of herbs to burn. Once summer had gone there would be little risk . . . and none at Darnaway, it being isolated enough. Lord, must one then either die of weariness or die of plague?

She was glad James had given her Bothwell to come down to, she could pass the time collecting gear to ride again south, when it pleased her and if there was no other diversion. She would become like him, restless and never settled, passing always from one abode to the next. She wondered how it would be when the English child came, and if he would be obliged to take up permanent residence somewhere. She did not think it would be at Stirling; Holyrood might suit. Things would be different then for all of them, she thought, looking round. James had his bastards hereabouts and reared them happily together with the sons of Highland chiefs whom he had promised to bring up, and the young foreign prince, Christiern Denmark, who had been sent to Scotland for his education. He lounged now nearby, a large-boned child with thick, sandy-fair hair; he was precocious and understood everything anyone said, replying in an accent which had at first amused her.

James, James, James, she thought, was he one man or a hundred? No one knew . . . she least of all, who should have known him as well as anyone. At Stirling he had vanished for a time every day and had been found in his laboratory, compounding messes of herbs and potions with which he would dose sick folk that came. He dissected birds and geese that were brought to him, trying to find out how they flew; he was convinced, he once told her, that man could fly if he could learn to design the wings. "You'd be better finding the Elixir of Life," she told him idly. She had heard Walter speak of that and how philosophers and alchemists had wasted God knew how much gold trying to find the Elixir, but it was never found. And James had looked grave when she spoke to him of that and walked up and down the room, talking and gesturing with his hands.

"The Elixir will never be found," he said, "or if it is, will cease to be desirable. How would we use our youth if it were impossible ever to grow old? If one has excess it is wasted . . . but the ills which man has brought upon himself, these may be healed. It is the things which are discovered on the way toward a goal which are of value, not the goal itself." And he had gone on talking and not looking at her and she had felt for once as if she were a person, someone whom he might have known, instead of only his mistress whose mind mattered nothing, as long as her body was fair.

But such times were rare and as a rule she was nothing more to him.

She looked at him now, noting how he had grown and broadened with this last year from near boyhood into adult magnificence. The wild lad who had roamed the Galloway moors was gone, and in his place there sat the friend of France and deliverer of Denmark, with the long labor of his conquest of the Isles and Scotland past. He looked like a king on a card, she thought, until one saw the eyes, which were alive. His laughter was charming, his words polished; he would fling with ease from French to Danish, thence to Gaelic and back to his own tongue again. The babel in the room was polyglot, between the followers of Christiern and the followers of the Isles.

A great king . . . and she his official mistress. She saw her own rich gear, leaning back on the cushions. She wore the square-cut bodice of the new style and her hair was hidden under a little round coif. A pendant hung on a chain about her neck with three drop pearls, depending from a double J in silver; J for Janet, J for James.

James.

She smiled at him, thinking how he was moody at times. There was that old affair of his father's murder, making him do public penance twice a year . . . and always, secretly, in his own flesh. She knew of that now, having seen the place on his body where the chain chafed it. He had never spoken of it to her. Then at other times he would be gay. No one could predict it, or him, and the only way she had found was to laugh, and make him laugh.

"Your play, madame."

She cast a card gracefully. During the time that her thoughts had assembled she had not lost track of the game. She was lucky at cards and in all games of chance; he pushed the chits toward her absently. She wondered if he were diverted or bored, and if they should play again.

"It is late," he said. He turned toward the window. Outside, the sound of music came; he went and flung open the casement. The music flooded into the room and as soon as she heard its wild abandon she knew who the player was; one of the stranger, the bizarre foreign folk who had ridden north that year from England. Their handsome brightly clad women, with gold coins jangling at their ears and about their throats, had danced the other day before the King. The Counts of Little Egypt, they called themselves; all their men were kings. They had been feted and received wherever they had been, France and the Empire and Hungary and back, through Greece and the country of old gods to India, where with the dry dust blowing in the Ganges basin were their origins, shrouded in time. James went often among them and strove to learn their tongue, but the things they told him were, he said, secrets and he would not divulge them. "Like enough it's their women you're after," Jan told him, herself seeing the attraction of the oliveskinned, dark-eyed queens.

He smiled, denying it. "An Egyptian woman is faithful to her husband," he told her, "and their virgins are chaste. Any Gorgio—outsider— attempting them is killed."

She snorted. "They'd not kill you. They owe you food and shelter."

But he shook his head. Later she found that he had been admitted to their brotherhood by a queer rite, a mingling of his own blood with that of a chosen man. Wherever they passed now he would be one of them.

Watching, she felt his affinity with unknown things, the night and the strangers. His shadowed face, with the beard jutting, looked down on to the place where the fiddler played; the music swelled more wildly, in loving and lament. She felt the chill of it strike her bones; why did they play for him so? She went to the window and laid her hand on his arm. "James—"

He turned to her; he looked like a stranger. She closed her eyes for an instant against the changed pale face, which frightened her. "Why do they play for you so?" she said. Back in the room the courtiers yawned and diced; they were nothing to him now, any more than she. Dear God, why did he leave her behind with fools? Had he forgotten their beginnings, the way she had found the hills and secret things, riding to watch the god send fire at Midsummer?

She felt his interest. "Why?" he said. Her opened eyes found him looking down at her, as when he had spoken to her of the Elixir. The novelty of being a person again fired her; she flung her head back and looked him between the eyes.

"Because they play as if you were already dead. Are you a living man?"

"I?" he said. The brooding eyes still held hers; she could not tell his thoughts. Suddenly he laughed. "They have cast my fate and the manner of it, and so they know," he said. "What do we care for such things?"

His eyes, half-closed now between lazy lids, surveyed her. She was a picture to warm any man's blood, richly gowned with the light behind her; a crystal, swinging in her ear, flashed fire. Swiftly he possessed himself of her hands. "If you deny that I live, I'll prove you wrong," he whispered.

"Then tell your visitor to have done with his dirge, and play a dancing tune."

She turned with him to the window; he gave her gold and she flung out the coins. The Count of Little Egypt's face in the darkness laughed up at them; she saw the flash of his teeth and the glint of gold rings in his ears. He broke into a running, dancing tune and her heart leaped for gladness; the power of the alien, secret folk to draw the King away had aroused resentment in her. They would have conjured his heart out of his body, she thought, leaving only a shell.

But now again he was her laughing lover. That night he was hers as never before; alone together, the darkness in the room relieved by leaping firelight, she was able to tell him at last of Beltane, and what had befallen her since and the cause of it. He had always taken pleasure in her as a thing of beauty and desire; to be, as he had told her, loved in the way he loved gems, smooth silks, carvings and paintings and other fair flesh. But now she was herself for him and she felt he knew of her; and turning to each other again in gladness she heard his voice, as it had sounded for that other.

"I did not know," he told her, "that you could hear that tune."

For a while between them it was Beltane.

Her life was to be measured by those rides north. Later His Grace
was to achieve it in a single day, flinging himself down for sleep on an
inn table in Tain. But now all was leisure and gaiety; it mattered little
enough when they won to Darnaway, judging from the laughter and
welcoming faces that thronged for them on the way. A royal progress,
she had once thought the farewell to Galloway; this, now, was a Roman
triumph, with the sound again of the mule bells, the chatter of many
tongues in the King's train, the dark-faced Moors and mulattoes that
had come, the scented Frenchmen and long-whiskered Gaels, all riding
past at a jaunty pace. Always she would remember the laughing King,
his long straight hair blown backward under the great broad hat, riding;
the jests and brilliance of his talk; his kindness, even on that day in
Arbroath when they had ridden away from the train and he had bought
her two mantles, like any knight for his companion. But it was seldom
they were alone, being everywhere met by friends, old and new; northern
lairds and their wives riding forth to meet them, hosts vying with one
another for their entertainment; hunting, dancing, listening to tales or
the high weird song of the clarsach players; sailing on the Cowie Water
and the wind-chopped breadth of Spey; feasting out of doors in the *al
fresco* manner of the Florentines. For this was Italian weather, continuing
warm into autumn. Further south, the pestilence still raged, in the cities
and the poorer streets of towns; men died like flies and there was nothing
to be done except wait for winter, with its sharp cold. The King made
the round of his justice ayres: Aberdeen, Fintry, Elgin, Inverness, Tain.
The Lady of Bothwell was ensconced at Darnaway on the twenty-first
of November.

She sat in the great hall after they had all ridden off, seeing the sparks
rise in the hearth with coming frost. The logs burned brightly, giving
off an aromatic smell; reminding her of the pines in summer, and the
sun's slant down on to the carpet of brown needles, as she had ridden
there with James. Everything in its own manner reminded her of him;
turning, looking over her shoulder into the gathering dark, she saw the
fire's gleam on the silver saltfat, the great beaten-work dish he had sent
her as a parting gift, knowing she loved silver and gold. And wine he
had sent her, saying she should lack for nothing. It is easy enough for a
man, she thought, to say good-by, with a kiss and a gift—and lonely when
he has gone.

And he had gone, bending down from the great white horse of Huntly's gift to kiss her farewell; and the last she had heard had been the echoing hoof-beats down the long road between the pines. And now there was no sound at all in Darnaway, except the hammering of builders in the stillness, as they wrought at some new matter the King would have done.

During that time she first made discovery of a new thing.

His Grace had given her candlesticks in silver gilt and also silks for sewing. Rather in the fashion of the time than from any real desire, she made an altarcloth. The upward-gazing faces of the angels on it reminded her of the Apostles in the King's Book of Hours that he carried. She had often felt a curious interest in that part of James, one of the many that she did not know. That he fasted rigorously she knew, keeping the calendar; during Lent he would go to the Franciscans Observants in Stirling as a lay brother there, doing the humblest tasks and attiring himself in the rough gray gown and sandals of the Order. She remembered how Wil Dunbar had written a satirical poem on it, begging him to return to Court.

The contrast of the gaiety and austerity in the King's nature intrigued her. His mother, they said, had been a near-saint, fasting always and doing penance, and his father was melancholy. Jan had shrugged her shoulders when she heard and made some sardonic rejoinder; but the thing remained with her. That she would never see him thus she knew; at Lenten times he stayed away from her. She recalled the thanksgiving pilgrimage to St. Ninian after the birth of their child; he was as pious, she remembered, as though it were a prince. There was no doubt that God would have an eye to bastards, when all was said and done; was not the saintly Bishop of Aberdeen, William Elphinstone, said to have been such?

She thought of it all, as the tall flames flickered and stilled above the candlesticks in the chapel at Darnaway where she had placed them; the gold thread of the altarcloth glittered in the faint light. Above, the walls seemed shadowy and bare, vault after vault rising into high darkness. It came to her that she would have His Grace's painter, Piers, come and ornament them. The tall silent figures rose in her mind to the imagined sound of singing. She'd have a body of choristers, boys gowned in black and white, as the King had them in his Chapel Royal in Stirling. It would give her pleasure to listen. . . .

She raised her head, aware of the reality of the stillness. As once on the moors she was conscious of a second presence, denying and yet confirming the creed of Beltane. Scraps of her early training came back to her, coupled with remembrance of the faces in the King's book. She remembered when she was a child being afraid, she had forgotten why, in the chapel of gray stone at home, kneeling there with her face in her hands.

But it is long enough since I laid aside all that, she thought. It had been a matter of course with her to forgo meat on Fridays and to go to confession and receive the Host, and she had a pair of beads the King had given her of greenstone, with a St. Ninian medal of silver and one also of St. Columba whose armbone lately, in a certain town, had relieved it of the plague. The beads slipped through her fingers now, silently; she must have been saying the words for long. A gentleness was about her, nourished by the calm air; she was aware that she was again pregnant, and she felt that she desired this child deeply; he of all her children would have had a joyous begetting. He should not, she thought, be born in Darnaway, here among the mists and cold and the sighing pines; already her spirit craved for Bothwell and the south.

She rode once again about her farms and saw the King's foresters; she was an able steward and, she knew, almost as if her conscious thoughts had told her, this would endear her to him still, long after other endearments had ceased. Having seen that all was well and the winter over, she packed her gear and made ready to come south. His Grace was in Stirling and she sent him word; he was busy with preparations for the English betrothal. The document had been signed in Glasgow in the previous February; they were saying how all the splendor of thistles and roses and unicorns on it had not lured the King's eye from the main issue, which was that Henry Tudor styled himself therein King of France. James had refused to sign until the mistake was rectified.

"He's able enough for the clerk, then," she thought, pleased. More than ever she missed the news of Court, the hub of things. Here in the north it was too far to ride except on matters of urgency; such as she heard would filter first by way of the Huntlys, His Grace's kin and hers.

James wrote to her seldom. Now and again his man would come riding north with inquiries for Moray, or instructions regarding the farms. She was able to write back that Moray grew apace, the sharp air of the north suiting him well; her prayer had been answered and the oval-faced boy resembled the King. She took her time about sending word of her second pregnancy to him; it might, she thought, cause him to forbid her undertaking of the long journey to Bothwell till after the child was born.

When at last she set out she took the distance slowly; the King's rule had made the roads safe. Closing her eyes against the swaying of the litter, she let her thoughts run back. How long was it since she had ridden thus, nearer her time than now, and poor Ag's caterwauling coming to her from the far end of the box? The King had done generously by David as she had prayed; now with his royal marriage and the making of him an earl he was very different from the lazy laird of Lesswalt, anxious only for peace and to doze by his fire at the day's end. And Mag, her little sister, the King had married well; she dressed in silks now and lisped about Court like any countess. Ah, she'd done well enough by them, she, the black sheep, that they'd despised, even Helen coming to her to borrow money one year when the crops had failed on Robert's farms. And she had been glad enough to lend it so that Helen would go home again and she could forget the half-resentful, half-curious glint in her eyes. They had not paid back yet and she would see that they did so, and with interest; did they take her for fruit to be squeezed? But she had been sorry for Helen, stuck down there in Galloway among her cows and hens and children; it had been the life that she, Jan, had given her all to escape from, and had done so.

"Am I the better for it?" she thought.

She looked at her hands, lying slackly in her lap; an idle woman's hands, taper-fingered, of the color of pale flowers. A great cut jewel lay about the thumb; the nails were almond-shaped, long and fine. Easy enough now to see she did no more spinning.

She smiled, thinking of the tale of the cottage girl who spun straw into gold and became a queen. Well, queendom was beyond her means, and she did not desire it, being content as she was. "Yet am I so content?" she thought. Watching the gray roads swinging past it came to her that she was not; always, she thought, in her own heart, the restlessness would lie that had made her once fling caution to the winds, and jettison Lochinvar. "What do I want, then?" she asked herself.

Bothwell welcomed her and she set her energies to straightening the house and garden. James had taught her much of the art of gardening as they practiced it in England and France and Italy; showing her the manner of grafting fruit as he had himself done with the famed Black Friar strain of apples the Dominicans had given him in Stirling. His great garden there now boasted fine crops of ripening fruit, hoarded in golden rows over the flat, drained space that had been a marsh once, near the scene of his father's murder. Jan had apple trees at Bothwell and also a herb garden; she liked to talk with the King as to the merits of herbs and their healing. She knew that the folk outside spoke of her as a witch, and laughed. "They will say that of anyone they do not understand," James had told her.

Now she found the rosemary thick and, remembering how he had begged cuttings from her when they should have grown, she sent them to him. His continued silence was beginning to perplex her; she wondered if by chance he were angered with her for coming south so soon, although such a course was unlike his reasonableness. He had written, kindly enough, of his pleasure over the new awaited birth; but had not come himself, and she felt a longing to see him. She knew herself for a fool and hid her hurt that he should take her for granted. Some new face would have charmed him, or the thought of the English alliance possessed his thoughts for the time being; later he would come to her. She accepted the situation, and passed the days calmly; gardening a little, sewing garments for the child. Moray she had left at Darnaway but Gordon's daughter was with her; the child was too stupid to be a companion but she had grown used to the sight of her about the house, dressed in the stuffs her father or the King would send her. James had a predilection for all children and sent gifts to small Janet along with those to his own, and she was dressed now in a gown of French tan stuff that he had sent to Darnaway.

Ramsay rode over one day and came across Jan in the garden. The sun was hot and she had sheltered her skin from it, tying a broad white kerchief over her neck and coif. She was advanced in pregnancy and aware of not looking her best; a prickle of annoyance caught at her when they announced him. She straightened, pushing back a wisp of hair from her eyes; the gesture reminded her of Elizabeth Drummond.

Ramsay struck her as nervous and ill at ease. He fidgeted about the bed where she was working, plucking at the leaves of a mallow plant till she was constrained to tell him to stop. His eyes she saw were restless; jerking from side to side as though someone followed him. He resembled more greatly the out-at-elbows exile from England than he had done for many years; his sleekness and prosperity had left him, although in what manner she could not decide; he dressed as richly as ever.

"Come in, and we'll have ale," she said. She spoke curtly, by no means pleased yet at sight of him. But his voice when he spoke held none of the old mockery, and she prepared to be sorry for him; he was a waif, she thought.

"You are less glad to give me ale than if I had been another, I know well. But I had thought there would be no harm in a word with you, and a sight of you. The Court is dull these days."

"Lacking its brightest star?" she mocked. "The King would give me fair warning of his coming, and not discover me in my oldest gown with a clout tied over my head. Take these for me."

She handed him the tools; he took them, regarding her. "As always, you await fair warning?" he asked her.

The look in his eyes aroused disquiet; that he had come for something she knew. "As always," she said warily. Would it be wise to tell him to his face that she knew him for a timeserving jackal?

"Then you wait in vain."

"So?" she said. The mallow leaves, torn and scattered about the path, occupied her; she thrust at one with her foot. "And my lord of Trarinyean has ridden down all this way to tell me."

"Don't mock me, Jan."

His voice was troubled; in spite of herself, a sardonic twist of enjoyment came to her mouth. James and his women! "Forest?" she said. Katherine Forest, that silly, pretty, fair-haired giggling creature, the daughter of a Court official whom my lords had once put in James' path, was still, she knew, visited by him sometimes. He was too kindhearted to desert a woman, and she was not envious of that fool.

"Not Forest," said Ramsay. He began, like her, to thrust at the leaves with his foot; a little trail was left on the path with the mark that his spur made. He would not meet her eyes and she felt that it was difficult for him to speak. She was still certain that he had come for no good purpose.

She jerked impatiently away. "Who, then? Am I a queasy girl? If it's some new—" Dear God, she thought, am I to be vaporish at this day for his drabs, when I spend half the year up in Darnaway?

"No, not—not new, Jan. It's—it isn't that. Don't upset yourself, for God's sake! I should not have come to tell you, but I thought—"

She rounded on him. "Out with it. Words I can stand, but not when a man stammers at me like a fool. Who is this woman? Do I know of her?"

"It is Margaret Drummond."

Sickness; the sound of his words like cool dropping water. The sun was unbearably hot; it glared in her eyes. Almost she felt them blinded, and through the haze of brightness Ramsay's voice went on.

"You are not well; I beg your pardon. Shall we go inside?"

"No." Resentment that he should have seen her pregnant came to her; he would sully the unborn child with his eyes upon her. The knowledge was strong with her that he had come to say this; that he had a purpose in saying it hammered in her mind. The garden seemed suddenly foolish and half-tended, the flowers withering in the sun.

"How did he meet her again?"

She was angered with herself for asking, and with all those who had kept this from her. She, the King's mistress, had no interest in the King's love. She had her castles, her children, as Marion Boyd had; like Marion Boyd he would marry her off, when he had done with her, as he would be; done with all women in the end, except one, to whom he would always return while she lived.

While she lived. . . .

"What am I?" she thought. Inexorably, Ramsay's voice went on.

"He met her again by chance. There was no more to it than that. It was not an impossible thing; His Grace rides often alone. They say he first came upon her dressed as a common man; and so it was again, doubtless. There is fair hunting in the Perthshire hills. One cannot stem the Tay." His voice sounded amused; she heard it as from a distance.

"You are certain. . . ." That, then, would be why the King had not written. That would be why she was here alone, her child expected; here, when she should have been hid in Darnaway.

"Did you never wonder why he took you up north—so far from Court?"

"The English bride comes next year. Every fool knows that. You are an old woman, my lord; what if he did see her again? There is the child, a girl."

He was regarding her lightly, hands on hips; admiration and amusement in his eyes. "Jan, Jan, you're a child yourself in the way you fight battles! He has not seen Drummond's daughter since she was christened."

Suddenly he drew nearer to her, talking softly and rapidly as he had done that night in Stirling Castle. She felt his physical repulsion less now; was it that she had become used to horror? Remembering, she saw the white rose garden; the lovers lying, the silver gown. The child had been conceived that night. She had envied Margaret Drummond her child, and her lover.

"You think that I deceive you, that I exaggerate to cause you pain. Of what use would that be to either of us? You and I have had our run, Jan; he owed me a debt and he paid me with land, and now I am as another and ride on his errands. You were another woman, any woman, for his night's need; had you not quickened and Angus borne you off by force, you would have been no more heard of. The King has done all in his power to rectify matters for you as for me, but he has never loved either of us."

No, never, never loved her. Never Beltane. She had never known it on that ride north, with the deft loving of his hands' touch; the way his shift had been fine as silk to her cheek which lay against it; the warmth of his body close to hers. Of the many beds in which they had lain on that road she must recall nothing, nor of the time they had lain under the stars on grass and he had loved her as the Egyptians loved, with his hands in her loosened hair. "You're lovely," he had whispered, with the night wind stirring the trees. "You're such a lovely thing, Jan, lovely, lovely. . . ."

But never "I love you." And she wasn't lovely now. The years cast back to when she was heavy with Lochinvar's child and had sworn that no man should ever have her so again; it would have been better if she had kept to her oath. She saw her face now under the broad white tied kerchief, flushed and without cosmetics like a nun's; she should have been a nun, let no man use her ever.

She heard Ramsay talk on, hardly taking in the words. Henry Tudor. What had Henry Tudor to do with her bruised heart? Henry was a king who used women and men as well; Henry had used James. What had Ramsay to say of it? "Henry Tudor is concerning himself with their new meeting, so much having been spoken of this thing that it has become known in England. He deems his daughter's betrothal lines so much paper; you must have heard the talk once that Drummond and the King were wed."

"There was no foundation for that talk," said Jan harshly. She had found her voice and her senses again; the thought came to her to defy him. "This is my pledge of the King's love," she said, and laughed; he did not hear her. "Whether there was foundation or not, the thing must end," he said, "or no princess makes her way from England north, to be called a concubine."

"End?" she said. Insensibly the thing came to her, drumming a warning in her ears. She did not know if it were that or her own blood, beating.

She looked at Ramsay; he seemed to her a thing small and pitiful, too small for the great names of which he talked. "What favor do you wear in this," she said, "that the fate of England so incenses you?"

For an instant a gleam, an ugly look, she thought, showed in his eyes; then it was gone and she wondered if she had imagined it. Smiling, he bowed over her hand, raising it to his lips with the earth still on it. "Your favor, if I may," he told her.

Jan looked at his bent dark head; the scent of the essence he used rose to her. "I neither sell my favors so lightly, nor do the concerns of England exercise me so that I will do as you say," she said. It had been a shot at random, but she saw him step back as though he had been struck. She remembered the hunted lost look in his eyes as he left her.

When he had gone she felt her knees trembling, and knew that it was with anger. She got herself back to the house and there she wrote to James. There was no woman, she thought, could be altogether what she had been to him; there were things that would never be forgotten, for a hundred Margaret Drummonds and in a hundred years. What if he had met with her again, walking in the Perthshire hills? The White Rose was dead, those days were dead, and *she* the mother of his son, and she— Dear God, was she still at all fair? She had them bring a French mirror to her; stripping the coif and kerchief, she saw the color of her hair. It tumbled to her shoulders in the old way, spiraled in brightest bronze. She'd have them dress it as the Italian women did, two high horns of Minerva, no coif hiding it, when the King came down. She'd make him remember her again, forgotten as she had been all those months in the north. Dear saints, she'd make him take her to Court—once again—only once, before the Queen came! They'd see then whether or not she could oust Drummond, after the child was born.

But before that James must come.

She put all her longing in her letter, hardly concealing her heart.

When the man had ridden off she felt better, making them light a fire although it was summer, warming herself before it and drinking spiced wine. The great thumb-ring of His Grace's gift flashed at her from her outspread hand. She'd wear that, when he came, and her crystals in her ears, and her green gown. She'd have the minstrels brought as she had done that time in Darnaway. They should sing for him and the girls should dance, with wreathed flowers in their hair. Ah, he'd forget Drummond, with her pale toils!

When the reply came it was written from Falkland.

Jan read it and then cast it into the fire, and word went round that the Lady of Bothwell had run mad. The reason for it was not known, but it was guessed at, and some who disliked her were glad and others regretful—in particular the hunting grooms, who thought her a spirited lady. In the great hall of her domain was no sound; above, her footsteps were not heard on a floor strewn with rushes. For that she was there they knew, pacing like a tigress, up and down; she had said nothing at first for rage; later the words came.

The room had a high window. By it a child sat alone, regarding her solemnly; Gordon's child, at seven years old, her face placid and dough-pale beneath a little hood of velvet. She was too stupid to understand what things were wrong and, unknowing, had no reason for fear. She sat with eyes round as an owl's, and as the sounds came, listened, but did not understand.

"Falkland. *My* Falkland. He's taken her there. They sit together there, and I am cast off." In the rich room, from wall to wall, the words were flung again, none caring. "I'll kill her," raged the Lady of Bothwell. "I'll kill her. Kill her. I will do it with my bare hands, with poison, with a knife. Kill, kill—" She flung round, in her restless walking; saw the child staring calmly, and went across and brought her hand flat across its face. The child fled, wailing. "That's roused you, has it, you bitch?" Jan called after her. "Go to your fool of a father, who can't breed others and will make you his heir. Go—go—and let me kill her, kill, kill, kill!"

The voice, and the sound of her raised and beating hands, carried out to the garden where the rosemary still bloomed. Its strength was fading now, so that the dry flowers strewed the ground, and their scent rose headily.

That summer a rider came to Bothwell with news from the north. Margaret Drummond and her two sisters had sat down to breakfast at Drummond Castle in Perthshire and by night they were dead, it was said of poison.

II

Voices came to her, sounding through her sleep; faces, voices, jumbled together and then at times singly, so that it seemed as if they came close about her, all eyes fixed accusingly on her in that room. Spens came, risen from the grave with the blood dried on him and his white face blank; Angus, with the three years' penance heavy on him and his beard snow-white, the look in his eyes as it had been for her, that day when they led him away. Ramsay watched, with his eyes that frightened her; his hands reached out to touch her because of something she had not done; he was lost as damned souls are lost, because she would not aid him.

They howled at her for vengeance and yet made no sound; their voices one with and yet apart from the others that came. Her mother was there, bound up with the pain that tore apart her body; she screamed at her to leave her be, and then she was back again in that other time, with Ag's crying in her ears and the Earl spurring his horse and saying there would be no time to reach Kilmarnock. Tears ran down her face at the thought of Bell; and it had been all useless, because he had not saved her from the pain, and the child was to be born again as a punishment, she thought, for having given birth to that other. But Marion was angry and would not help her now because her eyes were swollen with crying; and the other faces, weak and foolish, goats' faces, Kilmaurs and Lochinvar, came again and went, each one bodiless. Gordon's child wailed because she had struck it; or was it the cry of the other? And always there were the voices, calling and crying about the walls. "Burn her! Get her out! Burn her! Drown her!" And they cried that she was a witch and again that she must burn, and she felt the heat of the flames on her body from the Beltane fire. The crowds that called for the carline called for her, and they would cast her into the fire; she saw their faces, wolfish and white with hate, and heard their crying night and day so that they left her in no peace.

She could not remember the ceasing of the pain or the coming of drowsy weakness to her body, or the settling of present and past so that they resolved each about their own center. She was nothing and no one, lying at last alone in the great bed with the child in her arm, whose wailing she had heard, but now she saw that it slept. There was horror in her mind whose cause she could not fathom, and then seeing the white scared faces of the waiting-women she knew, and remembered; the way they cast glances at her, as if while they thought she still slept she could transform them into horrors, serving the devil; fear filled the room about them and the crying beyond the moat outside came clearly, so that it had not been alone in dreams. She turned and tried to see beyond the child's sleeping head, dark-red and still damp, to the window. The mist had come down and drifted in curled wreaths into the room; a summer mist, full of damp odors from the marsh, of pestilence and death. The voices outside came muffled, bodiless out of the mist; she heard the words at times clearly.

"Burn her! Burn the witch! Burn her! Drown her!"

Women's voices; the women of the whole world gathered, to have vengeance. They would tear her body limb from limb. She was too weak to plead for help, or move; when she lifted a hand to call for wine there was no strength in it and the arm fell back, thin and white, on the bed.

"Burn the poisoning whore, the devil's own. Burn the proud woman!" Poison. Poison. When had she spoken of that?

It came to her that Margaret Drummond, who had been afraid that night in the garden, was dead. Had she been afraid of love or of death? She saw the bodies, the slim flesh the King had loved, putrid and swollen with the death that bred in them; flies were about them in the heat of summer. Spens dead, Drummond dead, together in her mind; blood and foulness spreading, slowly, from them to her; it touched her where she lay and she could not withdraw from it, and she sobbed in disgust and terror but no sound came in her throat. The child lay by her and she tried to save it, shielding it from the foulness and destruction, and the thought saved her. It was a girl and tiny, warm, cradled in her arm as once James' head had been; James' daughter, with his dark-red hair. She would keep the child in memory of James after his death. The Egyptian's dirge had played death for him, for a man not dead, whose love had died. From now on he would not send for her nor come to her, a witch who must burn.

"Burn the witch!" the voices cried. She lay still, hearing them. After a while she began to mutter prayers, anything, repeated over and over in the manner of a rosary. She found the action helped her and the repetition, often without sense, of the well-known words relieved her terror for a while. She had been nothing and no one, a body without strength and mind without power, unable to help herself or to save others dependent upon her. She told herself presently that she would win through; always, as that night in Angus' stronghold, she had known that, somehow, her will would win.

Strength returned to her body slowly, hindered by a fever that followed the birth. There was no word from the King and she had no news of him. What was the nature of his grief she knew not and dared not think; remembering the chain, she feared that it would be violent. She prayed that if he believed the things that were being said of her he would send her for trial and she would see him face to face. But she was the mother of his son and as such above trial.

Caesar's no-wife, she thought, who must not be heard. Her eyes these days had the glint of a wary animal. Added to the fear of what awaited her without was the fear of treachery within, and that they would poison her food. The hangings of the bed at night were full of moving shadows. By day no one came near. That there was nothing she could do she knew, other than conserving her strength.

By degrees the crying outside abated, but she had always the fear that they were there, waiting for her, in the mist. It lingered on about Bothwell Castle, thickest in the early mornings after the dew; slowly rising and abating by noon, so that the trees and buildings became substantial again, having resolved out of an island of floating mist. She began to associate the unreal world with herself, and saw solid shapes as shadows.

She looked at herself one day in the glass, and was shocked to find how her flesh had shrunk. A gaunt haggard-eyed thing; what man would look at her? She sent for paint and painted her face; her eyes above the rouge glistened greenly. For an instant she wondered if it were not as they said, and she a witch, who by a spell having wished Margaret Drummond dead, she had died, and horribly. She walked that night about the ramparts, accustoming herself again to the fall of heights; seeing herself, a thin dark-cloaked figure, a ghost among ghosts, with only the dead for remembrance.

She must get away from here, she realized. It was in this way that one would run mad. She felt that from below they watched her; but no sound came from the marsh. Next day she called for her litter and set forth in it, the child with her; looking neither to right nor left through the undrawn curtains, as they bore her away from Bothwell.

Of that ride she remembered little, frozen with fear as a beast is, surrounded by enemies. The world had become so alien to her she could not tell its thoughts; she had no word of late events. She would not have them close the curtains; if, she thought, attack or violence came, she would have warning. The dusty roads wound on, with the wind stirring in the grasses.

Once, a body of peasants stoned her. They were soon scattered, the men-at-arms riding hard at them with spears. She remembered their hostile faces and the way the stone had struck one of the bearer horses, causing it to whinny and rear. She heard the cursing of the attendants and felt the lurch of the equipage unmoved; but she was angered because of the child, whom they might have harmed. It lay in her arms and slept peacefully.

They went by country roads, avoiding the towns. She surveyed herself curiously, aware of her lack of courage. It was as though she garnered all of it for her meeting with the King. She thought of him as someone whom she had never seen, a stranger. As they neared Stirling she passed his outriders on the road; Focart and Doule, men she knew well; they saluted her with wooden faces. She pictured the buzz of talk that would be when her coming was known, and flinched from it. "Draw the curtains," she told them. Folly enough, she admitted, with her lozenge embroidered plain for all to see; but she could not longer endure the thought of prying eyes.

"The King will see my Lady of Bothwell."

She had felt an uprush of relief, having had in her mind that he might refuse to see her. Now, with the waiting, all that was gone; clearest in her mind was that other time she had come to him, and watched the tiny figure on the hearth tiles, advancing.

There was an usher in her way; she brushed him aside, throwing, as she hurried across the room, her veil back from her face. The King was writing at the table and as she came in he looked up, once, briefly; nodded, and went on. The secretary was there, shuffling papers in the background. She began to talk, pulling off her gloves.

"I must talk with Your Grace. I implore Your Grace's protection. They are saying—do you know what they are saying? That I killed her—"

Clearly, in her own mind, as she spoke, came the picture of a woman maddened with rage and jealousy; up and down, up and down, feet making no sound on the straw-scattered floor; snarling, a tigress. "I'll kill her!" And the words floated out into the garden.

"He's heard," she thought. Aloud she said, "They are saying that, but it is not true. Have I ever lied to Your Grace? I swear that it is not true, and that I did her no harm. My God, are you listening to me?"

He went on sorting papers. He would gather them into a neat pile and then pass them to the secretary, and Whitelaw would go through them again and check them while the King signed more. There was a kind of relentless efficiency about the relation between the two acts, synchronised like the workings of a clock. "I talked of it," said Janet. She had begun to pull at the fingers of her gloves, there in her hand. "I said I'd like to kill her, which was true enough. I dare say at the time I would have done it, had she been by me, but in a swifter way."

She laughed a little. "Does Your Grace believe me?" she said. "They say that poison is a woman's weapon." Then she told him about the voices she had heard, calling about the walls at night to burn her for a witch. "I'm afraid of that," she told him. The gloves hung limply. "There are things I could stand, but not that."

She stopped, and began again. "I couldn't come for long." Had he remembered about the child's birth; had he ever fathered her child? They

said that they had brought Margaret Drummond's child to him and he
had spoken to it gently enough, and then sent it away. The child was still
too young to understand. "Often I hear them when they are not there,"
she told him, "the voices. With the damned mist that rises, nothing seems
real. I hoped to find Your Grace real enough; so I came." But you aren't
real, she thought, in horror; you aren't a man; you're a shell.

"So I came here." Her voice rose and broke. "Do you hold me in no
belief? At least let me stand my trial, and I'll put it to the proof; flesh
and blood I can face, but not shadows. How do I know what they say
of me, when I have not heard?" She had noticed, with the quickened
perception of detail which someone in fear possesses, that his hand had
stopped shifting papers. "You were afraid," he said. It was the first time
she had heard him speak.

"I'm not asking for your pity," she said savagely. The flooding of emotion had receded, leaving her like a brusque child. "Only . . . to have
my word taken. I'm not saying I didn't *want* to kill her. If everyone got
what they wanted there'd be fewer of us women. But I didn't do it." She
broke off, and flung the gloves on the table.

"No one has any proof," said the King precisely. He sounded like a
clerk. She stared at him, her horror mounting. "*James*—"

Carefully, the secretary gathered papers. He had not been told to go.
The slight sound jarred on her and she rounded on him savagely.

"Take your cheese-face out of here!"

Whitelaw, the Dean of Glasgow, looked from one to the other. The
woman looked, he thought, as though she would strike him. The King
raised a hand wearily, and Whitelaw disappeared, ruffled, into the outer
chamber.

"Thank God," said Janet. She went to the King, seized him by the
shoulders and shook him slightly. "James. James."

"Leave me," he said. His voice sounded tired.

"*No*. You can arrest me if you like—for treason, or . . . God knows!
It needs only that. How do you suppose I've contrived, waiting down there
with no word? How do you suppose I shall do, when the world sees you
won't receive me? If you believed I killed her—did you expect me to send
condolences—because I didn't—then charge me, have done . . . or if not,
let me be with you, so that their tongues are stilled . . . do you believe I
killed her, James? Do you? Do you?"

"No." It was almost a whisper. She stared at him.

"Then if you know so surely, you must know who—"

"Please go," he said gently. "Will you?"

"God's wounds," she said suddenly. She was silent for a moment. Presently she said, "Do you mean to kill yourself?"

She went round to the back of the table. "Let me stay," she said. "I'll be your mother or your nurse or your whore. I can be all three. There's no one else who can—now, after what has been. If you will live for England, for the English marriage . . . having paid so dearly . . ."

A great shudder went through his body. She felt it, her arms about him by the chair. "Having paid," she said, "the reward will be yours—through England, but not only so. You will be a great king, my dear; I hope to see you so. What was it you once said to me about the Elixir and our youth? We've squandered it, maybe; we will no longer be ourselves. But I can bring a little comfort to you."

She glared at him suddenly. "There's only one thing I won't do and that's go," she said. "Unless you send guards."

"Please go," he said again, as though she had not spoken. "I can't listen—yet."

Suddenly, he covered his face with his hands.

III

There began for them a new relationship which was to endure the test of time and change. That was to come soon; preparations for the English marriage progressed, inexorably. The Earl of Bothwell went south, with Dunbar in his train, to stand proxy for the King in cloth of gold and marry Margaret Tudor in St. Paul's. The friar-poet returned wordy with praise about London and boasting of a new dawn, the marriage of the Thistle and the Rose. These emblems were seen everywhere, inset in glass in the King's banqueting hall, decking the streets in time for the wedding as once the White Rose had done; woven in gold thread into white damask, to be fashioned into spousing gowns for both King and Queen.

Jan saw the Queen's gown, stiffly disposed on its stand with the gold thread glittering. The small figure who would fill it seemed no more than a doll. She found herself unable to accept the reality of Margaret Tudor and suspected that the King did likewise; the meticulous thought, which he began to take for every detail, was for no living woman of flesh and blood. Jan watched him choose the cloth of gold for cushions, the velvet to deck the Queen's rooms; particular as to the fringing, which must, he insisted, match that on the great bed of state, which the child would bring with her north. He had chosen the Queen's crown, having

it made lightweight in order not to be a burden with its formal arrangement of many-colored stones. He had every item of the ceremony
planned; the ride into Edinburgh, the free wine in the streets, the jousting by Hamilton of the Black Knight's day; the resplendencies of the
Cardinal Virtues and the winged angels singing on high wooden towers,
who would hand the Queen the keys of Edinburgh when at last she
reached the city. His own gear was magnificent, the coats and harness
fringed with gold, the shirts pearl-sewn; mantles lined with martrix fur,
a cap with a ruby on its pin. The new device, a unicorn, which he had
chosen for himself, was carved in stone on Holyrood's new towers; and
the allegory of that beast, which could only be captured by a maiden, he
accepted, with his growing acceptance of the new reality.

Jan felt the shadows lengthening at the day's end. She could not rid
herself of this feeling, nor herald, as Dunbar did, a new dawn. Only she
knew of the wakeful dark hours, and of how the King would toss in an
uneasy sleep, sweating and shivering from some dream of foul death
and twisted limbs, images that came with the slow healing of the mind.
Of his other hurt, his father's death, she knew little; but that, and this,
were more than any man could endure without a scar. At times the
wound that was hardly healed would open again; then even she could
do nothing with him, and he would ride out alone.

But he trusted her, in which fact she took pride. That summer she had
charge of the children at Stirling; her own and his, and the rest by
various mothers. She took a wry pleasure in them, seeing his likeness in
the bright tossing hair of the girls, his strength in the boys' limbs. The
eldest son, Alexander Stewart, aged nine, was now Archdeacon of St.
Andrews; he was sweet-natured and lovable and she grew to have an
affection for him, particularly as he displayed fondness for her small Earl
of Moray. Jamie, who adored him, would trot after him everywhere,
garbed in a little scarlet coat; their chief entertainment was the cow and
calf the King had bought for them at Stirling, and the peacock in the
great garden. There were more animals, Jan told them, in the park at
Holyrood; a horse with a red tail, from Spain; and a bear that could be
stirred up with a stick.

"There used to be a lion here," said Sandy gravely, "but it died with the
cold. When can we see the bear and the red-tailed horse? When the
Queen comes?"

Something in her snapped. "You little bastards'll see naught of the
Queen, or anything there is to show!" she told them. Afterward she re-

gretted it, seeing their hurt eyes. "Take comfort, then," she said to them, "no more will I."

She knew well enough where her place would be. Her part would be done when he went from her to his wedding; she took some little credit to herself for the change wrought in him. "This marriage," she had told him, "is what every jack-of-trade and publican and common man has looked for, for long. It's their wedding, not yours. The clothes you'll wear are for them, the pageants and resplendencies and wine are for them, and the bride's for them, when they line the roads to cheer her. Everything you do will be remembered; smile at them, and they'll go off their heads with joy."

She remembered his staring at her, as on that night in Falkland, as though there was something about her he had not known before; the picture of the commons had come to her, jostling and sweating as she had seen them that day at the Baresse; she remembered how she had longed then to be one of them. "Forget yourself," she told him, "even if it's only for a day. Make it one day to remember—and never say I told you so for my own good! The King's whore'll be well north and away at Darnaway, not leaning out of a balcony stance in the Canongate with streamers to throw, dolled in gauds!"

But he begged her to stay in Stirling for a time. Fear, she knew, was with him for the change; the English, hard-eyed in their new assessment of him and his country, and the unknown child-bride of scarcely fifteen. She had seen a portrait of Margaret Tudor which had been sent north; blue-eyed, yellow-haired, pink-cheeked and expressionless. The simile of a doll again recurred to her and she wondered if it were more merciful so; no person, no real person, could mean much to James any more.

And least of all herself. She had no illusions about their relation. They were comrades, rather than lovers; he had needed her, as comfort unpersonified in the darkness, for a time; and she had needed him, as a refuge from those voices which would never be entirely stilled, but which by reason of his protection of her had been quieted, as she knew they would be. Beltane was gone, as the carefree lover of Speyside was gone, never to return; she herself had changed. She watched his magnificent train ride off, after one day spent with the little Archdeacon and herself, to the bridal; in Stirling Castle the flasks and pestles and ovens of the laboratory stood and cooled. She did not know when he would return, or what the future would make of him, or for him. That the past was dead she was sure, and the time for loving. In any case he had not loved her then and did not now.

IV

She stood by the window one day, watching the drifting leaves.

Autumn had come early and the nights already were chill. As once before, by night she would walk about the ramparts, wrapped in a cloak against the cold and seeing the lights shine below in the town. The time of her flight from the garden in the dark, of Ramsay and her fear of him, of Angus, seemed far away; in another world, that girl, who had been so eager, grasping at life with both hands. Now she was older; how much older? She would not measure it in years but in the passing of experience, leaving one content to sit and watch as did the very old. She was watching now, a woman with red hair in a brown kirtle, standing by the glass and watching the leaves.

September; a month since the King's marriage. All that time festivities had continued in Edinburgh, the thronging streets packed to watch Margaret Tudor ride by on the King's saddlebow, and to hear the bells ring out the day of the wedding. The King, they said, had made forty-two knights in Giles'. There had been days of jousting, with the opponents in red satin; and days of feasting, with the rich garb and great golden chains the Scots lords wore causing envy to Henry Tudor's Englishmen, who would go home and tell their master there were no savages in the north. And the Earl of Surrey, the gruff old soldier who had marched against James in the Perkin wars had invested His Grace with the Order of the Garter in St. Giles' and been seen coming out of the church with him arm in arm, the great golden George vying with rubies about the King's neck, and the pair of them laughing.

All was peace, then; although they said the young Queen was showing signs of temper, being homesick for England and not disposed to show affection or gratitude for the efforts of His Grace to please her. But one dealt no longer with men and women in the affair, but with chessmen on a board. She saw them all stiffly, carved in red and white. Henry Tudor, the Red King, back in Westminster, would be well pleased with what he had done.

The leaves drifted on and she allowed her thoughts to go with them, taking a queer pleasure in their lack of volition, their inability to go other than where the wind willed. For every leaf a castle for the Queen's dower, she thought; Methven, Linlithgow, Doune, Cockburnspath and Menteith and Dunbar and Stirling.

"Stirling," she thought, and grinned. Herself and the King's bastards had been snug enough, here in the Queen's castle, but soon it would be time to leave before Her Grace's visit. The place was already largely stripped of furnishings and plate, with their own corner of the household run on a skeleton staff; everyone else was departed to Edinburgh along with all those from the town who could beg, borrow or steal a hack or a bed to lie in. Stirling was like a ghost town, empty. She did not look to see it wake to life again. This would be a summer residence now—a pleasure palace, where he would come for change or for an odd hour with his herbs and simples in the laboratory. Holyrood, the new palace that he had erected on the site of King David's abbey, would be his home; near enough to Edinburgh, and not far from the sea, where he could ride down and visit his beloved ships. Falkland for hunting, Linlithgow for leisure and to watch the swans on the lake. Darnaway . . . for timber. She shrugged, and turned away from the window. She herself would depart to Darnaway at the week's end, and the children go to their scattered homes or to St. Andrews, where that wily prelate, Forman the Prothonotary, had them in charge.

She found a chair and sank into it, sitting there idly for some time with folded hands. The thought came to her that she would like to have seen James, once again, before she went north. That that was impossible she knew. Too many Englishmen still about, ready to ride down south and tattle to Henry! No, she must leave James to his sullen child.

She raised a hand to her throat, in sudden fear. She'd no desire to end as Drummond had ended. The thought would come to her sometimes, in the night.

Who did the killing? She wondered, for the thousandth time, how much Ramsay knew.

Sitting there in the chair, looking into the empty grate where no fire had been lit, she thought of him and the look in his eyes when she had last seen him. Her fear of him had receded, now that she knew he might be leagued with murderers. The paradox did not strike her as absurd, there were too many strange things. As though this action, or the thought of it, had assoiled him, she had the feeling that he did not now hate the King. It was as though James the Third's death had been avenged in his reckoning. "A dear vengeance," she thought, "one death by three others."

They would be well assoiled, those three sisters, she thought; remembering the masses that the King had ordered to be sung in Dunblane Cathedral daily, for Margaret Drummond's soul. He had ridden there one day in summer, alone; to see for himself the three stones of blue marble, there in the center aisle, and hear the singing.

"God rest her," Janet thought. She rose abruptly, and called for her woman. She would walk, before the light died, outside; Moray with her, who would beg as he always did to be taken to see the King's great new gateway, with the strong arch, so that one could come riding now straight up from the town. "Fetch me my cloak," she said to the woman, "and my son."

The woman stood looking at her. "What is it?" she said. Always she had the feeling of strangeness, a memory of the Bothwell horror in servants' eyes.

"Madame, my young lady is sick. She has a fever."

Jan spun round. "The fool," she thought. "Why was I not told?"

She brushed past the woman and mounted the stairs, to the nursery that had been His Grace's when he was a child. The old Norwegian woman who had cared for him then was still in service, her face flat and wrinkled under the nodding coif. The baby was in the cradle, flushed and restless, placed near the fire; a caudle, with bread for a posset, steamed there, and stirring it was one of James' daughters who had not yet gone, Catherine Stewart, the child of Marion Boyd. The firelight shone on her oval face, long limbs and bright dark eyes.

"She's fractious," Kate said gravely. She was always placid and older than her years, taking the place for the young Archdeacon of their mother, who had married and become occupied with a new family at Rowallan. "She has held her hands to her belly this past hour; nurse put a poultice to it. And she will not take food."

The child wailed. Jan put a hand to its forehead, feeling the heat. In her mind was a dread of the great sickness of two years ago, although summer was gone. What could one do for a child too young to say anything?

"Send for a leech," she said crisply. She had little faith in leeches, but they should say that everything had been done that could be so. She picked the baby up in her arms and cradled it, rocking it to and fro. Its breath came in sobbing sounds; its cheeks were crimson. After a while it quieted and she put it down, and sending for a bowl of herbs and honey she fed it with a spoon. Time passed; it seemed to her that the child was quieter, but later it made whimpering sounds, scrabbling at the sheet; its legs drawn up against its belly. After a while dark fell

and she had them bring candles; holding the light over the cradle, shaded
with her hand, she knew a stab of terror. The eyes, between long fringed
lashes, stared at her without recognition; they were fixed, and squinted
slightly.

Jan went to the door, still carrying the candle. "Why doesn't the leech
come?" she demanded.

She hardly heard what they told her; in her mind she knew the
child would die. She'd seen a child look so, once in Galloway; the
spotted sickness, they called it, and did not know of any cure, although
the leeches with their nauseating remedies would pretend that they had
found one. She wished most passionately that James might have been
here to tend his own child; he had such skill with herbs, he had healed
many, there was no saying but that he might have had a cure for this.
But he was not here, and no rider however swift would be in time to
bring him; and the child she had wrested from the dark hours at Bothwell, who had brought her back to sanity with its tiny, helpless needs,
would die; the only token of joyous begetting, her one pledge of the
dear nights on Speyside, and that time when the Egyptian played.

"I could have spared even Moray," she thought, "or Gordon's fool."

The leech came after two hours more, from a blood-letting on the far
side of Gillies Hill. He placed hot cloths wrung in vinegar on the child's
belly and gave it a powder of amethyst and cupped its blood. It was all
useless, as she had known it would be, and in the early hours of the
morning the baby died. She could not trust herself to write to the King,
and sent instead the servant, Fleming, to bear him by word of mouth
the news. Poor James, she thought, no longer free to ride, as he would
have wished to do, from Edinburgh for her comfort and his own; he must
not even show that anything was amiss, in the middle of the bridal
festivities. She wondered if he had loved the child as greatly as she. The
depth of her own sense of loss astonished her. She lay on her own bed
weeping, as though it were someone long known who had died; and
could find no will to prevent the tears from running down her face.

She went to Darnaway and there found, as once before, a thing to
comfort her. The King's painter she had caused to come north once,
painting as she had desired them the dark and venerable figures of saints
on the chapel walls. She had taken pleasure in the sight of them and
in that of the candlesticks, and the little choristers garbed in white and
black that she had had taught to sing, as the King's own choir did in
Stirling Castle. But now she had her own dead and she spent much

time in the chapel telling her beads, with Moray beside her—he had from the time he could understand been, she told his father, a little beadsman —and together they would pray for the dead child's soul and have the priests sing for her. By the time the King's letter came she had recovered greatly from her grief, but not so completely as to be other than glad of its tenderness, which surprised and pleased her; as did also the news that he would come north soon.

V

His Grace made in the next year a devout pilgrimage to the shrine of St. Duthac in Tain, having been accompanied from as far south as Perth by a procession of friars, in honor of the gold and silver reliquary that he was to present to the shrine. He had left the Queen with a program of hunting parties, and it was whispered that his haste to reach Tain would be less than usual, as also the speed of his return. Certainly the King, who usually rode like the wind, matched his pace to his company on this occasion; those who saw him would remember the changed beard-less face, startling in its pallor against the great broad hat he wore. They told the tale of how the young Queen last year had sent for her women to cut off his beard, and how he had submitted to this good-naturedly, paying the ladies with a gift of twelve ells of cloth of gold as a barber's fee. It was thought that the change suited him, showing the oval of the face, and the brilliant eyes, more clearly. His garb, as contrasted with that in which he had often enough ridden the roads in his bacherlorhood, was magnificent; the hat he wore, after the fashion of the Flemings, had forty ells of yellow ribbon looped about its brim. It was said that his rich-ness of dress and manners had impressed the English nobles greatly. Ah, but, they whispered, he'd brought no Englishmen on this ride!

Jan waited at Darnaway Castle, knowing that he would come. She was poised outwardly, and assured; but under her gown of sea-green satin her heart was racing wildly. She moved up and down the long room at Darnaway, hearing at every turn her skirts' rustle, feeling the swinging weight of diamonds in her ears. There was a mirror in the hall, clearer and finer than the one that had hung in her father's castle, all those many years ago; the woman looked at her as she passed by, a tall woman with flaming hair. Had she remained haggard, she wondered, after that time at Bothwell? Would he think her worn, provincial, flam-boyant, after the sleek Englishwomen from Henry Tudor's Court, and his bride of fifteen? She peered into the mirror, seeing the laughter lines about her eyes; ghosts of wrinkles, deepening when she smiled; the veriest hint of age. Above them her eyes shone. "Bring more candles!" she called to them. "Bring all the light you can!"

The Earl of Moray, stiff in his best clothes, was brought to her. "Bide quiet and don't move, or soil your gear," she told him. She scanned him curiously thinking that he was the quietest child she had ever seen. There was none of her stirring nature in him. Dear God, when I remember how I was a little devil at his age, running about with the grooms, and thrashed weekly! But there had been no need for her admonition about taking care of his clothes and being quiet; he was always so. She saw his grave stare at the glitter of her rings, and held out her hands to him and laughed.

"Stare your fill, then, at your bedizened mother, who hides her lack of youth by a bonny show of gems."

The Earl reached out his small fingers gently, stroking the rings. He was fond of all beautiful things, a dog's shining coat, jewels and flowers, and the swift movement and wild bright eyes of animals. He loved his mother but feared her; she was, he thought, like the shimmering ice queens in the old Northern folk tales that the King's nurse used to tell at Stirling; her eyes were as green as deep water with the sun in it, and her gems glittered and silks shone and she was beautiful, but not always kind. He dared not speak to spoil this moment when she had spoken laughingly to him, without carping. He was uncomfortable in his best clothes and lonely, as he had often been of late, for the other children's company at Stirling Castle, especially Sandy's. But this moment, with his mother shining like a green flower above him, must not be spoilt. He sighed with happiness, leaning against her and breathing the sweet smell of the herbs she used, that they had dried in the garden last summer.

"Mother when do we go back to Bothwell?"

Her brows drew together and he realized that he had displeased her. His mouth drooped; it had been the herbs that made him think of Bothwell, where the rosemary grew so sweetly. But she did not scold him and only asked if he were a hundred years old, and then she broke away from him and went to the window and looked out.

Bothwell, Janet was thinking. Why had the child reminded her of it? It was lonelier here than the Dead Sea, but her fear of what had befallen at Bothwell made her afraid to visit the south.

Nothing left now but to grow old, she thought, here, in the chilly winters.

She looked out; it had seemed to her that she heard horsemen. She could see no one, but a medley of moving, brightening torches on the road told her; he had come! She laughed at her thoughts of a moment before; to grow old was not yet.

"Did he give me a castle set high on a hill in order that I might watch for his coming?" she thought. Her hair glowed in the candlelight behind her; watching, the child thought it was made of fire. "Your father has come," she told him. Her voice sounded strangely light. From below the long winding of a horn came, and the sound of horsemen riding. His mother stretched out a hand to him and Moray came gravely and took it, remembering the thing of which his nurse was continually telling him, that he was the King's son. He walked forward, his hand in his mother's; the hall seemed unendingly long. How short his legs were against his mother's. He wished he could imitate her long strides, taken among the rich hush of skirts that he knew. Moray looked straight ahead of him, very stiff and erect; conscious that he must be on his best behavior, he, the King's son. Then that was forgotten in a bustle at the end of the hall, and amid the great blaze of candles, stir and movement, and voices raised, and laughter; and a tall man came through the open doorway, wrapped in a cloak, with his hat still on his head, although the other heads were bare.

The Lady of Darnaway swept forward with her son. "Your Grace does me honor!" And swiftly, with a superb arc of movement, she dipped to the ground in a curtsy, green skirts billowing like waves of the sea, slender body and flaming head bowed. And the tall man raised her and kissed both her hands and then her mouth, and suddenly Moray saw she was like a girl again, flushed and laughing, with her eyes shining like two stars.

"Is this my son?" The Earl made his bow, as he had been taught; he was frightened to find that he did not remember the King. Stirling seemed long ago and he had been smaller then. But raising his eyes from the uncomfortable stiffness of his silken clothes he saw friendly dark ones regarding him, laughing yet sad. Why was the King so sad? Moray forgot his clothes and grinned shyly.

"You've pleasant cheer, my dear, and the night's cold." His father had drawn his mother's hand through his arm and was leading her away. "I'll be glad of—a draught of your dark ale."

And then they both laughed joyfully, as though there must be some secret between them. Hands laid themselves on the Earl of Moray also, to take him away; he had been seen, had played his part creditably, and it was past his bedtime. He climbed the stairs unwillingly, straining his ears for the sound of the swiftly loved voice. He heard the low correct words of his mother. She would be talking grandly, he knew, for the sake of the servants. There was one thing, though, that he had heard, when she had forgotten her great state in surprise; although she had quickly reclaimed herself again.

"God's blood, my dear, they've bearded you! There's a sorry case!"

But after supper when they were alone Jan knew there was something he had to say.

She waited, knowing they would come to it; and meanwhile talking, chattering with her mouth full of pins, divesting herself of her own garments because, as she said, her woman had left her.

"She stole, and I beat her. That was all there was to say. Then she went, and I have not got another." The green gown rustled to the floor. "They won't stay here."

"It's not the place, it's the mistress," he remarked. "I never knew anyone who could keep servants for so short a time."

He picked up the gown and smoothed it out, arranging its folds over a chair. "Your Grace makes a most excellent waiting maid," she told him. "Where learned you the way of it? Or were you born so?"

"I believe I may have been," he admitted. He turned and watched her, stroking idly as he did so the velvet bands of the gown sleeve with a gesture that reminded her of Moray. Jan shook out her hair, so that it came loose over her shoulders; ran her fingers through it, to shed its weight, and came to him.

"I won't comb it tonight," she said, and smiled up at him. "Quickly, Your Grace. I've wearied for you."

But he held her away from him gently, grasping her by the shoulders. "Jan—" he said. He frowned, troubled.

"What is it?" she said. She slid her hands upwards over his chest, smiling secretly; she looked like a dryad, green eyes slanting behind the heavily tumbled hair. He heard the low sound of her laughter. "The journey has wearied Your Grace?" Her eyes mocked him. "I'll sing you to sleep," she promised.

He spoke suddenly, and turned his face away. "Jan, you must marry."

She had stayed quite still, hands against him as they had been. Pres-

ently she had laughed again, a high harsh sound, making him wince
suddenly. He turned and walked away, keeping his back to her, and
she went to a chair and sat down. Turning, so that her body twisted,
she leaned over the back of it, chin on elbows, and watched him. There
was no reading her expression.

"Your Grace is paying me off," she said. "A pensionable servant—
with the reward of a complacent man. That's cause for laughter; it would
have been less so of—"

"*No!*" He wheeled round on her. "Listen, for God's sake, to me; I will
explain, if I can."

"Your Grace will have a hard task."

"Heaven knows it isn't easy!"

She snuggled her chin on her folded arms, and smiled at him. "There
is a clause in the Darnaway deed that occurs to me, made in the days of
Your Grace's heat. 'So long as she shall remain without husband or
other man.' Does Your Grace remember?"

"I remember everything," said James.

He turned, with a gesture of appeal; she was never to forget the look
on his face. "Can you recall everything you have done for me, and still
think I could ever forget? You've been my light when my mind was
dark, you've brought sanity and even laughter since . . . you've been
my lovely mistress, my dear comrade, my good friend. You've been kind
when I needed kindness, and a devil, as now, when that would pall. I'd
not part with you for any consideration. Do you understand me? But,
for the times that have changed—"

"The King is wed, so I must be so too, otherwise the tattle will fly
south when Your Grace rides north. Is that the way of it? How well I
understand!"

She mocked him, but her heart was wrung for his trouble. "There's
little I would not do for Your Grace," she told him. In her mind was relief
that she was not to be discarded, pensioned off, as Boyd and Forest had
been, kindly enough; "but, Dear God, I could not endure to lose him!"
Also there had come swift regret, when she thought that she might lose
Darnaway; she had not sufficiently cared for her possession until she
thought it in danger of forfeit. Now she saw it for what it was, a refuge
from the tongues of the south, in Bothwell and Galloway; her own domain, far from the reach of the Queen. Here she had been a queen in her
own right, riding the forest paths; there was no other place that would
serve her to the same degree. She went to him, twining her arms about

his neck; persuading him to sit by her, to tell her of the matters he had arranged. That he would have done so she knew well enough. "Who is the man?" she asked him.

He frowned. "It need make no difference who is the man; this is no marriage. That had to be understood; I'll not share your body. This is protection only." His eyes darkened; he had not forgotten the tale of howling witch-voices in the Bothwell mist. "I'm no longer free to protect you as I was wont."

Jan laughed at him. "Is it a troll I'm to wed, or a leper or a hunchback? I have a curious fancy to know of it, whether or not we ever meet again after the ceremony." The ridiculousness of the situation overcame her and she dissolved in helpless laughter. "Oh, James, James—"

"John Ramsay."

"All kings are lawyers," she said wryly. In her heart had hammered a sudden fear. It seemed as though she had always known, although she could not have done so. Had there not been an affinity between them, ever since that time at Stirling, in the garden? She examined curiously the prospect of being married to Ramsay, thinking how a year or two ago she could not have endured it.

He watched her; she thought she saw relief in his eyes that she made no scene. She remembered that he would have tantrums to endure at home, and the thought blotted out all lesser issues; while he was here, she resolved, he should have peace. She heard his voice again, light with thankfulness at her acceptance; his hands caressed her with gratitude.

"Listen, then," he told her. "It will be for your good, this thing; John has a house that he'd share with you, in part gift, in the Cowgate of Edinburgh. He'd be willing to do so; you could live in town." He began to talk gaily of her dreary complaints of the winters north; the expressive hands gesticulated, his eyes shone. "Never say it isn't the best thing for everyone! And John's a soldier; he'd look after you."

"As well be looked after by a goat," she grimaced. Her eyes narrowed suddenly. "What interest has Ramsay in this, apart from the money you've paid him? He stands to gain less than I."

James shrugged. "He has a desire to live at Bothwell."

A memory came to her; had not Bothwell been Ramsay's, something of the kind, in the late King's reign? "He lost his lordship of it in exile, when the earldom became Patrick Hepburn's." But Hepburn had Hermitage Castle, which had been Bell-the-Cat's, instead of Bothwell, which was hers.

She started to laugh again; the coil of affairs amused her. "How many birds does Your Grace kill with one stone?"

He seized her, and shook her; she saw his eyes alight with laughter. He was so swift in transition from sadness to joy that he was many men in one; no wonder he had many loves, none knowing the whole of him; the Elf-King, the sun-spirit, the monk, the passionate lover; her carline with the long-fingered hands and long bright hair, her Egyptian, the King of Scotland.

She called him these and other names; mingled with her love for him was now a yearning, like that of a mother over her son. In their tender loving of that night the young alien wife was forgotten; he lay in her arms as though he had been always hers. Such times she knew would be short; he would be gone soon, back to his palaces and new concerns, his Central Court of Justice that he had opened, his ships that he had built. He had put two newly born infants on an island in the Forth with a dumb nurse to tend them, and would row out in a year or two to find out what language they would speak. He was convinced it would be that of Eden, and he had told her of it and she had not laughed. Dear James, she thought, always trying new notions, sure that even the disproving of a thing was knowledge acquired. She wondered in that connection how she would fare with Ramsay. "I'm one of his experiments," she thought, "as much as anything."

She looked down at him asleep and fixed the lines of his face in her memory; the fine curve of the mouth, relaxed now, showed a hint of sadness. She wondered if he ever gave himself time to think of Margaret Drummond, and if the restless filling of every moment of his waking day was in effect to drive out that and other griefs. Well, she could thank herself that she had been the one to help set him on that road.

He was a great king. But for now he was her child, lying as the dead baby had done with his head against her shoulder. She wondered if he would find himself free to visit her in Edinburgh, and decided that he would not; he was kind to the homesick girl who had come from England and, no matter how much of a trial she might be to him, he would be courteous to her in her own capital city. But there would be other things. And meanwhile, before he slept, he had promised on his return to find Jan a new waiting maid. "I'll give the thing in charge to Denton, the Queen's Mistress," he told her. "She will know what to do."

The picture he aroused in her mind made her shake with quiet laughter, carefully so as not to wake him.

VI

At first, Janet found her marriage a success.

Ramsay's house in the Cowgate was pleasant, with compact rooms and at the back an orchard. According to the terms of their marriage settlement, she was to share it jointly with him, together with certain other property about the town. On one of the few occasions when she saw Ramsay, other than at the actual ceremony, they appeared together in Court for this purpose, and the deed was signed. It suited her to have a place in Edinburgh, although Court circles were tacitly barred. She began by degrees to create a set for herself, of old friends and new; Walter Kennedy, as in former days, was much about her. He borrowed money once or twice, and sampled her wine; brought along his friends, including Dunbar once, whose reaction amused her. The friar-poet was under the Queen's patronage, and it was not to his interest to be seen about the King's mistress. He was ill at ease, and never came again; she remembered his little observant eyes, flickering from side to side of the room and back to herself, and the way he clasped his hands over his rotund belly under the priest's gown. He was, she learned, in an agony of love for Mistress Musgrave, the Queen's waiting-woman, who mocked at him but kept the poems he sent her, couched in identical floral terms to those he used to the Queen; these, and the verses he sent to the King concerning his own financial state, and the rhyming correspondence with Walter, occupied his days. Jan bore him no ill will for his desertion of her, taking a malicious delight in saluting him openly in the street if they happened to pass one another on the causeway.

She saw the Queen once. There was a balcony in the Cowgate house and on it she had grown into the way of sunning herself, on days when it was warm enough to sit out of doors; passers-by in the street became used to the sight of her, acquaintances doffing their hats as they rode by. She was growing old, she thought, in the delight she took in watching the world pass by: once it would have been torment to her. But the jutting roofs of Edinburgh she had grown to love, knowing their every outline and the way the street lurched down, narrowly, from the giant bulk of the Castle to the King's new towers; and the bustle of life that went on below, starting from early dawn; cry of Leith fishsellers, up and down the street with their wares; clothmen with bales for sale; peddlers with ribbons. Often a minstrel would come and then she would be reminded, poignantly, of the Egyptian fiddler at Falkland; but never one played so sweetly as he, and she learned that the King had given the queer folk a letter to his kinsman, John of Denmark, asking him to treat them honorably when they should pass overseas.

One day she was sitting in the afternoon sun, her feet resting on a long-saddle that she had had the servant bring from within. She felt lazy and disinclined for exertion, and when the cavalcade rode down the street she hardly glanced up. When she did so she saw a plump girl mounted on a white palfrey, her dark-gold hair parted smoothly under a velvet hood; as she rode by her small blue eyes roved, curiously hostile, over Jan. Their eyes met and the girl rode on, and by the quality of the train which clattered after her, their high English voices raised, Jan knew she had seen the Queen.

Of His Grace she saw little or nothing, as she had foreseen. She hardly regretted it, so varied and full was the life the new Edinburgh offered. All the talk now was of printing; an Edinburgh merchant, Walter Chepman, had financed a press, and his associate, Andrew Myllar, a dark thin hollow-eyed young man who had been a printer's apprentice in Rouen, was to set it up. His Grace, it was said, took a passionate interest, going down himself often to Chepman's shop in Blackfriars' Wynd and smearing himself with ink-balls, garbed in a leather apron like any 'prentice-boy. She was glad that he had this interest in outside things, tiding him over the blows that still fell; that very year the young Queen's son that she had borne him died, and the rejoicings that had attended his birth were so many husks on the wind.

Spring came, and the blossoms in the Cowgate orchard whitened and then fell. Ramsay appeared occasionally; she would know of his presence by the sight of his horse in the stable, or a chance meeting with him face to face on the stairs. He spent, she knew, much time at Bothwell, preferring it on the whole to town. Jan shrugged; what he did was no concern of hers. Soon she also would go to Bothwell for the summer; the plague made it advisable to leave town in the heat.

When the Court departed to Stirling, she packed her belongings and went. She was untroubled by ties at the moment, the Earl of Moray having been left at Darnaway with his nurse. Soon, she knew, the King would have him to St. Andrews, to school there; a consolation for the absence of Sandy, who was to depart in the autumn to the University of Padua. "I want him to have the finest teachers that Europe can provide," James had said, his eyes blazing. He had walked up and down the room, gesticulating with his hands, telling her how Sandy should be sent first to

Rotterdam, to the queer thin scholar Erasmus whose nose was like a pen, and whose brilliance of logical thought was the talk of continents. Sandy, James was convinced, would be a light to the Church as St. Ninian had been; he was pure, gay, chivalrous, kind; skilled with a lute, although he was so young; adept at fashioning verses, a fluent speaker of tongues. "And he loves God. When I am dead he will be there to guide those whom I shall leave. I have every trust in him."

She had laughed, at the same time as the thing tore at her heart. "Why, you are not yet thirty-five, and you talk of dying!" she teased him. But he had regarded her with those bright-dark eyes whose depths held many things, and she had spoken of it no more.

Moray, then, would be provided for, following where Sandy led; she had no fear for him. Gordon's daughter concerned her little, having spent as was her wont a great part of the year with her father's people at Lochinvar. Gordon's mother had married him to a widow out of Kyle; the marriage was not a happy one, and it was said he had failed to provide her with children as she had been fruitful before. He clung with great affection to Net, whom he would make his heir; until she was of marriageable age she was to spend a part of every year with him, and after that to go to him altogether. "And God send help, or a stout tocher, when they come to search for a husband for her," Janet thought, "for a plainer pudding I did never see." At times it seemed to her impossible that she should have given birth to that child, so unlike her in every way.

She rode down to Bothwell ahead of the baggage train, glad of the chance to feel the wind tearing through her hair as she rode at speed, outdistancing the grooms who came behind. So had she often ridden down with His Grace, the pair of them making the dust fly on the summer roads behind their horses' hooves. There was no other woman who could challenge him so; he had taken pride in her horsemanship, as in everything else about her. She rode now, long feather streaming from her hat, curls back-blown remembering that time in Galloway, when she had ridden to Whithorn with young Adam Boyd, on the Arabian colt; remembering Speyside, and the way they had raced the sun. "After we're both dead they'll remember how we rode, the King and I," she thought. It seemed to her that James was with her now, his eyes bright and laughing in the shadow of the hat, his hair whipped by the wind. "Well, so we'll ride again." She held her head high, her lips smiling. There would never be true age for either of them. Meantime she felt better for her light amusing winter, better and on terms with the world. And soon he would come again.

The children playing among the hawthorn bushes saw her ride by; they crossed themselves as they had been taught to do, looking after her fearfully. She laughed aloud, seeing the gesture and the wealth of blossom, like snow, on the trees. Let them say what they would of her! There was no mist about Bothwell now; the dark she had left behind.

Ramsay met her in the hall and raised her hands to his lips; he was smiling the small, closed smile she had learned to associate with him. He welcomed her to Bothwell and the manner of his speech amused her. "It is as though," she thought, "he welcomed me to his domain."

Later she found that this notion persisted. He had himself, she discovered, styled "my lord." The fact intrigued, but did not greatly surprise her; Sir John Ramsay and the Lady of Bothwell sounded admittedly ill matched for man and wife. She accepted that, with a twist of the lips; at the evening meal she mocked him with it.

"More wine, my lord of Bothwell?"

He did not smile, allowing the servant to help him gravely to more wine. Over it, she found him a cultured enough companion; their acquaintance was the same, and in discussion of it they passed the hours pleasantly until it was time to go to bed.

The days that followed passed, in the same manner, quietly; it rained, and in her single turn about the garden she found it lush with weeds. On sending for the gardener to upbraid him, she found that it was a new man. She frowned; there had been several changes in the staff that had not escaped her notice.

Later she sent for the steward. "I don't like your new man."

The steward's face betrayed nothing. "The gardener, fool! Have him dismissed."

"My lady—"

She was annoyed with his indecision, standing there; she thought he looked sullen. "Has there been a plague here, that all those whom I employed are carried off? Find the man who was here, who had skill with herb growing. I'd not have parted with him for three rose nobles. What is that you say?"

The steward muttered that it was not his concern. "*What?*" said Janet again. She looked at him standing there, weight shifting from one foot to another; the livery he wore was soiled and his chin unshaven. "You impertinent fool," she told him roundly. "Mend your manners, and your dress, and answer smartly, and obey orders, or by God I'll find another steward! I've suffered you long enough."

The man flushed above his linen; the look in his eyes was not pleasant. "Lord Bothwell will be responsible for that, madame. I'm in his employ, not yours!"

There was a silence.

"Then who," said Janet, dangerously quiet, "is Lord Bothwell?"

She was waiting for Ramsay when he returned that evening.

During the interval, she had schooled herself to be calm. It was not, she thought, a matter to make an issue over; Ramsay was probably as ignorant of it as she had been. It was natural for the servants to be under some misapprehension; the position, to them, must appear to be as it was in other households. Now that she had dismissed the steward, giving him five hours to collect his gear and go, there should be no more doubt among them as regarded circumstances. At the same time she determined, as tactfully as possible, to drop a hint to Ramsay about his position here.

He came in about seven o'clock, his dog at his heels. He had been riding all day in the rain, and his hair hung dankly; he shook, carefully, the water from his hat, so that it showered from the soaked plume over the floor. For some reason the gesture irritated her; she drew a long breath.

"Why can't you do that outside?" she asked him. "The straw's sodden, and will rot. Ramsay, I want to talk to you."

He smiled, and flung the hat in a corner. "Have you supped?" he said. "There was no need to wait for me; I come and go at all hours. I had a meal, in any event, at the inn in Lanark."

"I care not where you supped; we don't count every bone here!" said Janet crossly. "You can sit down; I've some matters to discuss with you. Sit there, by the table."

Ramsay lounged to the fire. "Your temper's frayed," he said. "These logs burn well; I had them brought from Newton." He stretched out his hands to the blaze.

Her eyes narrowed. "You've made yourself at home here, have you not?"

"Why, so I think. It takes time to arrange all in order. Another year—"

"Have you taken leave of your senses?" said Janet suddenly.

She sat down in the chair; the shock had made her knees weak. Ramsay continued to warm his hands, his smiling profile black against the flames. Whatever she said, she knew, he would still smile; he was like a cat, she thought. The remembrance of the white cat he kept upstairs in his rooms came to her; it was often here, rubbing itself against his legs.

Ramsay turned to her suddenly. "There is no need for you to stay."

The voice was gentle; what was it that made her shiver? She could no longer see the face, turned with his back to the fire. For an instant it seemed that, with the flames behind him, he was the devil; she remembered the other time when she had had that notion of him. Now, for the first time, the knowledge came to her that she had married him; it seemed that she had never had time to grasp the fact before. I've married Ramsay, she told herself, incredulously. The reality strove for recognition.

She looked at him. He had raised his head, and was staring into the far end of the hall, toward the shadowed stairs. The lines of his mouth, seen now as the fire leaped, had slackened; the yearning, lifted profile reminded one of a boy. He was a boy, in fact, she realized; here, in Bothwell. She laughed aloud. "Does your dead King return to you here, and bring you fairy gold? This may have been his gift to you, John, but there have been others in possession since. I'm in possession now; I'll thank you to remember that. Have your ghosts, but leave me my direction." She would have said more, but he swung round and faced her; the look in his eyes was that of a caught wild animal. "So you say," he said. Suddenly it seemed as if all that lay in his mind was loosed and he talked to her as he had longed to talk, for years, to any man. Lauder was before them, with the dark bodies swinging at the end of ropes; the dead King's cries came again, and the memory of his earlier laughter. "He gave me this land and castle to be mine. I had no home and he made me a home. I had no father and he loved me. He saved my life once; I don't forget that. They took away his gift to me after he died but that alters nothing." And he babbled on about the right of a dead hand; no man now living had power, he said, to take Bothwell away from him.

She heard him, half in pity for his madness and half in a kind of fear that his wish might be realized. Darnaway she had thought was dear to her only when in danger of losing it; how much more so was Bothwell hers, that she had loved and whose garden she had tended! She'd not lose Bothwell to any madman's whim.

"You are insane," she said to him. She stood and faced him in the firelight. It seemed to her that she was stronger than he; her fear receded.

"The King's my protector," she told him. No dead hand there! "He'll come and de-lord you, my lord Bothwell, to your deserts. These are things I could tell."

"What things?" he asked her. Suddenly fear was with her. Why had she mentioned that? What could she prove?

As if he knew of the swift advantage over her, he came over and seized her wrists. "You bring your lover here to cover your whoring with my name, and I'll school you," he said. "I won't have that—here."

"The King's servant!" she sneered. She was very much afraid. The touch of his fingers, as always, repulsed her; she fought to free her wrists.

"Let me go, you—" For answer he struck her in the face; lightly, continuously, with the free hand that was not occupied with hers; she felt her cheeks flame, and the sickness he inspired in her rose till her strength quailed.

At the same time she heard his voice. "I'm not your tame dog. That was what you both expected, wasn't it? To bring him here . . . as you have done before. He killed my King and he shall not cross this threshold again. Elsewhere you can do as you like. You have your sty in Darnaway and the house in Edinburgh, which was mine. It is fair enough exchange for a woman like you, with a past like yours."

"You spy—you *murderer*—"

Ramsay ran his free hand through the meshes of her hair. Having grasped it, he jerked her head back; his face swam above her for an instant and then his lips were on hers. She endured, half-fainting, the contact of him; the acrid smell of wet leather rose from his coat. Finally he released her, laughing.

"You have married me, you know," he said. "Shall we leave each to his own way?"

She did not answer, huddled in the chair where she had fallen, her arm against her mouth.

For some weeks she remained quiet.

Fear had been with her before in Bothwell and for a while she relived that time again. By day Ramsay avoided her; meeting him, in the hall or on the stairs, she would withdraw her body, holding her skirts aside to avoid their contact with him. By night she slept with candles lit, fearful that he would come to her in the darkness. The things in her mind were beyond reason; every least action was magnified. A step outside the door made her start, the fall of the leather curtain against a draft making her blench for fear. So had Margaret Drummond been in the days when she was afraid, and she herself had scorned that fear, saying that she would never know it. How wrong she had been! And always there was the damned white cat, his familiar, she thought, sidling about one's feet; its great lost eyes, luminous in the dark passages, following her. Ramsay loved nothing on earth now except that cat. Often the wish came to her to destroy it, but she was too much afraid.

She would not leave Bothwell, having the feeling that did she do so it would be his, irrevocably; a thing that could not be explained. There was, she knew, no course in law that would wean a wife's property away from her husband. The wife herself was property, even the King having no power to alter that. Ramsay knew that and James, in trusting him, had taken no thought . . . but how could he have done so?

And so it was for Ramsay to hold that threat over her, hoping by the very force of her loathing for him to drive her out, or else break her spirit so that she no longer opposed his plans. She wondered what the feeling was of Ramsay toward her; not lust, as so many men had felt it; he could have had her before now. The thought of that made the nausea rise in her again. He despised her, she thought; had always done. That, then, was all they had in common; a desire for the good things of life, and mutual contempt.

And a wife could give no evidence against her husband in court, and even if proof of what she suspected were found. . . .

It was then that the plan came to her.

Ramsay went to Edinburgh for a few days toward Christmas. He would know her safe, under the servants' watching eyes; everything she did would be known. She had the feeling of smallness of an insect under a great glass dome, the sky; waking and sleeping, her every movement noted, the times she climbed upstairs or down. If they asked, she would say she had gone to look at her charter; it lay in the great chest in the room that was now Ramsay's. She called the steward to her, knowing he had the keys.

"I have a wish to open the deed chest in my lord's chamber. Be good enough to bring me the key."

If the man refused, she thought, she would strike him. She had been constantly aware of his smug presence, ever since the day she had dismissed him and he had appeared the next day at the table while Ramsay sat at meat. But if he had any suspicion in his mind he did not voice it; possibly the fact that she had asked openly for the keys disarmed him. He came, nevertheless, and stood by her, while she knelt by the lock.

Jan bit her lip; there would be little enough she could take away, while he remained there. She rummaged among scrolls and documents, reading an idle one here and there; no sign was there of her charter, but she found the deed of gift of Trarinyean.

Her lip curled. He can keep it, she thought, his rickle of stones. The King's signature was at the bottom, among others. Nothing else was there

except piled deeds; meticulously arranged, with the prim tidiness of
which men like Ramsay were capable. Once she came on a small bundle,
wrapped in black leather; she slipped it into her wide sleeve, the steward
seeing nothing.

"That is all, and you can tidy these." She took pleasure in watching,
feeling the small hard bulk of the theft against her arm. The fact that
the Bothwell charter was not to be found disturbed her little; he must
have sent it to his attorney, she thought, and she could remember the
terms well enough. If need be she had a weapon she could use against
Ramsay, but the thought of that made her quail. There had been so
many years between then and now, and so much suffering; she did not
think she could open it all again.

But there was a thing she could employ. Opening the package, later
when she was back in her own chamber, she found a jewel. It was of
crystal, set about with gems; she knew enough to tell that they were of
great value. The shape of the thing was oval, backed with flat gold;
on the other side, the heavy convexity of the crystal contained a portrait.
Through it, magnified by the curving thickness, the shrewd eyes of
Henry Tudor looked at her. She stared at the pictured face, seeing the
words written in the gold; a date in summer of the year before the King's
marriage in 1503.

Bell-the-Cat stretched himself, and idly surveyed his eldest grandson,
who sat opposite him at the fire.

Outside, the snow had stopped, and the great drifts lay thick and still
against the windows. He cursed the cold, which made his bones ache;
he'd never had them put in French glass panes, like the King. He'd do it,
maybe, if he were a younger man; as well be upsides with Stirling and
Edinburgh. They said the Queen's folk had been impresssed with the
prevalence of glass windows up here. Well, they'd had time enough to
get used to that, and other things; he'd heard James was paying their
salaries all these years, as Henry Tudor was too close.

"Well?" he said, not listening to what Archie was saying. Below came
the scuffle of footsteps; his wife, scurrying about. He scowled at the
thought of her; a mouselike woman, nothing to her but "yes" and "no";
poor sport at board and in bed; her own servants bullied her. Nevertheless, he thought, she'd sooner bide down where the servants are than come
where I am. He grinned, maliciously.

"I'm glad that amuses you, Grandfather," said Lord Archibald Douglas
in a pained voice. "For my part, I find it trying."

He crossed one shapely leg over the other, and placed his fingertips together. "Don't do that, don't do that," said the Earl testily. "Like a damned clerk."

The young man unclasped his fingers quickly. In the light of the fire, his sulky good looks were enhanced; the pouting lips, which were thought by many to be a little too feminine, and the carefully essenced hair. He wore a riding gown of orange camlet, furred in narrow bands; the new fashion, which was to make toes broader, sleeves wider, and chests padded heavily, became him; as did the little, ultrafashionable high ruff, not yet seen in England and imported from France. My lord jerked his arrogant chin.

"I don't think clerking would appeal to me, Grandfather. It's true there is little else left. For men of ambition to be detained at Court, licking the King's boots in hope of promotion—I'd as soon enlist myself in France, with Bernard Stuart; they still have their wars."

"Then why the devil don't you?" said Angus. "You've talked of it often enough."

Lord Archibald smirked. "The Queen could ill spare me, I think. I escort the poor girl in the absences of her husband. For a woman who is condemned to bearing children year after year, none of whom live—"

"Have a care what you're saying," Angus growled. "Her Grace can spare you well enough. I've not forgotten the time I spent in the King's jails for interfering with his delights."

"Dear Sir, even that would be a diversion, fined as we are even for a skirmish in the Border country, and even the Isles quiet, so that there is no choice but to end like Father, collecting petty rents in Ettrickdale."

"Bide your while," said Angus. "Your marriage'll help you. You've not been allowed to make a damned gowk of yourself there, as I was."

The boy moved impatiently. "Patrick Hepburn cares for no one but the King, and his daughter wearies me. I detest weeping women, and that is all she does all day."

"If she weeps, you know she's occupied," Angus grunted. "It's the ones who don't weep who are the danger."

"Danger," murmured Lord Archibald. A slight frown creased his smooth brow; there was a resemblance between the two faces at the fire. "There's little of that. Take yourself, Grandfather; when were you last on a foray?"

"You can mind your own damned business as to that. Disturb the King's peace if you will, in your own way; leave my ways alone."

"You've made little enough from them, sir; you and Grandfather Drummond, who hoped to see his daughter Queen of Scotland. Does he think of that now when he hears Mass in Dunblane, and of where the King's peace brought her?"

"Mind your manners!" roared the old man. "You've a mischievous tongue, by God!"

He rose abruptly from his chair, and turned about the room. Archibald Douglas watched him, his lips curved in a tolerant smile. How white the old man's getting since his spell in jail, he thought; his beard's white as wool.

Aloud he said, "Aunt Margaret, whom I well remember, was the price paid for ambition. Her story—and her fate—has not quenched that same in me, my lord. Women are pawns, however one looks at them; the Queen is so."

"You're not as I was," said Angus. His great height filled the narrow room. He looked at the boy with eyes that held something of scorn. "You'd be Her Grace's lapdog, then. Get out; I'm weary of you. Go and see your grandmother; take your women's talk to her. I don't know what you wanted of me." He spat into the rushes.

"Money," said his grandson engagingly. He rose, with a lazy grace. "I'll go, as you've no use for me," he said. "Come war, and you'll see my sword; come peace, and there is little left but dalliance." He lounged to the door, casting an eye on the window as he passed. "In that respect, there's a lady below. To see Granny?" He cocked an interested eyebrow. "She looks a trim enough ship all white rig and gilding, like the King's new vessel in the Roads of Leith. George sent his respects to you, sir; I had forgot."

"George and you are tarred with the same brush, timeservers both; I've no use for either," muttered the Earl. Lord Archibald bade him a graceful farewell, and made his way out; he was obviously in haste to meet the lady.

Bell-the-Cat went on walking the floor, to stave off his irritation and because of the drafts. He'd have them bring logs, piled logs, to warm his bones. The rooms at Douglas were ill to heat, here in the snow. He bellowed for the servant, who came running; the giving of orders and the bringing of the logs occupied his mind, making him forget the things of which Archie had just spoken, which disquieted him. He'd no wish to have his line end as the Boyds had ended, heads struck from shoulders on a block, and no more a proud name! Ah, but the days when the Douglases had lorded Scotland were far off now; the silly Tudor wench would be ruled by her husband; there was little danger, while the King lived.

While the King lived . . . Why had he thought that?

There was a sound at the door; his wife stood there, with scared eyes. "Come in," he roared at her. "Don't stand there as if it were a river bank and you a bait a fish would swallow. Drop the curtain; the draft freezes my bones. Has that young jackdaw gone?"

"My—my lord, there's a visitor." Katherine Stirling swallowed; she always found that the effort of addressing her spouse made her throat cease to function. "A woman," she said flatly. "She desires speech with you."

"For God's sake give her her silver, and tell her to go!" roared the Earl. "Why trouble me with such?"

The Countess flushed. "It is not one of—" she began. She looked at him helplessly. "She is dressed like a lady," she ventured. How could one describe the creature below?

"Send her up," barked Angus, "if it's the only way to get rid of her—and you." But the Countess had disappeared.

The Earl went back to the fire again, staring down into the logs which were beginning to burn. Time was, long ago, when the assignation would have intrigued him; all women had done so once, things of challenge and mystery that had to be conquered and set down. But now all was flat and stale and he was old, a chilled old man; hands stretched to the fire and then buried under the side slips of his gown, for warmth. Then he turned to the door, hearing the hush of skirts; and having done so felt his blood run swiftly in him, an instant, before the years closed back.

For whoever he expected to come sweeping into the room, her silver-gray cloak falling sheer from shoulder to heel, blown back with the speed of her coming; and with a hood to match whose gray fur framed her face, it was not Janet.

"I had to come, Bell. Believe me, I had to."

She was standing with her face tilted to his in the old way, hands again on his shoulders as if she would have drawn his head down. But in his bitter hurt he had nothing to say, would not look at her, after the first, or trouble to disengage her hands.

"Bell, I'm in trouble. Such trouble as no one would dream; you've got to help me, there's no one else to whom I can turn."

"Has it taken you eight years to think of that?" he said, and turned away. "Go back to your husband, or your lover. It's naught to me."

"Angus, it's Ramsay I've come about. You must hear me. It is a matter of too much vileness—" She bit her lip. "That wife of yours wasn't going to let me come up," she said. "Let me sit down, Bell; I've ridden from Bothwell today, in the snow."

He looked at her; the fur of the hood was beaded with fine drops, and the hem of the cloak was sodden. "Sit, then," he said to her. He stood away from her, looking down into the fire. "What of Ramsay?" he said. "What in God's name possessed—"

"It's no marriage," said Jan wearily. She was sitting back in the chair, with her eyes closed. For the first time he saw that there were violet shadows beneath them, and that her face was thinner, and drawn. "Indeed so?" he said. Janet laughed rather wildly.

"No, and he's used that fact to—to—" Her face crumpled suddenly; she began her soft crying, sitting in the chair. "Help me," she said again. "For God's sake, Angus, help me; I'm desperate."

"Fair words," he said. He went to the table, and poured her wine. "Drink that," he said, going over to her. She took the flagon, and tossed it off; the gesture lightened him. "So you still take your wine like a man?" he told her. "You've changed little."

"You've changed much, Bell. You're older and harder and your hair's white." She glared at him, still crying.

"I'm wiser, maybe." His voice held steel. He went to the window, looking out at the banked snow. "What would you with me?" he asked her.

In this room, he was thinking as her voice went on, in this very room I hung her with jewels, once. It had been snowing then, too. He was surprised at his own lack of feeling, remembering. "I'm old," he thought.

"So Ramsay covets Bothwell," he said at last. "That could have been foreseen. What have I to do with it?"

"Bell, oh, Bell, listen to me. It's not that, it isn't only that. I would have endured, somehow, I suppose, at the end, if that were all; gone to Darnaway, obtained a separation from him. At the time I found the thought ill to bear, and so I looked, as I said, for the charter, to see if there were aught—" She rose, suddenly, and came to him, where he stood by the window, and put the package into his hand. "I found that," she said. "Don't you see, in God's name?"

Angus stood looking down at the portrait, saying nothing.

"See?" he said at last. "England and our country are at truce. You

can't convict a man on evidence of a brod. Ramsay's in comfort enough
now to have forgotten exile—and dreams of revenge." He laughed, and
closed his fingers round the crystal. She stared at him, then snatched at
it, wildly.

"How blind are you, Angus? Does Henry give away diamonds to a
spy?" She threw back her head and stared at him, fixedly; her great
straining eyes reminded him of a fox, caught, seeing death; he had
watched one once, never forgetting it among the many deaths he had
seen of men. "They say," said Janet, "that Henry is so mean his robes
are trimmed year in, year out, with the same piece of vair fur. The train
he sent with his daughter to Scotland are living on James' charity. When
Ramsay was in England he nearly starved on the miserable pension
Henry allotted him." She laughed; the sound was like a sob. "No, Bell,
those diamonds are for a signal service; look at the date, and recall . . .
Or were you, dear Heaven, in prison still? I can't remember; but I
should have thought that news would have reached you, even behind
four walls. Oh, Bell, when I remember what I went through at Bothwell,
with the voices calling to get me out and burn me, and all the time
he—he—the English-paid rat, had received his poison!"

"Poison?" said Angus stupidly. He stared at her.

Jan took him by the shoulders and shook him. The tears were running
down her face. "On that day Margaret Drummond died. It was safe
then for the King's daughter to come out of England, and for Ramsay
to go back to Bothwell and live his dream again. Can you understand
now why I came?"

He had taken her back to the fire and tried to calm her, shocked with
the tale of things to a forgetfulness of his own anger, acting as he might
have done years back, when Margaret Drummond's death was a new
thing. She leaned back against him and cried like a child from relief and
sheer weariness. It was as though they had said farewell yesterday, to
meet again. Angus saw himself sourly; she's cozened me again, he
thought. He supposed it would always be so. Deep in his mind was the
memory of Margaret Drummond's quiet beauty, seen once in her father's
castle in Perthshire, the time he had ridden north to marry his son George
to Elizabeth Drummond. To have destroyed and stilled that beauty was
a crime as great as Lauder, evening scores with the man-boy with oddly
light eyes. "But there's no proof, or shred of it," he told her, "and never
will be. *This* means little."

"Proof?" said Janet, and shuddered. "I've sat in the same house with him, eaten at the same table. Ever since I found—that, I've watched him, knowing it had been in my mind all the time from the beginning. I dared not let him out of my sight; I used to wonder what he would do if he found it was gone, knowing by that that I had guessed. He came back for a few days, then went away again. He's much about the King."

"Have you said aught?" Angus asked her. He was frowning.

"No; d'you take me for a fool? I said nothing, only watched. I used to watch the food going into his mouth and it made me want to vomit. I thought till my head turned; then I came to you. If you killed me, I thought, you'd do it openly; with your sword, or fling me over the wall." She moved her head on his shoulder. "But to die like a rat, with poison . . . Bell, I heard at the time how they found them. It wasn't a quick death, they were in agony from the morning until night, when they died. They had to bury them quickly because the bodies swelled so. She was a beautiful woman and it was a filthy way to die. I used to thank God kneeling that James hadn't seen her then. He loved her, you know; not me." She turned, suddenly, and looked up into his face. "I'm telling you all this, Bell," she said. "Why don't you stop me? But it's good to get it told."

"Ay," he said grimly. He was looking at the flames.

Presently he began to discuss with her, crisply, what she was to do. "Get north to Darnaway," he told her. "No—" for she had begun to disclaim—"it will be better so! Take guards, for God's sake; if you can't trust your own you can have mine. But get north, and don't return without word from me. There will be no need to add to things." He frowned. "And leave the brod with me." He took it from her.

"What will you do?" she asked him.

But he would not tell her. "Get north," was all he would say. "Tomorrow; or tonight. I'm only praying your steward, that you speak of, has not told him of the theft of his gaud. There's another he keeps by him, about his neck; he looks at it night and day."

She looked at him, with puzzled eyes. "You seem—" she began, then changed her mind, and began to mock him. "And Bothwell?" she said. "Am I to creep away, and leave him master; next time I come not to be admitted save at his good pleasure? I'll hold siege about the gate, Bell, with your men."

He glanced down at her, with something of the look in his eyes that he had reserved for Lord Archibald Douglas. "I do this not for your sake," he told her. "Have no fear, I'll save you Bothwell; am I likely to forget how you came by it?" He put her from him, suddenly, and rose and finished what they had to say from his own side of the hearth.

A week later, he rode to Bothwell Castle.

He was magnificently dressed. A doublet of crimson, buttoned high to the throat, showed points above such as the King wore, of fine lawn. His boots were of Portugal leather; from his hat's brim there curled down a great black plume, showing against the whiteness of his hair and beard. He looked like a majestic old god, a Wotan or Jove; the sword he wore, girded to a belt embossed and studded with silver, was the one he had swung to kill Spens and heavy enough for four men's strength. He rode as he had always done, like the devil, with his cloak flying behind him; his men wound his horn at the gates of Bothwell, which opened to let him pass.

Ramsay had ridden out, and he said he would await him. There was a gleam of pleasure in the blue eyes; did my young cock, Archibald Douglas, think it so long since he had been on a foray? He imagined that his appearance would cause Ramsay some little surprise.

Ramsay came in at last slowly, as if the information that Angus was waiting for him had put him on ceremony as the owner of Bothwell. His light eyes were wary, but his manner was pleasant enough. Angus had been standing on his arrival, the great hat with its dangling plumes still in his hand. Ramsay motioned him to the fire. "Sit down, my lord; I'll have them bring wine."

"You need not for me."

Angus swung his hat gently, one arm leaning on the mantel overhanging the fire; blue eyes fixed intently on Ramsay's face. "We are neighbors, my lord of Bothwell," he said. His voice was like silk.

Ramsay said that he regretted his wife was from home. "You're acquainted, I believe." He leaned idly against the table; the two of them were like duelists, waiting to begin. Suddenly Ramsay laughed.

"I wonder when we last spoke?" he said. "Could it, my lord, have been in a certain room in London, with five men present; the year my lord was spoken of as being at Amiens? Much was decided in that room."

"But little accomplished, as you'll know, having had longer fare of Harry Tudor's bounty than I, and staying the leaner for it."

Ramsay's eyes narrowed. "Why did you ride to visit me?" he said. "I do not care for talk at cross-purposes. What's been has been."

"Ay. . . ."

Suddenly the Earl's face crimsoned. "My arm, my lord, is the span of your waist, I'm thinking. We cannot alter the past, but, by God, we can ensure that there is the less of vileness in the time to come! Provoke me not; I'm hard to hold, it is not easy . . . You are listening to me?"

"Intently." Ramsay had begun to wonder if the old man were not a little childish. He swung, idly, his weight to and fro, on the table's edge; remembering how, not so many years ago by human reckoning, this old man had been the object of his fear. Many a dream he had had of him, the hangman, with his cruel blond hair and loud rough tongue, and hands like a butcher's, pulling at the ropes. And Cochrane, Rob, whom Ramsay and them all had loved, who could raise a house to seem like a palace out of air, who cherished fine silks and the glow of gems on gold, and could make the King laugh, had changed suddenly. Ramsay remembered the jerking congested thing on the rope; his hands clenched together, wet with sweat. If he could have killed Angus then!

"How can I serve you, my lord?"

"Get out of here."

The voices seemed far away. Had they come from themselves or others? Ramsay brought himself back to the present day, to the old man by the fire, to reality. "My lord?" Childish, the old Earl; rude-mannered, as all men of an older day. The times were past wherein he had gloried.

"I said get out of here," said Bell-the-Cat. "Go back to Ayrshire, where your land is. What serves it to batten on a woman who's not wanting you? Go, and leave her to what's her own; her gratitude'll not harm you."

Ramsay had begun to laugh, in the high soft sound he used like a girl's. "So Janet ran to you, after all these years?" he said. "There's something there not canny."

Angus stood quite still; the veins of his face and brow were prominent. "The sign that we used in that room, that day, was the Scorpion," he said. "There is another that I can give."

"My dear sir, you may give me all the signs of the Zodiac if you so wish. Come, sit down, drink wine with me."

He smiled persuasively. It was a triumph, this, over the golden beast he remembered; to come to this, to senility, ridicule, decay of the mind while the body still pursued its functions; an old animal, to be held up and laughed at at fairs.

"There is a creature not unlike the scorpion," Angus said. "My lord of Bothwell is fond, I believe, of it as a breakfast dish. It does not harm him as it has harmed others."

Ramsay stared at him. "Some years ago now," said Angus, "you went down, my lord, to the Fishmarket at Leith; there you bought crawfish.

They were sent to a lady in gift, as often gifts went by riders from the King's houses to the west; fruit, often, from Linlithgow. And she was not cautious at receiving these, for your name was not on them. She accepted them, Ramsay, and the next day—"

"Shellfish are not safe to keep from one day's end to the next," said Ramsay. He had begun his rocking to and fro on the table's edge again; his lips were tightly compressed, and there was a whiteness about his mouth.

"By that day's end, they were dead, those three bonny girls, bloated and forsaken; by my God in Heaven, the killer will be judged!"

"You rave, my lord," said Ramsay coldly. He was brushing a speck of dust from his sleeve.

"She died last," said Angus. "She dragged herself from the room where they were to the room upstairs where help would be found; they found her on the stairs. It sticks in the throat of a man who's seen many bleed and die. May God rest their souls; may you rot, with him that sent you. Do you wish me to shout this thing to the housetops? Would you rather that?"

Ramsay passed his tongue over his dry lips. "You'd not dare," he said. "Your house would come tumbling about your ears. There are great names involved."

"I had not expected," said Angus slowly, "that you would own to it. Such a crime, which does not come within the nature of clean death, is foreign." The eyes regarding Ramsay held the deepest contempt. "My God, did you carry out their orders to the letter? I'd hardly credit any man so vile as to think out the deed thus alone. You're a pitiful thing, Ramsay; less than a man; less than a dog, serving your master. A dog has faith and you'd none. There was no sum of money large enough to justify such a deed; and surely not a glass brod set about with stones."

Ramsay had risen. "You go too far, as that bitch went," he said. "I'll—" Angus' hands closed on his throat.

"Now hear me," said the Earl softly. His hands compressed Ramsay's throat a little; he looked at the congested face, and laughed. "Had it not been for the King's peace, whom you ill served, I'd throttle you like a dog now," he said. "Do you mind Lauder Bridge? I should have done it then."

Ramsay's hands clawed frantically; Angus detached one, seized him, and shook him like a rat. His eyes blazed with a kind of a joy; how long since he'd acted thus? "I can deal with any who come," he said. "And now for the death of those three girls I'll tell what I would do, for they were kin to me. It would not be found safe for you to ride out, my lord of Bothwell—" he spat out the words—"beyond the confines of what you're pleased to call your estate; for I have a sword, and my sons also." He laughed, showing his teeth. "Your tripes would litter the road. Hear you me?"

He flung Ramsay from him. "That's for what's past. For the sake of what's to come, and with Lauder Brig in the balance, I'll strike you a bargain; for, rat that you are, I think you caught in the net as much as any, with no choice but to obey. Am I right in that?" He stood with eyes blazing at Ramsay, who had righted his balance and stood feeling his throat tenderly. "Ah, God's blood, keep your hand from your blade!" said Angus impatiently. "I'd win it from your body in a trice."

"What do you want of me?" said Ramsay thickly. His throat felt bruised and the blood hammered in his head. "Leave here, as I've said," replied Angus, "and with speed. You've other places to lay your head."

"This is mine owing to my marriage," said Ramsay sullenly.

A slow grin, old and wicked, spread across the Earl's face; he began to laugh. Words, that brought a flush to Ramsay's face, came to him; he laughed on, as though he watched a show. Suddenly Ramsay hid his face in his hands and began to sob. The knowledge of his own degradation came to him; he sank down, weakly, in a chair. "Marriage?" said the Earl. "This—marriage—must cease."

"What right have you to say it?"

Angus told him.

There was silence. Ramsay regarded the Earl helplessly from his chair. His face in the light of the hall looked peaked and white, like a boy's.

"So it has all been useless," he said.

He looked around at the hall, at the shadows which had been reality. What was there for men like him? Already his aspirations and dreams had faded and left him, stranded and a trifle ridiculous, in the glare of day.

"For God's sake marry," said Angus, not unkindly. "A tongueless woman if you can contrive it, who'll give you children. It's a barren thing, stolen goods; you've been too long alone."

Ramsay smiled wryly, thinking of the stolen beryls of Lauder; did Angus still wear them? The Earl, now, tossed the black leather package into his hands; clapped the hat on his head again, and turned to go.

"It's a wise man within, maybe, but not a bonny one," he said. "Serve him no longer."

"I have served his purpose," said Ramsay. "He has no more use for me."

"Then take the diamonds out, and sell them; or string them into a necklace for your wife, when you marry." He pulled his gloves on. "How long will it take you to pack your gear?"

"Not long," said Ramsay. He was regarding the other expressionlessly. "I wonder which of us is the bigger rogue?" he said.

"I am," said Angus bitterly, "and the bigger fool too." He turned to go, passing without haste through the door, his cloak swinging behind him like a bishop's. He did not look back; Ramsay stood watching him, and presently heard him ride away.

That autumn the marriage between the Lady of Bothwell and Sir John Ramsay of Trarinyean was annulled without reason given. Next year Sir John married again, a rosy-faced girl from Wemyss whose father's lands were adjoining his. He never saw the Lady again, nor spoke of her; nor she of him.

Part Five

THE GLOWING ASHES

1509–1513

I

A MAN was riding up the road to Bothwell one summer's day. He rode, not recklessly as His Grace had made it fashionable to do, but with caution; guiding with a plump firm hand his horse over the ruts in the road. Behind him were his serving men, who would sound a decorous horn as he approached the gates of the Castle. It was Gordon of Lochinvar, who had ridden over from Kenmure in connection with some business of his daughter Janet, aged twelve.

He was dressed with some plainness, for he had no desire to draw attention to himself. The Lady of Bothwell was notorious; so much so as to have become almost a legend in the district, which saw little of her. She kept herself close; coming out, they said, on days of storm to hunt like a man, tearing through the winter woods with mud on her cheek, and her hair flying behind her; followed by pages and serving men gorgeously attired, the Queen of Elfland's train. Gordon primmed his lips, thinking of the names the ignorant had for her, her beauty or her wantonness making of her a fey queen or a hellish witch, who rode also at night on the devil's mare and turned the milk of cows. But he and those about him knew well enough what to make of such tales, seeing in them only that the Lady of Bothwell grew old, and the King came less often to visit her than formerly, having troubles enough at home and abroad to make him forget the idle pleasures in which previously he had been wont to indulge.

Gordon thought of some of those troubles, running over methodically in his mind the news from the North, where a full-scale rebellion had just been put down, engendered by the last descendant of John of the

Isles. The Borders, too, were unquiet; it was thought that the new King of England, Henry the Eighth, was less inclined for friendship than had at first been supposed, and indeed did all in his power to foment ill-feeling, on the Borders and elsewhere. The English had murdered His Grace's Warden of the Marches and would not give up the murderer; they had intercepted and killed His Grace's sailors at sea, and kept the ships. Ah, there were troublesome times coming; and all to no purpose it seemed, the English marriage that had seemed to promise peace, this half-dozen years back. There was not, even, a living heir to show for it, the Queen's children that had been born having every one, soon or late, died feebly. And although Lochinvar's warlike neighbors about Galloway rejoiced at the thought of riding to war again, he did not so; he was a peace-loving man and had looked forward to growing old with his child, Net, about him.

He wondered, now for the first time in all these years, what the mother would look like now. Net he had seen twice yearly; she resembled him; there was nothing, not a trace, of the wild enchantment that had trapped and humiliated him, so many years ago that it seemed a lifetime between then and now. He, a staid middle-aged man, should have no cause to remember it, except as a blessing which had sent his child to him, his wife bearing him none. He knew that she blamed him, would have said Net was none of his, except for the blessed resemblance that made the issue without doubt. And soon Net would come to him altogether. It was because of that that he rode over today. Already, with the nearing of Bothwell towers, the irritating uncertainty grew on him, making him less assured than he had been; what would she—Jan—look like now?

She would have changed. The torment that had come to him in dreams would go, and he be glad of it. He had never mentioned its presence to a living soul.

They led him to her in the room in the upper part of the castle. She was by the fire, and her appearance shocked him; she was thin enough to be haggard, her skin sallow and tightly drawn over her bones; by contrast her eyes seemed large and brilliant. He felt compunction stir him; had this been the ogress he feared to meet, this ill woman? She smiled at him, stretching out a hand from the bench which he took and kissed; it was like a claw.

"You've come at an ill time," she said, "but I stand on no ceremony and I have not painted my face. It's an ague that takes me in the summer heat; got, I think, from the damned flying biting things on Newton marsh. So the King says, who is my physician. And you've come late; we're near neighbors. Why have you not been to visit me all these years?"

He saw the eyes watching him, with a gleam of enjoyment. He felt himself flounder, as he used. Damn her and her witch ways! he thought angrily.

She smiled still. "You'll take some wine?" She rose, and poured it, for himself and her; the glasses were French, of ruby-color. He took it gingerly.

"I am not used to such fragile ware," he ventured, "but to honest leather."

"It gets very black and foul. The Lord of Aubigny, who died, as you know, last year while over here, brought these to me. His dearest wish was to visit the shrine of St. Ninian, but it was never fulfilled."

They talked a little about the wonder of St. Ninian and of how the King had cured a sickness of the Queen's by making a pilgrimage there on foot from Edinburgh.

"They say she was cured at the time he left Whithorn. But no prayer to St. Ninian has brought them a living heir."

He was surprised at the concern in her voice, which faintly embarrassed him. As if she read his thoughts, she laughed.

"Think not that the King and I are now aught but friends. Time's past for loving. He sent me sweetmeats when he heard I was sick; he is very kind to me."

"And you suffer yourself to be left?" said Lochinvar. Her eyes danced, disconcerting his.

"My lord of Angus consoles me."

"She's quite shameless," he thought. A flush rose to his face. "I have come about the child," he reminded her. "You had my letter?"

"I have had several letters. You want her now?"

There was a monkey, gray and furred, swinging on a chain near the window. He caught sight of it for the first time and its movements fascinated him. Its bright dark eyes surveyed him with a sad-comic look; we are both here, it said. Did she fill her time with such toys?

He realized that he had not answered and turned again, to find her regarding him. "Jan," he said. "She's here—Net—now?"

"Below—somewhere." The voice was casual. "Do you want to take her with you? I was uncertain, from your letter; I remember that was the arrangement. If her gear is ready she can go."

Still he hesitated. "How is—is the Earl of Moray?"

"Moray's to school in St. Andrews, with the Prothonotary and Lyle's son. He is to follow Sandy Stewart to Padua at the end of the year. The King will have them all turned to clerks and preachers. Even now Moray looks at me with grave eyes."

"Then—you will be alone?"

She shrugged. "There are consolations, which no man would savor. If I want to lie back with white of egg and lemon juice on my face, I can do so. I was about to, when you came in." She grinned at him. "Don't let that haste you away."

The monkey stirred and whimpered on its perch. "Jan—"

"Yes?" she said, and her eyebrows flew up. You bore me, the look told him. He shifted awkwardly.

"Jan, I—we wondered—if you do not want to part with the child."

"Why?"

"It could be arranged," he said, not answering her. "I—we, my wife and I, have discussed it; she's fond of Net, but she—"

"Does not relish the thought of another woman's bastard, and will not have my daughter in the house? Is that it?"

Still her voice held that irritating amusement. He hastened to disclaim, feeling his dignity in danger. She was feverish, he told himself.

"No, no, that is not it!" he assured her. "As you know, we have no children. My wife would be only too glad—"

She smiled again, but not unkindly. "Did I frighten you so much, Sandy, that you were unable to beget another heir? Poor lad, I did not mean it."

Her eyes, against the light, crinkled with laughter. Lochinvar's mouth set primly. The blood drummed in his head with rage and ridicule; he could not fight his anger down. His voice when it came was louder than he intended. "My wife and I were moved by some natural compassion. We considered the loneliness of your state, and how it might be that the comfort of the child would console you. I came to make you the offer that the arrangement for the heirship should stand, but that Net should remain half the year with you. I do not think this offer ungenerous, knowing what had gone before. I am not a vindictive man."

Janet Kennedy laughed. She threw back her head and shook with laughter, clasping the carved bench ends with her ringed hands. "You?" she said.

Suddenly she rose to her feet. "You little rat," she said. She went to the door and called for the servant; Gordon remained, white with shock, in his chair. Feet were heard, scurrying on the stairs; soon the door opened. Janet, a devil in whirling yellow skirts, faced him again, eyes lit with fury.

"Now you hear me—" she began; but the manservant's scared face appeared. She addressed him in a voice that was surprisingly calm.

"Fetch the Lady Janet Gordon's cloak and put it on her back. Pack such gear as she now needs, and prepare the rest to be sent after. And have her wait this—nobleman—in the hall; he'll not detain her. Hurry!"

The man disappeared. She faced him again. The interruption had taken the force of her fury; her words now to him were idle and almost disinterested. "You see how much your child means to me?" she said. "Take her, and never let me see her again."

"Jan—"

"Oh—Jan—Jan—your lust's as hot as ever! If I were to have you lie down on the bed with me now you would do it, you plaster hypocrite— how I loathe your kind! There are too many of you in Scotland; one day it'll be the country's doom, when all true men are under the earth. I pray I don't live till then."

She laughed suddenly, seeing his staring at her. "Take your child, and your pity. Bring her up to breed other pudding-faces. It's not the flesh without that matters, God knows, but that within is stolid too . . . like you. My loneliness, you say? I'd rather have a lifetime of loneliness, having been true to myself, than a single hour of your company. Go now."

She swept toward him and turned him by the shoulders; her thin fingers showed surprising strength. Bewilderment and anger were with him; what had she meant by being true to herself? The knowledge that the servant must have witnessed his discomfiture infuriated him; he lost control, shouting at her as she bundled him out at the door.

"Perhaps now you'll see to what you have brought youself!" he said. "The careful woman who guards her household has laid up treasure for herself, but not you! You're ageing, madame, and your lovers have left you; the King has seen that he lived in error, and visits you no more. He was at Kenmure this summer with my wife and me and—agreeably inclined, and there was no word of you, and no move to visit you, as far as I am aware! Thus it is that—that the proper order of things is established in the end, and you, who scorned to marry me, are left here a laughingstock!" He freed himself at last from her thrusting fingers, turned in the doorway, tousled and flushed, and reiterated, "A laughing-stock, madame! I bid you farewell!"

"Do so, then!" said she mockingly. Suddenly she stood still in the doorway; the light was behind her, shining in her hair and making her face hidden. He stopped, in his descent of the stairs, seeing her; her voice when it came was quiet.

"If we'd our lives to live again, I'd have mine no different."

He turned again, and hastened down the stairs; he felt a fool for having waited. She had never been for him, that elfin creature; he had wasted a lifetime lacking her. He would never know whether his love or hate for her had been the stronger, or whether or not he regretted the fact that they would never meet again. He tried to cover the doubtfulness of his feelings with the standards of every day, but they would not apply; she had stripped him.

"Give my love to the King when next he comes to Kenmure, and tell him I laugh loudest of all," she called after him. "And that I'd not change for any man!"

Going down into the hall, to where his daughter waited, the words followed him; bemused as he was, their sense did not come to him then. Laughter? She would laugh, but at what? A laughingstock, he'd called her, he remembered. She had always laughed, in the days when she seemed like a flame. She was like one still. And she'd not change—had not changed, she said; not for any man. Well, God knew, she'd packed more into her life than most men in a hundred years.

Flaming Janet. Thank God she hadn't married him! "It would have been the same," he thought. "She'd never have settled down."

The thought occupied him all the way from Bothwell to Kenmure, with Net riding square-cheeked and silent behind him. There were two kinds of folk, that was all, and there was no doing with the other kind. But nothing could touch them at all.

II

It was the ninth of September, 1513.

Bell-the-Cat sat by his fire and listened to the beating rain; he sipped, every now and again, a cup of mulled ale they had brought him, and stretched his feet in their furred slippers to the warmth.

Every now and again the wet would gather in the chimney and drop with a hiss on to the fire, and his head, which had been nodding, would jerk resentfully, and then the quiet would settle down again and he would almost sleep.

Almost, but not quite; for his thoughts were active. They increased in proportion as his body weakened with age, so that for many hours of the day now he would sit thus, huddled before the fire, saying nothing except to growl and order, when it was needed, to the page who waited in the shadows. Then the boy would come forward; he was a young boy, too young to have gone with the King to war. Here they were, the pair of them, too old and too young. He thought of that, seeing the firelight shine on the boy's fair head. He snapped his fingers.

"My lord?" The boy came obediently. He could not be more, Angus thought, than ten years old. All *his* life now, or what was left of it, he would be surrounded by children and old men. He jerked his head toward the floor.

"Sit down by me. Say naught; I'd have your company but not your tongue."

He turned again to the fire. He was uncertain why he had called the boy. Behind them, the room lay vaulted and dark. When had he sat in such a room, waiting, hearing the sound the hawks made as they preened their feathers, high above; seeing the shining of their red eyes in the darkness? Hawks and jesses, to ride out with by day, red-hooded and with tiny bells at one's wrist. There had been some news that came. . . .

He moved restlessly, knowing his mind wandered. "I know well enough of what goes on." He heard his own inner voice make the flat, defiant statement, convincing himself that he had not grown old. Ay, he'd been at that Council a month or two back when Bishop Elphinstone had risen and gone out weeping because they called him a crazy old man, he being the only one there who had spoken up against war with England. And he, Angus, had shouted and taunted with the rest of them, not caring very greatly for the French or the Auld Alliance but anxious, as it were, to associate himself with the general opinion.

The King, they knew, was not anxious for the war.

Angus spat into the fire. Of what avail for a man to work himself nigh to death in pursuit of an ideal there was no attaining? James had done that, laboring through the night with dispatches to France and the Emperor and the North, attempting his cherished idea of a League of Christendom in Europe, when all that Europe wanted to do was tear itself apart and share the spoil. Henry of England was at France's throat, spread out now in his golden tent before Térouenne. He'd spent all the money the old King had left on warships and fighting mercenaries and gilt armor. Henry wanted war as a game, like a young cockerel spoiling for the fight. It mattered little enough to him about his sister's marriage to a man who was pledged to aid France.

"All these are high matters," grunted the old man. The difference to him was that, after all these years of peace, Douglas men had ridden out again to war and he unable to go with them. He and a child, left alone in a hall of slumbering shadows. Three weeks ago he'd seen the boys ride off, led by his son George, stiff and ill at ease on his black charger, with the blazon carried above. He'd never liked George, or the way he always made a virtue out of necessity. Now, even, he'd not deny that he'd rather be at home with his wife and his bailiffs and his sheep. There was no saying but that he'd fight well enough; but without the joy in it that oneself would have had.

The old man grinned, showing his yellowed teeth. "George'll meet the King and tell him that he fights because it is his duty, and that face of his smooth as duff, which will try His Grace sorely."

Young Archie would be there, too. He'd a fair notion of the kind of fighter his own grandson would make. Archie had left his wife, Bothwell's daughter, in labor at home, riding off to leave her without much regret. Somehow one had the notion that nothing much amiss would happen to young Archie, whatever else befell. He was like enough to what he, Bell-the-Cat, had been when young. He'll ride back, he thought, no matter who else does not return.

The words made an echo in his mind and he raised his head swiftly. What had made him say that, so easily taking it for granted that others would not return?

There'll be losses, he thought, to reassure himself. God knew, with the size of the army His Grace had taken south, foregathered that day as they had reported on the Borough Muir; and the French kickshaws, the cannon, of which he was so proud, and Mons, who could shoot a stone the size of a loaf—small wonder if there were a blow struck, some losses. What was he thinking of? This was war, not a child's affair like that of young Hume at Brownrigg this summer, when he'd tumbled like a fool into an ambush of Englishmen among the whins. Angus grinned wickedly; Hume had been his wife's lover, and he rejoiced in his discomfiture.

Old as I am, he thought, I've never been a fool. But if a man was born thus there was no altering it. Hume had lost the King many spearmen and saved his own wretched hide. Nobody wanted him when he came riding home. It would remain to see whether he would redeem himself in the battle that must by now be joined.

No word for many days. . . . The last he had heard was that the King's men had taken Norham, on the Tweed. The river, they said, had been high with rain. Foray weather! It was still in his heart to regret that he had not ridden with them, although he was old. "I'd have shown them an arrow shot still, a blow with a sword."

Four hundred of them, Douglas men, riding out under the crowned-heart banner behind George and his sons; and the Glenbervie men with William, grim-mouthed under jutting basnets. He had watched them go forth to the Borough Muir with banners flying in spite of the rain. Passing by they had saluted him, the old man who was done now but who had led them in other days. He'd held his hands over them like an archbishop, wishing them well, feeling the blood warm in him as they rode by, the sons of the men who'd followed him to burn Bamborough in the late King's wars.

That had been long ago . . . and Wood, the great sailor, smiting the English then over four seas, was sitting now at Largo eating his heart out because the Scots fleet had sailed without him and he, too, was old. So many old men . . . and if none returned of the army, as he had said, who in God's name would govern Scotland?

"Ah, why think of that?" he growled. To think of a thing was to wish it.

The rain dripped in the chimney. Outside the wind had risen and there were the beginnings of storm. It would be whipping about the King's tents tonight, straining the girths that bound the waxed silk. His Grace had always preferred living in tents to living in castles; Angus recalled the many times hunting when he'd taken his pavilions with him. And those French engineers, who guarded the cannon, would sit in the pavilions by him and talk of the way to wage their curious formal war.

"The time will come when sword blows and a man's strength are things of the past. Everything now is this cheating folly, this measuring of the distance a fistful of powder can be made to fly, annihilating an enemy that no one need ever see." There would be no joy in war when such methods came to be in general use. Wars would be waged by men like old Henry Tudor, dead now and rotting in the new tomb he'd built for himself at Westminster, with the pen fallen from his fingers and his son squandering all he had saved. No one would ever come to close grips with an honorable foe; there would be no more honor because the need for it would have been destroyed.

But tonight. . . . How were they faring now?

The King fought for honor, Angus thought. The tormented face of James rose before him. Thinking of him now, it seemed he was the only man oneself had ever loved. The boar's mind hunted round the thing and could not explain it. They had shared a woman; men had done so before and been no better friends. They had made war on each other in open and in secret, and long years ago the King had sent him a Christmas gift of a black velvet gown after digging ditches round him at Tantallon.

"I helped kill his father and I hanged his father's friends," Angus thought, "and he diced with me after."

There was no explaining James Stewart . . . any Stewart. He found his thoughts center about that slim figure in French armor to a degree that he had not spared for any other—except one.

She . . . where was she tonight?

Did she sit by the fire, as he did, or kneel in her chapel praying? That half of her had bewildered and intrigued him, coming as it had so late after the other things he knew of her. He could see her clearly now, lips moving and parted in prayer, long hands moving over the beads the King had given her, eyes dark. She'd pray for James, whom she had loved; for his son, who had ridden to battle with him. Those two were more to her than her own son, now at Padua. Women were unpredictable creatures; the legend of motherhood altered them not at all. It had altered her not at all.

Flaming Janet. The thought crossed his mind that she might have given him sons. He wondered what they would have been like; tall, maybe, with the color of the hair between her red and his gold. They would not have been old enough yet to ride with the King; here, sitting by him like this page who sat. She, herself, sitting by him here. . . .

He shook himself free of it, as he had once not been able to do. She would never sit by him again. Loving enough, they'd been together, all these years; like a man and his wife, an old man, past young loving. But now he was old and shadows were as strong to him as reality, and there was no need for her to come in the flesh. "Time's past," he had said to her once, "for loving."

He remembered her eyes, swimming with tears out of pity for him because he knew he had grown old. "Too late for that, Bell!" She held out her hands to him. "But—to comfort each other!"

She had been his comfort and he hers, but tonight she was not here. He watched the page boy's head absently. Strange how one could accustom oneself to the fading of a long-known desire, as though with the body's ageing all colors changed from bright to dull, the eyes no longer enduring them. She knew of it, hunting there alone at Bothwell among the yellowing leaves. Older, both of them; was it better to grow old, or to die? There were some, he knew, for whom age was not conceivable. He had never been able to think of the King as growing old, as if a man nearing forty could transform himself in men's minds to perpetual youth by virtue of that Elixir he had sought and had not found.

"He never found it, though he spent much gold."

Who was it had told him of that, grieving a little as though it were their loss? Jan. Jan had been with the King in Stirling when he brewed his concoctions and studied herbs, and she'd laughed and cried at the tale of the wings His Grace had tried out, made of feathers. The man who wore them had sailed down from the battlements of Stirling Castle and broken both his legs. There'd been little time for all that lately. What would happen now, when the King came back from war?

He found that he could not think of the King as coming back. A chillness, deep in his bones, was with him; fostered, he told himself, by the draft from the night outside. The storm had not grown yet to its full strength, and later a moon would rise. He could picture the silver light flooding and tossing over the floor with the clouds that passed. But now the fire leaped high, and he should not be cold.

"I'm idle," he thought, "and have been sitting here too long."

Still he couldn't bring himself to move. The door opened and a woman came in, moving with stiff uncertainty through the half-lit dark of the hall. Angus scowled; it was his wife, he thought. Then he remembered she had been gone for years; gone, she had, with Hume, and left him. He had not regretted her going, but the indignity scalded him; he to be laughed at! She was living somewhere in the south now, with the son she had borne Hume. Angus' teeth showed; in the old days he would have killed Hume. "As I killed Spens." The remembrance of that fortified him.

The woman came forward into the light and he saw that it was George's wife Elizabeth Drummond. She wore riding dress and her skirts were whipped and sodden with the storm. She moved mechanically, as one who is very weary; the firelight shone on her face and showed it a mass of tiny wrinkles. She came and sat down by the fire, stretching out her hands to the warmth.

"The child is dead." Her voice came dully; it was as though she were speaking of some happening far away and scarcely known. Angus stared.

"The child?" he said. He had been so wrapped up in his own thoughts that he had no idea who she meant. He watched her profile, staring at the flames.

"Archie's child," she said. "Your great-grandson. It is not thought that the mother will live through the night."

He turned the thing over in his mind, slowly, savoring its possibilities. "The young die," said Elizabeth, "and the old go on." Suddenly she bowed her face in her hands and wept. Angus watched her silently in a rising impatience. They always come to me, he thought, and weep.

Suddenly he rose and spat into the fire and said, "If it had happened to me in youth that my wife had died in childbed with her first-born, I'd have been able to make my way in the world. And that's what Archie will do, mark you my words." He became aware of her horrified eyes staring up at him. "Why so?" he said. "Would you rather he was killed in battle? He'll ride home."

"Who is to say who will ride home?" she wailed. "At the time the King's army left Edinburgh there was plague in the town, and not a soul in the streets to bid them farewell."

"They'll not die of pestilence, but of my lord Surrey's spears." He turned and began to stump with difficulty toward the door, jerking his head to the page to follow him. "Tell them in God's name to saddle horses," he muttered. "I ride out."

He heard the agitated flutter of her skirts behind him; always they were about him, the women, coaxing him back to the fire. "My lord can't ride in this storm," she said persuasively. "Where would you go?"

"To battle. What the devil is it to you?" But he allowed her to lead him back to the fire again. Outside, the rain still beat against the walls. He settled down and listened to it and thought how when they would let him go he would ride down into Galloway again and collect his teinds for the monastery of Whithorn, where he was justiciar. The air there would be clean-swept and the land green and pleasant. Jan's land, Galloway. He never went there without remembering her.

He thought of the gray buildings standing in the light of the sun and how there, where there would be no woman to trouble him or weep over him, he might stay for a while. There would be no sound there but the sea, washing about the White Isle where Ninian had landed and the King had knelt so many times on devout pilgrimage. He grinned. That baggage, Jan, had reaped her benefits of that devotion. Whatever befell now she would be settled for life; at Bothwell, or Darnaway, where she'd made the farms flourish and the forests green with wood for

the King's ships. Galloway no more for her, but she was remembered in
the very air there. He'd bide there for a while, to see what had befallen.
No monk he, like the Black Douglas, ending his days at Lindores! Only
for a while; and then home again, for the dividing of the spoil. There
would be something to tell of tonight, in this storm.

He raised his head and sniffed the air, as an old hunting dog will do.
"The roads will be thick with mud," he said. "Pray God they get the
guns out." The wild rain, hurtling against the stones, came to him like
the rattle of spears. Outside, the sky would be like a sheet of water; he'd
not ride tonight. But tomorrow, when it was clear, he'd ride to Whithorn;
they should not stop him going there.

He slept soon, nodding forward against the fire. George's wife sat for
a while and then rose and crept away. She was like a creature whose
thread of direction is lost. She made her way aimlessly to the room above
the gate, where soon they would come riding to tell her that her son's
wife was dead. She was conscious of coming change and it scared her,
and her bones ached and it was damp. She would be glad to get back
home.

She shivered, remembering that there might be no one left to take her
home. She had had the feeling, unexplained to herself, that she would
not see George again. It was not like George to have a soldier's death;
he should have died in sleep, nodding like that old man beside the fire.
She had turned once to watch Angus as she mounted the stairs, seeing
the white hair and beard luminous with the firelight behind them. He
was sleeping peacefully; by him was the great sword with which he had
killed Spens, and his hand would search for it when he wakened.

Her heart smote her for him, knowing that he would wake alone, as
he so often did, in the dark of the empty hall. But there would be many
in Scotland now who must accustom themselves to loneliness. Tomorrow
news would come of Flodden Field, and of George's death and the King's
and many others. She dropped the curtain softly, denying the unease
that lay with her, praying to the saints as when in doubt she was accustomed to do. She was a plain woman without the fire of fancy, and
what the King and the Egyptians had known she could not foretell. At
the hour when, far south in a Northumbrian bog, the King took his
last wound and fell, no other sign was given to her than the screaming
of the wind as the storm rose fully, and the rain flailed hard enough to
batter down the walls.

The Lady of Bothwell knelt at her beads, telling them with the clear intensity of one who has for so long repeated the words that they have passed beyond lack of meaning into fullness again.

Above where she knelt, a dark thin bowed shape with head veiled, other dark figures, of Piers' painted saints, stared down at her. The impersonal knowledge in their eyes spoke of things which had to be accepted, like the coming of old age and the fact that the King had ridden off to war. Of one and the other she had known for long, and now that they had come she was able, through long schooling, to hide her grief and appear calm, even though now in the chapel she was not alone. There were many women who had come here to pray, for the souls of departed sons and lovers and husbands. She felt the strength of their silent prayers behind her; they made no sound. All over the country there would be chapels filled, now that the banners were sewn and farewells made, and no more left to do but wait for news.

She closed her eyes for an instant, aware of the women. They at least had bidden their men farewell; they would have a memory, if the worst befell, of a last rough caress on mouth or cheek, a word of thanks. She had not that, not even the consolation of having seen the King ride to war. Among all the white faces behind glass in Edinburgh's plague-stricken streets that day, hers had been lacking; there was no place for her there, in that city where once she had leaned out from a balcony as he rode to war and thrown a white rose. The time was past for white roses.

"Time's past for loving." Who had said that? And yet, how richly they had loved! What other woman would not have given much for a single one of her memories?

Even so, they're all old, she thought. She wondered if as she herself grew older they would draw nearer in apparent time again. A very old woman speaking of the past thought of it as yesterday.

"Let me grow old then, and my hair white." She was astonished at the fierceness of the tears that rose. Other women could kneel passively, hoping that God would send the best; but she had always known within herself that James would not return.

He knew, she thought. How long had that been so, and had the Egyptian's playing that night been his early warning? They said of him that even when he was born his father held in great fear the casting of his new stars. What did it mean to be doomed, so that there was no escape; denying the Christian teaching of free will which with half his heart he had followed so passionately?

Back, always very far back, the memories ran. Many years ago she had watched him course about the needfire and be chosen the scapegoat, the carline on whom, for the sins of the whole people, should fall the just wrath of angered gods. They had not known, the shepherds and the men about the moor that day, what it was they chose; a harmless ploy to them, its significance forgotten. But she knew now that the carline bore the griefs of the world as God had borne them on the Cross. She remembered the face of James as she had last seen it, the dark tormented eyes reflecting something of the hopelessness to which men's stupidity and greed had brought him, after long effort. The young golden cockerel, Harry of England, ascended; the fey King of Scots would go down in darkness, few recognizing his worth. They would remember him because he died bravely, not because he had lived kindly. After many years the striven-for things, the printing press in Edinburgh and the wings for man to fly, the jousting for golden prizes and the magnificent marriage, even, of the Thistle and the Rose, would be forgotten. And no one would remember the matters in which he and she had had their delight; the long rides north in wind and starlight, the chatter of many tongues along the road; the brave colors and heartwarming laughter, the mules in scarlet leather harness fringed with little bells, that rang gaily as they rode along. Small things, unfelt at the time, but looking back she saw them; they were all of her life in this world, and who could vouch for the next?

I'll not be his in heaven, she thought, so this is the end.

Coming out of the chapel she heard the wind rise, and felt its strength as it blew against her. The challenge of the storm stayed with her, knowing the King far south this night among the wind and rain. She had them fetch her cloak and she wrapped it about her, and then went out alone. She did not care what they thought of her, the mad woman of Bothwell walking by herself among the Darnaway forests. She had never been afraid of natural things.

The storm rose and the hurled rain as she walked drenched her face and hair, loosened and blown back as it had used to be when she was a girl striding in Galloway. During the time that she walked against the wind the thought of Angus came to her; she wondered how he fared this night, and whether he had heard news. He had, she knew, been for the war with England. It must have irked him to be found too old, at the last, to ride.

Douglas men, Kennedy men, following the King to battle. Her brothers and half brothers were close by the King's side. Ramsay would have fought, she heard, but he was an ill man. She spared a thought aside for

Ramsay, idly as for one long dead; his wife, she heard, had borne him a son last autumn, and she had been glad when they told her of it, thinking that now the torment in his mind would be stilled. A strange homeless creature, a waif, like herself; his task, like hers, was done.

The men of Darnaway had gone. She had ridden with them a little of the way, giving them her prayers and a sewn banner, and silver for the road. They had louted to her and kissed her hand, and then they had gone and she had turned back to comfort the women, giving them the use of her hall and chapel till the men should return. Throughout Scotland they would be waiting thus, little colonies of women and the aged who could not ride to fight. Her thoughts flew to Edinburgh and she wondered how the Queen fared, left alone in an alien country and again, they said, near her time. Of all the children she had borne the King only one, a boy, had lived.

"James the Fifth," she thought wryly. How was one to continue in this acceptance? The only way she found was to walk on, and on, hard against the force of the storm, pitting her strength against it so that she had no time to run mad. It rose and howled in the treetops, bending the great pines so that they groaned aloud. Tomorrow many of them would be found prone and naked, white strands upthrusting into the calm day from a great jagged hole in the earth. The pride of Scotland torn up, her courage felled and uprooted. Dear God, she had thoughts like Walter Kennedy who had been dead for years!

"*Timor mortis conturbat me.*" Those lines Wil Dunbar had written for Walter, and the hundred other dead poets who now were shadows on the grass. He, too, had danced for the world, and now found that the world was leaving him. How could it be the same for anyone, after the King had gone? There would be laughter again but it would not be the same laughter, and everything on which the sun had shone would be poorer, sadder gray. Gray women, mourning for the men who would not come back. Gray Scotland, mourning for her King. And she, too, would grow old in the remembrance of it, the years shedding grayness like dust on her skin and hair.

"You've been my light when my mind was dark, brought sanity and laughter. My lovely mistress, my dear comrade, my good friend."

The words came to her clearly, sent hither again on the swiftness of the storm. That they did not come from his present thoughts she knew; a fey man, near to death, would have his mind fixed on a single goal. But once he had said those words to her, and she took joy in remembering them. They had been her valediction, a fitting one and all that she could have desired.

"It matters nothing that I could say no farewell to him," she thought. Their hours together were precious, beyond space or time. In a world grown dun after his death her flame would still burn, warming a little with its brightness the chill of the new day. She'd not change for Lutheran saws or any new morality! She'd live as she had always done, take pleasure in color and warmth and light. She'd grow old in her own way, remembering him.

"I knew him as well as any. Can anyone else say that?"

She turned and pondered it wryly, resting against a tree trunk a little removed from the force of the storm. Storm all her life had been, and she recognized the fact and liked it. Even her love had been strife and battle, a warring of body and soul. She looked now at the line of sky that lay between the pines, seeing the little, angry red streak that showed the last of the sunset. Far south there was a battle ended, and something of that dead peace after storm came to her mind. She loosened the sodden clutch of the cloak about her shoulders and made her way down, carefully, picking her way along the path by which she had come. There would be comfort in Darnaway and mulled warm wine to drink at the day's end. She would not sit in the hall with the women who talked of grief, but upstairs in her chamber where so often the King had come to her, and pray for him and for the young Archbishop, his son, and for Moray in Padua. "God grant he bear the news bravely. God send him safely home."

She was certain of what would befall. The strength in her rose above the battling wind. Darnaway's lights beckoned to her, and she gathered her skirts high like a countrywoman and strode home.

Genealogical Tables

STEWARTS
TUDORS AND PLANTAGENETS
(Simplified)

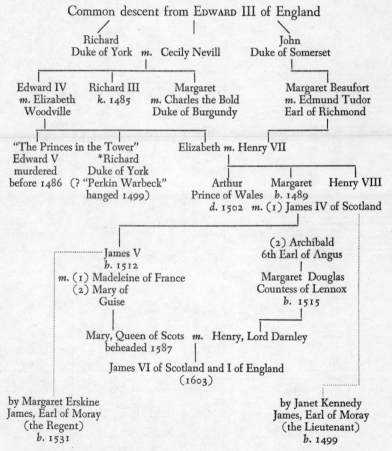

Common descent from EDWARD III of England

Richard
Duke of York *m.* Cecily Nevill

John
Duke of Somerset

Edward IV
m. Elizabeth
Woodville

Richard III
k. 1485

Margaret
m. Charles the Bold
Duke of Burgundy

Margaret Beaufort
m. Edmund Tudor
Earl of Richmond

"The Princes in the Tower"
Edward V
murdered
before 1486

*Richard
Duke of York
(? "Perkin Warbeck"
hanged 1499)

Elizabeth *m.* Henry VII

Arthur
Prince of Wales
d. 1502

Margaret
b. 1489
m. (1) James IV of Scotland

Henry VIII

James V
b. 1512
m. (1) Madeleine of France
(2) Mary of
Guise

(2) Archibald
6th Earl of Angus

Margaret Douglas
Countess of Lennox
b. 1515

Mary, Queen of Scots *m.* Henry, Lord Darnley
beheaded 1587

James VI of Scotland and I of England
(1603)

by Margaret Erskine
James, Earl of Moray
(the Regent)
b. 1531

by Janet Kennedy
James, Earl of Moray
(the Lieutenant)
b. 1499

* The identity of "Warbeck" is still in dispute. In the renunciation dictated by
Henry VII which he was forced to sign and read on capture, he is described as
being the son of a Flemish boat-builder.

THE BOYD, DOUGLAS AND KENNEDY CONNECTIONS
(Simplified)

Main characters in story in block capitals
Bastard lines ....

Robert, Lord Boyd *m.* Mariot Maxwell (before 1451)

Thomas, Earl of Arran
m. Mary Stewart,
sister of James III

Archibald
m. Christian Mure

Elizabeth
m. ARCHIBALD
5th EARL OF ANGUS
("Bell-the-Cat")
1468

Annabella
m. John Gordon
of Lochinvar

Alexander

JOHN, LORD KENNEDY
m. (1) Elizabeth Montgomerie

James

Margaret
m. (1) Alexander
Lord Forbes
(2) DAVID, 1st EARL
OF CASSILIS

4 others

Marion
Mistress of James IV
(later *m.* John Mure
of Rowallan)

ADAM OF PENKILL
m. Helen Kennedy
1531

(2) ELIZABETH GORDON
widow of Nicol
Earl of Erroll

ALEXANDER

JANET
Mistress of James IV
m. (1) ? ARCHIBALD
5th EARL OF ANGUS
(2) JOHN RAMSAY OF
TRARINYEAN

Janet
b. 1496

HELEN

MARGARET
m. Andrew
Lord Avandale

m. (1) Robert
Graham
(2) Adam
Boyd
(1531)

4 others

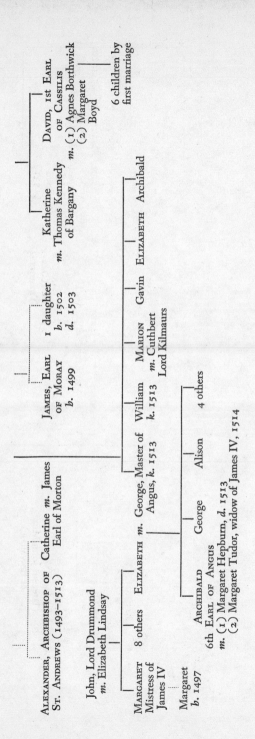

ALEXANDER, ARCHBISHOP OF ST. ANDREWS (1493–1513)

Catherine *m.* James Earl of Morton

James, Earl of Moray *b.* 1499

1 daughter *b.* 1502 *d.* 1503

Katherine *m.* Thomas Kennedy of Bargany

David, 1st Earl of Cassilis *m.* (1) Agnes Borthwick (2) Margaret Boyd

6 children by first marriage

John, Lord Drummond *m.* Elizabeth Lindsay

Margaret Mistress of James IV

8 others

Elizabeth *m.* George, Master of Angus, *k.* 1513

William *k.* 1513

Marion *m.* Cuthbert Lord Kilmaurs

Gavin   Elizabeth   Archibald

Margaret *b.* 1497

Archibald 6th Earl of Angus *m.* (1) Margaret Hepburn, *d.* 1513 (2) Margaret Tudor, widow of James IV, 1514

George   Alison   4 others

Glossary

assoil absolve; expiate

ayre small courts of justice held by the King on itinerary

bannock a cake made from wheaten or oat flour, together with milk and eggs

bothy (*bothies*) hut(s)

brig bridge

brod framed picture; likeness

carline scapegoat, used in the sense implied here; a year-fool; chosen one

chiel servant

clarsach a form of old Celtic harp

curch kerchief

dagged cut in points or slashes

gangrel vagrant

gaud ornament; trinket

gowk a laughingstock; a silly fool

handfasting betrothal

hippocras highly spiced wine

jess (falconry) a short strap secured around the leg of a hawk

justiciar a high royal official; judicial officer

keeking peeping

kickshaw toy; bauble

kist chest

long-saddle   early name for a settle

lout   to bend; bow

mammet   a doll; pet; favorite; plaything

merk   Scottish silver coin, worth approximately 13s-4d

martrix fur   the pelt of an unborn or prematurely born lamb

murrain   a plague affecting cattle

needfire   the new fire kindled at Midsummer and regarded as the gift of the gods

pirning   embellishment of plain cloth with gold or silver thread

rax   to wrench, pull; used as here, to increase the speed of rubbing of opposed surfaces, in order to kindle a flame

raddle   paint (their cheeks) with red ocher

reiving   stealing; thieving; robbing

rickle   a loose heap

rose noble   former English gold coin—first issued by Edward the Fourth in 1465—so called from the rose stamped on it

saltfat   a vessel for salt or salting, as saltcellar

sarcenet   a soft silk fabric, plain or twill weave

smirr   mist; cloud

sprat   small European herring

stockfish   fish dried in the open air without salt

straight-saddle   Joan Beaufort, the English queen of James the First, had brought the graceful fashion of sidesaddle riding to her husband's country. But for many generations older women preferred to ride astride, and for this purpose would have their skirts kilted and tied up out of the way

succuba   a demon, especially one assuming female form to have sexual intercourse with men in their sleep

teinds   tithes

tocher   dowry

tursing   truss; to pack up or off; to be off

upsetting   setting up in business (here used in connection with a christening ceremony)

vair   squirrel

warlock   sorcerer; wizard

whin   a spiny evergreen shrub often used for fuel and fodder (called also *gorse* and *furze*)

Bibliography

Accounts of the Lord High Treasurer of Scotland (ed. Dickson)
    vv. iii-iv
Dictionary of National Biography (ed. Lee)
Douglas' *Scots Peerage* (ed. Wood)
The Douglas Book
The Douglases (Hume of Godscroft)
Ellis' *Select Letters*
Fairbairn's *Book of Crests*
Frazer   *The Golden Bough*
Gregory Smith   *The Days of James IV*
Lindsay of Pitscottie's *Chronicle*
Registers of the Great and Privy Seals of Scotland
Scott   Notes to *Marmion*
Tytler's *History of Scotland*